TRUST

ME

ROMILY BERNARD

HARPER TEEN
An Imprint of HarperCollinsPublishers

Library of Congress Control Number: 2015940699
ISBN 978-0-06-222909-0

Typography by Joel Tippie
16 17 18 19 20   PC/RRDH   10 9 8 7 6 5 4 3 2 1
❖
First Edition

For Natalie Richards—I wouldn't be here without you

Is it still kidnapping if your mom lets them take you? Because it definitely feels like kidnapping—no matter how many times Agent Hart smiles at me.

"C'mon, Wick," he says, rebuttoning the front of his suit jacket because I won't shake his hand. "I promise you'll like where you're going."

Doubtful. That smile snakes chills up my spine.

"Bren?" I call, wincing when my voice cracks. My adoptive mom left me with Hart so we could "talk," but I'm *so* done talking. "Bren?"

Bren appears in our living room doorway, my duffel bag—already packed—in one hand. It kicks all the air right out of me.

"How long have you been planning this?" I whisper.

"It's not like that, Wick."

It *is* like that or she'd be able to meet my eyes.

"You'll like it there," Bren continues, her free hand going to her reddening neck. "Mr. Hart's program is specifically designed for teenagers dealing with loss. He can keep you safe—keep you out of trouble."

"I'm not *in* trouble."

Yet. The word hangs between us and Bren takes a deep breath. "Your therapist thinks it's for the best."

"We've been watching you together, Wick," Hart adds.

I flick my eyes to him, force myself to hold his gaze. The way Hart grins looks like a toothpaste ad, but I can hear the threat simmering underneath. He's daring me to challenge him.

What if I did?

What if I told Bren everything? I could tell her how it all started when Hart gave me the videos of my mother informing on my father, how the informing led to my mother's murder, how I found that murderer and made him pay.

I could tell Bren that I used to track down cheaters for money and that Detective Carson blackmailed me into working for him. I could tell her that my nightmares are so bad I'm afraid to sleep.

I could tell her I spent so much time being scared, I didn't know what it felt like to be safe until it was too late.

Hart steps closer. "We know how much you've been struggling. Your therapist thinks your PTSD stems from what happened with your foster father."

I stiffen. My foster father is better known as Bren's husband, or ex-husband, Todd. He raped a childhood friend of mine. It drove her to suicide; then he switched his attention to my sister.

And then to me.

I caught him before he could hurt anyone else, but the way I did it wasn't exactly legal and I attracted Detective Carson's notice. He threatened to tell Bren everything if I didn't work for him. I agreed. After the damage Todd's crimes did to Lily and Bren . . . well, how could I *not* have agreed? He was going to ruin what was supposed to be the rest of our lives.

I lift my chin a little higher. "Yeah, so?"

"Looking Glass," Hart says softly, "is a very special program. We can help you get back your control, your life. It's designed specifically for teens with your computer talents. You'll be safe there. I'm asking you to trust me—just for a little while."

I stay still.

"We really need to get going, Mrs. Callaway," Hart says, turning that full-watt smile on my adoptive mom. There's something plastic about him. It's the way his chestnut-colored hair doesn't move, how his shoes are shined. Hart's like a Ken doll come to life except for the bulge at the small of his back. Is that a pistol?

Hart's careful to always face Bren so she won't see it, but I do. What kind of counselor needs a gun? This isn't good, but if I tell Bren, what happens? Will he tell her everything he knows about me? That's worse.

"I want to get Wick settled before dinner," Hart says. "She'll need to meet the other teens, see the facilities—"

"What about Lily?" Saying my little sister's name conjures tears in my eyes and I force my chin higher. "How am I supposed to say good-bye?"

Bren focuses on her feet. "I'll tell her what happened."

She's really going to give me up. I blink; blink again because now my eyes are stinging. I know how this works. I've been through enough foster homes to understand how to leave. I knew this wouldn't last.

But I didn't know how much it would hurt. The pain is incandescent. I feel like I could walk around it, sling it across my shoulders, and carry it. Bren was supposed to be forever and I was stupid enough to believe her.

"Please, Bren. Please don't do this." The words shoot from me before I'm even aware I'm saying them. "Please don't send me away."

For the first time since Hart arrived, Bren looks at me. "It's for your own good, Wick. It's not just the . . . *acting out*." Her voice drops into a whisper and she edges closer. "It's not safe for you here."

My heart double thumps. "What are you talking about?"

Bren's eyes go past me and straight to *him*.

I step in front of Bren, block her from seeing Hart. "What aren't you telling me?"

"Show her." Hart again. He appears at my side, those shiny shoes quiet as cat feet on the carpet. "Be honest with her, Mrs. Callaway."

Bren does as she's told, but not before I see her wince. Was that "honest" dig supposed to hurt her? Because it did. I glare at Hart and Bren touches my arm.

"That boy you caught—the one who was trying to murder his father—he's dead." She passes me a police report. It's pages and pages of tiny font, but two words stand out: Jason Baines. He was a rising star in my father's drug ring and damn near killed me.

I shrug. "That's horrible, but it doesn't mean anything."

"Good point," Hart says. "I mean, people get shivved in jail all the time, right?"

I don't look at him. Can't. He put the slightest emphasis on "shivved" and now I know he knows about another shivving—one I helped make happen. I'm not ashamed I helped my father kill Joe Bender. I know what Joe did to my sister and what he was going to do to me when he was released from jail.

I am, however, scared for Bren to find this out.

"It isn't just Jason who's gone," Hart continues and there's the flutter of paper as he takes the report from Bren. "It's every single person who worked for your father. They're disappearing and—"

"Michael," I say.

Hart's brows twitch together. "I'm sorry?"

"*Michael*. I would prefer you call him Michael, not my father."

Hart nods. "Fine. This is just the beginning. They will come for you, Wick."

I flinch and Hart sees it. I hate that. Now he knows his words just climbed under my skin to simmer.

"'They'?" I roll my eyes. "Could you be any more vague?"

"Stop it." Bren thrusts herself between us and braces both hands on my shoulders. "I *know*, Wick. I know what you did to catch Todd was illegal and dangerous and—" Her voices catches and she has to swallow twice. "Mr. Hart says you've attracted some attention because of it. When your father went to jail, he left a vacuum. There are others who are going to take his place and they'll want you to help them do it. Mr. Hart says that's why Detective Carson kept coming around. He says you *will* be a target. He's very sure you're in danger."

That's because he's lying. I'm not a target. I'm not in danger. No one knows what I did for Michael. And I start to say so, but Bren cuts me off.

"I forgive you, Wick. I understand. When it came to Todd, it was my fault. I didn't protect you. You had to save yourself, but this time, I'm saving you."

"Bren, I—"

"Just *try*, okay?"

I nod. Honestly, when it comes to Bren, it's kind of automatic for me. I always agree because it's easier than telling her the truth. She can't even talk about the hacking I did to catch her husband, Todd, before he attacked another girl. And if she can't say any of that, what would the rest of the truth do to her? Once you learn something about someone, you can't unlearn it. And I'm not sure I want to find out what would happen. She's giving me an opportunity here. We can cover this up, pretend it never happened. I'm good at that.

"The point is," Hart says, rubbing one palm against his jaw, "you're prey now. You can't stay here. It's not safe for you and it's not safe for them."

My stomach lurches sideways. *Them.* Bren and Lily.

"If you come with me," Hart continues, "I'll make sure they're protected."

"So I go away forever?"

"No!" Bren tugs me closer, eyes glassy and bright. "Just for right now. Just until we decide what to do."

"Beyond the obvious benefits of keeping you alive, I'm offering you an opportunity." Hart takes the duffel bag from Bren and slings it onto his shoulder. "You have so much potential. Let us help you reach it."

Chills again. They crawl all over my body. Hart's acting like a friend, but he can't be. There's no way. Hart gave me the videos of my mom, said he wanted to see what I could do with "proper motivation."

Know what I did? In the course of six weeks, I brought down a pair of murderers, I discovered who my biological mother really was, and I saved my sister and myself.

I also helped kill someone.

Joe Bender was my father's right hand and my once-upon-a-time handler. He would've killed me, my sister, maybe even Bren, but I got to him first. I used Michael to take him down and Hart knows it.

Thing is . . . to blow Hart's cover, I'd have to destroy my own.

"Promise me you'll try, Wick." Bren's eyes are huge and shining. Her fingers link in mine, squeeze. "Please? Just do what Mr. Hart says and then come home to us."

I open my mouth . . . close it. Bottom line, everything started when Hart brought me those videos and now he's finishing it. If I go with him, I don't know what will be waiting for me and that's terrifying.

But telling Bren the truth? That's worse. Even if she didn't haul me straight to the police, she'd hate me. I'd trade the truth of what I did for my hope that she'll let me come home. If Bren doesn't know and I play Hart's game . . . maybe I could come back? Maybe we could be together again. I could be with my sister, my friends.

"I'll visit you soon," Bren whispers and tucks a strand of hair behind my ear. I have to fight not to lean into her. If I do, I'll fall apart. "I didn't keep you safe enough before. I'm making up for it now."

"It wasn't your fault—"

She leans close, touches her forehead to mine. "Letting him take you is going to kill me. That's how I know how lucky I am—because I'm losing so much right now."

"Mrs. Callaway?" Hart's trying for polite and failing.

His smile is gritted. "We really need to go."

Bren nods and follows us to the front door. She opens it, and briefly I'm blinded by sunshine. It's a beautiful day. The neighbors are out; one of them waves to Bren, but she doesn't notice.

Hart's hand goes to my shoulder. Like we're good buddies. Like this is fun and I can't feel the way his fingers tighten.

I swallow and my throat click-clicks. We're off the porch now. In the open. Panic flares in my chest. If I ran, could he catch me?

I slide him a sideways glance. Hart's considerably taller than I am. He looks fit too. If I ran, he *would* catch me.

And if he didn't catch me, where would I go?

My entire life is tied up in the computer in my bedroom—my viruses, my customers, my bank accounts. How freaking ironic. I've prepared and prepared for the day I'd have to disappear, and now?

My hands roll into fists.

"Promise me, Wick," Bren whispers.

"I prom—" Hart jerks me forward, steering me down the sidewalk. There's a town car waiting at the curb and beyond the town car . . . there's a dark gray Ford headed my way.

Milo. Panic makes me stumble. Our date. We were supposed to meet and now—oh, God. *Milo.*

His car coasts closer and the hum in my ears grinds into a roar. I want to scream for him to gun it. To run.

But then Hart will know there are others and he'll come for Milo too.

I force my eyes forward, focus on the house across the street, and one second . . . two seconds . . . Milo's car rolls into my line of vision. I watch him.

He pretends to watch the road.

Our eyes only meet once.

Once is enough. Milo drives on, dragging something from me as he passes. It limps behind his car and makes a left at the corner to follow him.

"Is everything okay, Wick?" Hart asks. He's watching me so closely. Did he see? Does he know? He isn't saying anything. What does that mean?

A driver in dark shades pops out of the car, takes my bag, and tosses it in the trunk.

"Nice ride," I say as Hart opens the rear door for me, our reflections stunted in the glass. "But I thought kidnappers preferred panel vans?"

Hart laughs. It's a buttery sound like something that belongs to talk show hosts and sitcom dads. "Smile, Wick. This is going to be fun."

It's all so spy-mystery novel, I feel like I should be blind-folded or something. But Hart doesn't move to touch me. He sits next to me, concentrating on his iPhone—scrolling through email from the looks of it and leaving me to watch the scenery pass.

Or rather, *pretend* to watch the scenery pass.

The only thing I can concentrate on now is Milo's face, that twitch in his expression when he realized I'd been caught.

And how we both knew we were over.

In some ways, there are advantages to dating someone like Milo: He knows this stuff as well as I do. We are the same and we know how this goes. The fact that he drove on should not hurt. It does not hurt. One of us was always bound to be caught.

But no matter how many times I repeat this, it still feels like I'm mumbling through a mouthful of glass.

I start to count road signs. We're heading north toward Atlanta, the driver weaving in and out of traffic. I can't see anything through the tinted glass partition, but I'd have to guess we're doing seventy—maybe eighty. Every time he switches lanes, my breath catches.

"Are we going to the airport?" I ask as the car hurtles toward the interstate turnoff.

Hart looks up. "No. We're going to midtown actually. We share a building with a few other companies."

"Is that where I'll be staying?"

"Precisely." Hart pockets his phone and tugs a set of manila folders from the briefcase between us. After flipping through the pages, he pauses, finger pressed against something I can't see.

"Tell me about Joe Bender," he says at last.

"He worked for Michael."

"And?"

"And he was shivved in jail." I stare through the window, watch putty-gray office buildings fly past. We're drawing farther and farther into the city. The streets are getting narrower, sidewalks clogged with men and women leaving work. Their eyes glide right past the town car. It's like we're invisible because we look like we belong. "I think Joe was waiting for a plea bargain or something."

"Did they ever find out who killed him?"

"No."

"Did you kill him?"

"No."

"Look at me. Wick? Look. At. Me."

I grit my teeth, turn to Hart. I'm careful to keep my face blank, but I can't stop my fingers from digging into the smooth leather seats. If he looks down, he'll see and he'll know.

"Let me ask it this way," Hart says. "Were you involved in killing him?"

"Of course not."

Hart twists to face me fully. "You lie beautifully." He turns the folder around and pushes it toward me. "Here. Look. This is what *we* think happened."

My stomach tilts. The entire folder is dedicated to me. There are pictures—Lily with me; Bren with me; my best friend, Lauren, with me—and reports. Someone had been watching, cataloging everything: my visit to Joe, Lily's attack by one of Joe's men, how I went to see Michael the next day.

That was sloppy of me, but I'd been too panicked to wait. One of Joe's grunts had jumped my sister on her way home from school. She was terrified and I knew Joe was getting out. He'd struck some deal with the Feds and once he was free . . . well, it didn't take much imagination to know what would happen next.

Yes, it was noted by the police that I visited both men. Yes, until then, I had never visited either of them. But without anyone knowing about Lily's attack, I was pretty safe. Lily covered for me, for *us*. And without anyone able to connect my visits . . . well, it was fairly easy to explain everything away.

Except apparently Hart's people *did* connect it. They figured out Lily was the hidden piece.

I close the folder, feel cold sweat roll beneath my clothes.

"Now," Hart says, leaning closer. "Tell me what really happened."

"Joe killed my mother. He knew she was informing on my dad—on *him*—so he dragged her to the top of an unsecured building, told her if she didn't jump he would kill my sister and me."

"And what did you do with that information?"

"I told Michael." It sounds so innocent when I say the words like that, but it's not. I did not put the knife in Joe's stomach, but by telling Michael, I might as well have.

"And you knew your dad would respond like that?" Hart asks.

"I had a hunch."

"Interesting. Do you think he loved her?"

I blink, try to fit my head around Hart's sudden detour. "Michael beat my mother. Badly. That's not love."

"Maybe for him it was. He could destroy her, but no one else could."

I sneak a sideways glance at Hart. Something ahead of us has caught his interest, and in this unguarded moment he looks different. Without the smile, Hart's face is hard, angular . . . watchful. His skin's pale and a little waxy like he doesn't see sunshine much. And as I watch, his right hand drifts backward, like he's thinking of going for his pocket . . . or his gun.

It stops, but he continues to watch the window. Whatever he's seen bothers him, but I can't tell what it is.

"Are we being followed?" I ask.

Hart considers me. "I want to lie and say no . . . but, somehow, I think that would be a very big mistake with you."

A tiny part of me likes Hart more for recognizing this. It would be a mistake because I could never trust him again. But I don't get the chance to tell him anything because just as I open my mouth, an SUV slams into us.

Our car fishtails to the left as the SUV plows into our right and keeps coming.

The force slings me to my side, the seat belt slicing into my ribs. I brace one hand against the seat and suck in a single breath before we're hit again.

Hart swears, scrounges for something on the floorboard. I don't know how he can even move. My seat belt is cutting into my neck, my stomach. I flatten one hand against the door and then the seat.

They hit us even harder this time.

My teeth jam together, crushing my tongue until I taste blood, and I still can't stop watching. I don't understand. This isn't a random accident. They're coming *after* us, almost pushing the town car sideways.

The SUV slows and our car straightens, accelerates. I

slump. Escaping. We're escaping.

Then the other driver guns it again. He rams us and I'm spinning above it all, watching my door buckle under the larger car's grill.

I twist, bracing both hands on either side of me as we're shoved under the shadow of an office building. Our car skids . . . skids . . . collides.

My head smashes against the cracked window. Pain. Colors burst behind my eyelids and I grab my head. Worse.

The air smells like gasoline and my mouth tastes like pennies. Hart moans. I force my eyes open. Blink. Can't focus. Blink again. Still can't see straight. Everything's smeary. Something's crunching.

Glass.

I shift, my surroundings snapping into focus. We've stopped and the SUV is reversing, bits of windshield spitting under its tires. The driver door opens and a guy in a black ski mask hops onto the pavement.

Walks straight toward me.

Panic hums in my ears and I scrabble at the seat belt, fingers numb. It clicks loose and I fall sideways. He yanks at my door. Won't open. He takes two steps back.

And then charges forward.

I shrink down as a huge boot kicks in the window, spraying me with glass. He uses one arm to knock the last bits away and then reaches into the car and grabs me. I shriek. He pulls me through the window.

My knees hit the pavement in a bright white pop of

pain. I kick both feet under me and slip. He hoists me up, half dragging me toward the SUV's passenger door. Through the window, I can see the silhouette of shoulders and a head. Someone else is in there.

Someone else is waiting for me.

I dig my Chucks into the pavement, hear something scraping behind us. Feet. Coming fast.

Hart hits both of us at a dead run. I land face-first, getting a mouthful of gravel, but even before I can spit out the bits, Hart's forearm is hooked around my waist. He flings me backward, pinning me behind him just as there's an unmistakable click in the air.

Pistol. Hart's pistol.

"You need to leave," Hart says. It's so quiet I don't think the ski mask guy could possibly hear it, but he must've. He retreats one step. Two. His eyes stay on me though. They never leave my face.

Because he's memorizing me?

Or because I should know him?

I scrape one hand across my lips and smell him on me. Cigarettes and the leather from his gloves. I gag.

Hart gestures toward the SUV with the now-cocked gun. "Go."

This time, the guy doesn't hesitate. He walks around the ruined front grill and jumps in the driver's seat. The SUV peels off and Hart turns to me, checking me so closely we're breathing the same damn air.

He put himself between us. He *shielded* me. This

isn't . . . it was never supposed to be . . . I swallow and taste bile.

Hart wipes a touch of blood from his face and grimaces at his reddened fingertips. He looks so much less plastic now, so much less together. If it weren't for the blood—and how that blood happened—it might be a much, much more approachable look for him.

We study each other in silence until Hart breaks first. "I warned you. Do you believe me now?"

Yes. Hot tears prick my eyes and I inhale hard, fighting them. "Who was that?"

"Hard to tell at this point. One of Michael's competitors? One of Michael's men? Someone else? All I really know is they're coming for you, Wick. Next time . . . they won't go so easy. There will be more."

"And that means you're going to save me? What if something like this happens to Bren? To *Lily*?"

"We'll stop them."

Our driver limps to my side, cell phone in one hand.

Hart ignores him. "We know what you did when you got those recordings of your mother," he tells me. "We know about Joe Bender and what you engineered." The statements should sound accusatory—at least hateful—but Hart's tone wobbles between guidance-counselor understanding and . . . just plain *proud*. "Do you regret what happened?"

What happened was I had Joe Bender killed. Why can't he just say it? Why can't I?

I did it to save my sister. Joe hurt her to get to me. The

murder should feel justified. It should be easy to confess.

I meet Hart's gaze. "I don't regret it."

"Good." There's a faraway whine of sirens and we both tense. Hart watches the closest side street, index finger tapping against his knee. "There are terrible people in this world, Wicket. They make nothing but misery. What if you could help that?"

My stomach sinks. "I'm not into playing God."

I've heard this line of reasoning before and it makes me nervous. The night Detective Carson escaped, he told me all about how he had wanted to make me a hero—that's why he blackmailed me into working for him. He thought he was making me Good by siccing me on people he thought were Evil. And the thing is . . . they *were* evil. He was right. But he was also deciding whose sins were the worst, who deserved punishment, and who deserved a pass.

"Don't think of it as playing God," Hart says, eyes still skittering over the side streets. Our driver returns to the ruined town car, holding his cell to one ear.

"Then what is it?"

He turns to me. "I'm proud of you. I'm proud of you for standing up. You did an ugly thing—the right thing is often ugly, and that's what makes it so hard for most people to recognize it."

We stare at each other. I want to tell Hart that's not really an answer to my question, but it doesn't matter anymore. Call it ugly. Call it the truth. Call it *whatever*. I'm getting less and less impressed with labels. The only time they matter is when you're figuring out the person who's using them.

"You can't tell anyone what a gift you gave to the world," Hart continues, watching me. "But I'm bringing you somewhere you *can* tell people—because we understand."

"I thought you were bringing me somewhere to keep me safe, not egg me on."

Hart's smile is thin, faint. Bitter. "Don't kid yourself, Wick. These people saw you. They *see* you. You are now known. You looked into the dark and it looked back. I know you know this."

I do.

"Why do you want me?" I ask.

"Looking Glass specializes in internet securities, virus removal—you're good at that, aren't you?"

Slowly, I nod.

"Please trust that I can help you," he says.

"No one ever says 'please' to me." Not entirely true. Griff does. Or he *did* once upon a time when we were together and I was pretending to be someone I'm not. I look at Hart and tell myself I don't care about how Griff is past tense, how Milo is probably long gone, and how my entire life as I knew it no longer exists.

Too bad I'm not that good a liar.

Hart sighs. "Yeah, I know. It hasn't been easy for you, but things can be different if you let us help you."

I hesitate. Hart seems so . . . sincere. I don't know what to do with that or the fact that I want to believe him. I pick gravel from my palms instead as the sirens grow closer.

"Boss?" The driver appears at the side of our car. He's holding his neck like it hurts and his eyes are wide. "Someone's reported the accident. They're maybe five minutes away."

"'They'?" I ask.

"The police," Hart says, and nods to the driver, who disappears around the front of the town car. "We have scanners in all the vehicles." He digs into his coat pocket, pulls out a packet of wet wipes, and hands them to me.

Guns and hand sanitizer? There's a joke about Boy Scouts and always being prepared somewhere in there, but my brain's too scrambled to connect it.

"I don't think I want to ask why you carry wet wipes around with you," I say.

"You're probably right, but unless you want a trip to the ER for that scratch on your head, I'd suggest you wipe off your face and take down your hair to cover that cut. We have doctors at the office. It's safer for you to be examined there."

It's not a bad point, but I still take the packet a bit reluctantly. Hart isn't what I thought. He's . . . I don't know. Probably best not to think about it. Besides, anything's better than being sticky so I spend a moment cleaning off my face and hands, barely noticing how the cuts sting.

"Ready?" Hart asks, straightening his clothes.

I nod, eyes pinned to another black town car approaching us. It pulls to the curb just as a police cruiser rounds the corner and heads straight for us. Another black-suited driver opens the door to the second town car. He leans against the frame, watching us and waiting.

"Don't say anything," Hart says as the police officer approaches. The car stops, lights still rolling. "Just let me handle it."

"Gladly," I say and hang behind. Hart and the driver talk to the officer, who in turn calls in another cop and a tow truck. There's a lot of gesturing: hands waving around, hands resting on belts, hands slapping shoulders . . . until one of the officers finally notices me. He nudges the first guy and they both wave me closer.

"Miss? Are you all right?"

"Yeah. Absolutely."

"Your father says it was a hit-and-run." The officer's eyes slide back and forth between us. Cataloging all the flaws in calling Hart my father? We look nothing alike, but I guess we could be related . . . if Hart knocked up my mom in his very early twenties. Still, the officer doesn't comment.

Because he really hasn't noticed?

Or because Hart lied so confidently it made everything feel like the truth?

"Is that true?" the officer asks.

Hart's gaze meets mine. His smile hasn't moved, but there's something in the way his shoulders have stiffened that reveals his worry. He doesn't think I'll go along with his story. He doesn't trust me even though he's asked me to trust him.

Trust me, he said. We're the good guys, he said.

I saved you, he didn't say, but it's still true.

At Bren's when Hart said he was one of the good guys, I'd wanted to laugh. This whole thing seems so impossible. There are no good guys, no such thing as heroes. I *know* this.

Then again, considering my previous track record of not recognizing a good thing when I had it . . . maybe . . . maybe?

"Miss?" the officer asks. "Was your father right? It was a hit-and-run?"

I look at the officers, lower my chin, and wobble my lower lip until I look like Tragedy Girl just trying to be brave.

"Absolutely," I say. "He's right. They came out of nowhere."

We leave our first driver to wait for the tow truck and take the second town car. The interior is exactly like the first, right down to the cup holders and the leathery smell.

"How many of these things do you have?" I ask, buckling the seat belt.

"Enough."

We pull away from the curb. Second Driver has a lighter foot than First Driver. I'm grateful. Between the smack to the head and getting yanked around, nausea is rolling up from my stomach.

"Shouldn't there have been more paperwork?" I ask, keeping my eyes on the police cruiser as we drive past.

"Don't worry. It's all taken care of."

I flick my attention to Hart, searching for anything

under his tone and finding . . . nothing. He's completely unconcerned.

"I appreciate what you did back there," Hart continues after checking the glass screen that divides us from the front seat. Once he's certain the driver can't hear us, he settles, adjusting and readjusting his jacket. "I'm glad to know you understand what we're up against."

"Honestly?" The word's awkward in my mouth, like it's made of only edges and corners. "I'm not sure that I do understand. Carson said that people would be looking for me and he'd been . . . protecting me or whatever."

"He was. It was a mistake of course. Detective Carson— with all due respect—didn't have the ability to protect you like we can." Hart pauses, staring into space and probably reflecting on the fact that Carson never got me rammed by an SUV.

"Do you know where Carson is?" he asks at last. "Where we could find him?"

"No."

"And you have no clues as to where he might be?"

I hesitate and I can't tell whether it's out of habit . . . or because I'm still not entirely on board with Hart. The safest thing to say here would be something along the lines of *I have no idea* and *No, Carson never said anything about where he might hide.*

It's also the truth.

But if they've been watching me, Hart might already know I went to Carson's house the night he disappeared two months ago. If it's a test . . . "I did see him—that last night, when they caught Ian Bay and his half brother. Carson was freaked. He kept saying people were after him."

Technically, Carson also said people were after *me*. Looks like he was right.

"He said something about the ATF finding explosives?" I screw up my face to look like a suitably confused teenage girl even though I'm not. I'm actually sort of, kind of at fault here, because around the same time Carson blackmailed me into working for him, I met Milo—a supergenius inventor who enjoys computers, spy equipment, explosives . . .

And me.

Sometimes it feels like we were made for each other. The whole thing started when I did Milo a favor and he repaid me by framing Carson as a terrorist. Which he wasn't, but when the ATF searched his storage unit they found evidence that Carson wasn't the honest, upright cop he was pretending to be, and just like that, I was free.

Or I was for a little while.

I don't bother elaborating even though I can tell Hart's waiting for it. There's no way they know about Milo.

And there's no way he's in danger because Milo's too careful. Not to mention, sniffing around his place is dangerous. Like can-get-you-blown-to-kingdom-come dangerous.

I rub both palms against my knees. "What do you want with Carson?"

"We have our reasons." Hart's gaze travels over my face,

my body, and snags on my hands. "Tell me about Griff."

The name is like a blow: fast, hard, and leaves me breathless. William Reed Griffin. Goes by Griff. Only.

Always.

I can't tell Hart how it was my fault. Carson was going to use him, ruin him actually. So I took Griff's place. I let Carson use me because I thought that would fix everything. It saved Griff, but it ruined our relationship. We haven't spoken in almost two months now—something I probably shouldn't be so acutely aware of since I've been dating Milo for almost as long.

"I don't have anything to say," I manage at last.

"Liar."

It should be an accusation, but Hart's smiling—almost laughing.

"There's lots to tell about Griffin," he continues and his smile is slippery, widening every time he says Griff's name. "I know there's more. You know there's more. We haven't been able to get a good read on him, but others could. Others *will*. As far as we can tell, the only time Griffin shows is when you're around. You disappear? He disappears. Makes me think you're the corrupting influence."

Probably.

Hart's gaze latches on my face. "Or that he wants to save you."

"It's not like that." *It's exactly like that.* I hold Hart's eyes and feel Griff's hands all over me, pulling me apart.

Putting me back together.

I wish I could forget that. Being with Milo helped.

"What do you want with Griff?"

"I want to know if he's like you—if he could use our help. Because I can help you, Wick. You just have to trust me. You have to be honest. Tell me about Griff. He's like you, isn't he?" Hart lifts his arm and I jerk—can't help it, hate myself for doing it, but I shrink—and Hart's laugh is a sudden sputter.

"Did you just flinch?" He puts his hand on the arm-rest as the town car accelerates into the far lane. We make a hard left turn onto a deserted side street. I've been so busy talking to Hart that I haven't paid any attention to where we are and now I'm truly lost. We're surrounded by nothing but concrete-and-glass office buildings. Everything looks the same.

"That father of yours," Hart says softly, so softly he could be talking to some frightened animal or threatening a gunman. "He really did a number on you, didn't he? I'm sorry I startled you. I'll have to remember that."

If he'd said that in Bren's peach-and-cream living room, it would have been a threat. Another dare. I would've retaliated. I would've lied. No point anymore though, right?

Even so, Hart's digging for a response. I just don't know what to give him. Play along? Agree? It's the truth. My father wasn't the only monster I've ever faced, but he's the only one who came for me in the light. I know this. Hart probably knows this. Why are things that are the truest so hard to say?

Our driver stops the town car at an underground garage entrance, and after a beat the gate lifts and we coast through a mostly empty parking deck, casting slanted shadows under the yellow lights.

"You look worried, Wick." The car stops, parks, but neither of us moves to get out. Hart tilts his head as he considers me. "Don't worry. You'll tell me all about Griffin eventually. One day soon, you'll trust me. Everyone does."

Maybe, but not at Griff's expense. Those are not my secrets to tell, and besides, this only proves that Griff was right: Once you make yourself useful to the wrong people, you're never free. I will gladly spend the rest of my life making sure that *never* happens to him.

There's a clanging to our right as a freight elevator descends into the parking deck. I watch through my window as it hits the pavement. The rusted doors grind open, revealing a five-foot-by-five-foot square of chrome and polished wood, security camera in the corner, and security keypad by the gate lock. I take a steadying breath, realizing I'm already trying to plan my escape route even though I know, if I go up, I'm not coming back down.

Hart opens his door. "Welcome to Looking Glass."

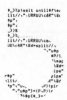

The freight elevator climbs and climbs and I count every floor. We're thirty stories up now and still rising, and even though I'm starting to sweat, I kind of wish I could see it. I've never been so high.

And we just keep going.

Hart's on his iPhone again, only putting it away when the elevator finally stops. There's a pause before the doors open, revealing a stark white foyer—shiny white floor and shiny white walls. It's like standing in a deserted Apple Store, and I can admit that my inner geek is . . . interested.

Hart motions to me. "After you."

It takes me a breath, but I push myself forward, walking off the elevator on spongy joints.

"Is that the new girl?"

I jerk, realizing there's someone to my right, and retreat

a step before reminding myself to hold my ground.

Hart steps off the elevator still tapping on his phone. "Oh, hey. Glad you're here."

"Where else would I be?" the girl asks without taking her dark eyes off me.

"Yeah . . . true." Hart stares at both of us, brows drawn together. "Alejandra, this is Wick. Wick, this is Alejandra—"

"Alex," she says.

"Alex," Hart agrees. "You two are going to be roommates."

Oh joy. Alex is a little taller, a little older, and staring me down like she's trying to decide exactly how she's going to kick my ass.

"I have a meeting that's just been scheduled." Hart squints at the iPhone's screen. "Do you think you could get Wick to the infirmary and then—"

Now Alex is backing up. "What's wrong with her?"

"Car accident. No big deal though, right, Wick?" Hart has that easy, plastic smile on again, and if I learn anything from being here, I want to learn that.

"No, no big deal," I say.

"Wick banged her head," Hart continues. "And got some cuts and bruises. Can you take her by the infirmary and then show her around, fill her in on how we do stuff? She needs to be with the boss in twenty minutes or so."

Alex buries both hands in the front pocket of her hoodie. "Fine."

Hart grins at me. "The driver'll bring your stuff up. I'll have it left in your room. See you around, okay?"

"Sure." The elevator doors close behind me and I try not to wince. Like Alex implied, it's not as if we're going anywhere. We watch Hart lope down the hallway, disappearing around a bend, and when I turn to Alex, she's already facing me.

"So what's your deal?" she asks, leaning closer.

"Deal?"

Alex's sigh is long and labored. "You're not one of *those* geeks, are you?"

"What does that mean?"

"The kind with personal-space issues and no social skills."

"No." *Well, not totally.* I cross both arms over my chest and glare at her, but it's a little hard to look tough since Alex has at least three inches on me.

"So you have issues?" she asks.

"Doesn't everyone?"

Alex's coffee-colored eyes narrow, but her mouth twitches like she might be amused. "C'mon."

I spend maybe ten minutes with the infirmary doctor, getting cleaned up and checked over before being told to "run along." It's every bit as condescending as it sounds.

"Charming, isn't she?" Alex asks after I get shoved back into the hallway.

I dry swallow two of the pain pills I was given and nod.

"I don't even know her name."

"No point. We cycle through doctors pretty quickly. The other guys are . . . challenging to work with?" Alex grins. "Yeah, let's go with that. Hurry it up or we're going to be late."

She pivots and stalks off like a supermodel on the runway, leaving me to trail along after her, my Chucks slapping against the shiny marble tile. The surrounding downtown buildings are close, but late-afternoon sunlight still slants through the windows, making Looking Glass's white walls and floors almost blinding. The hallway's lined with enormous abstract paintings. The blues and greens make my chest ache and we're almost to the windows before I realize why: They're the same shade of blue and green that always stained Griff's hands.

He drew in ink, but he wanted to work with oil paints.

"Hey." Alex snaps her fingers and I jerk my attention to her, cheeks going hot. "Stop gawking. We're on the fortieth floor. You'll be assigned a key card for access to this floor and the one above it."

"What's upstairs?"

"The cubicle ghetto mostly—computer stations and stuff." The corridor splits and Alex nods her head to the right. "Kitchen's down there. Technically, we're all supposed to help with meals, but after Kent spiked everyone's food with laxatives last year, Hart hired Mrs. Bascombe to take care of it."

My feet stall and I have to push myself to keep pace.

"Last year? How long have you been here?"

"Thirteen months, eighteen days."

"Where were you before?"

Alex tugs one hand through her ponytail, dark curls tangling in her fingers. "Around. I did contract work. Anyway, bedrooms, bathrooms, and common areas are on this floor."

We make another turn, hit another hallway. It's the same deal. Lots of glass. Lots of light. Cameras everywhere. I sneak peeks as we pass. Interesting. They're fixed, meaning they don't pan like other cameras do. It's just one continuous image.

Which can make them easier to trick.

Alex slides me a sideways look. "What are you? A senior in high school?"

"Junior."

"Ugh. I hated junior year. Anyway, it's basically glorified homeschooling around here. We check in with our teachers, get assignments, return the assignments, get a grade."

"Are they any good? The teachers, I mean."

"If you're smart enough to be here, it shouldn't matter." Alex pauses, and when she continues, she's trying to sound nicer. "I know it's a lot. You'll have course work plus the client stuff they'll assign you, but what else are we going to do, you know?"

We make another turn and return to the foyer. Basically, the entire layout is one big hamster-on-a-wheel circle and Alex's point couldn't have been made better. My entire life has been reduced to, maybe, eight thousand square feet. It's definitely not a prison, but . . .

"That's pretty much it." Alex faces me, hands still deep in her hoodie's pocket, and I notice again how old her eyes seem. They're beaten down. Tired. That doesn't happen naturally. No one starts life looking like that. Things have to happen. People have to do things to you.

I know. I see it every time I look in the mirror. Seeing it in her though? It's a sickening jolt. She's like me.

"You want to meet the others?" Alex doesn't wait for me to answer before swiping her key card through the elevator's security pad. The doors open and I follow Alex inside. We go up one floor, get off. No foyer this time, but the walls are still bright white and the abstract paintings are still enormous.

"Come on," Alex says and turns to the left. We go, maybe, twenty steps before the space spills wide, revealing a white marble-and-glass waiting area. Two long, red couches frame another set of brightly polished elevator doors. The whole place smells ever so faintly of oranges.

"We use the service elevator," Alex says. "When clients come to visit, they use this one. It goes to the ground floor rather than the parking deck. And before you ask, no, your key card won't work on it."

I nod, slowly turning. Glass walls stretch to our right and left, revealing open work spaces with wide banks of windows beyond them. It looks like a trendy office with computer stations pushed together in clumps and a long conference table next to them. Forty or fifty people could work here and yet there are only three guys on the entire floor.

Alex pushes through a set of glass doors and they all look up, look at me. "Boys, this is Wick." Alex turns her hand toward me and gestures toward the group. "Wick, these are the boys."

The two skinny ones wave at me. With their candy-colored graphic tees, they look like nerdy bookends.

"I'm Jake," says the left one.

"I'm Connor," says the right one.

"Nice to meet you."

"And I'm Kent." The last guy pushes away from his desk to study me, both hands folded on his Buddha belly. Kent's big—like linebacker big—and has caterpillar eyebrows. Every time he blinks, they shiver. "I'm sure you already know of me. Online, I'm Sever."

He pauses, waiting for that little revelation to sink in. Wow. Yeah, I definitely know him—know *of* him, I should say. The guy's a legend.

"I'm also hungry," Kent adds. "And I want you to make me a sandwich. That's how it works around here."

I shrug. "Not anymore."

There's a small cough to my left, and when I look at Alex, she's grinning. "Well, this is going to be fun," she says. "We work here most days. Kent's group leader."

"Which means you have to do what I say," he adds.

"And what a joy it is too," Alex says as I look around. It's a great space—bright and airy—but sparse too. There're only the boys, the computer stations, and . . . huh, no security cameras in the work areas. I check each corner of the room, eyes lingering even on the air ducts, and there's nothing.

"Looking Glass does a lot of consulting work," Alex says, a little louder than necessary, and when our eyes meet, I can tell she knows I noticed the lack of cameras. "Online securities mostly. It's how they test what you can do and how you'll build your résumé. Looking Glass benefits from our expertise and we benefit from their customer contacts."

"*If* she's good enough to stay," Kent says, taking a step toward me. I have to fight myself to hold still. The guy wears his weight like a weapon. "And don't think of trying anything on my network. I track everything. You sneeze, I'll know it."

"Good to know," I say.

"So what kind of geek are you?" Connor edges closer. His brown hair needs a cut and he's wearing too much Axe body spray. It makes my eyes water. "Obviously computers are your thing, but what's your specialty?"

I hesitate. "Viruses . . . infiltration . . . that sort of thing."

"Oh. They probably brought you in for that new account, the one with the virus problem."

Alex shakes her head. "Yeah, no time for that. She has to meet the boss."

Everyone nods, like this is the most normal thing in the world, and shuffles to his station. I look at Alex and she gives me a *well?* expression. "Any questions?"

"Not really."

"Good. This way." We go through the doors again and, this time, follow the glass wall around until we reach a rear hallway. We're facing yet another office building, and almost directly across from us, a lone guy stands, one hand at his ear, staring out.

Staring at us?

I slow. "Alex?"

"Yeah?"

"Can people . . . see us?"

She follows my gaze out the window and makes a dismissive noise. "No. Our glass is mirrored. Don't worry about it. He's probably just wishing he could jump. C'mon."

"Wait a second. *Look.*"

Begrudgingly, Alex looks and we both watch the guy adjust a small light with his other hand.

"Is that . . . a laser microphone?" I ask. "Is he trying to listen to us?"

"Probably. The buildings are really close, and our client list is epic. He could be a competitor. We sweep for bugs all the time though. It's not going to get him anywhere." Alex grabs my arm and tugs me along. "Don't worry about him. Worry about being late to the boss."

We turn at the corner and Alex knocks on the first door, opening it even though I never heard a response from inside. I trail after her, stepping into a low-lit office. After the brightness of the hallway, it takes my eyes a beat to adjust, and when they do, I stop dead.

The "boss" I'm supposed to meet? My therapist, Dr. Norcut.

Neither of us moves until Alex leaves and we're alone. When the door clicks shut, Norcut smiles. "Surprised?"

Surprised . . . speechless . . . *pissed*.

"Hart said you were a bit rattled after the accident," Norcut continues. "He thought we should wait to chat. I disagreed." Heavy curtains are drawn across the office's windows, dipping everything in shadows. Norcut moves to my right, and briefly her voice sounds like it's slithering from the dark. "I'm so glad you decided to join the program."

I heave myself forward, blood thumping in my temples. "I'm not really sure I had a choice."

"True." She shifts again, coming around the side of the desk so we're face-to-face. Norcut's blond hair is brighter in the shadows. It makes her look illuminated. "Will you sit down? Please? Like you said, it isn't as if you have much choice."

Stiff-legged, I take the farthest-away armchair as Norcut goes to the first set of curtains, pulling them back to reveal an impossibly blue sky marbled with clouds.

"Our program is . . . unique." She takes the chair next to me and turns sideways so we can face each other. "What did you think of the others?"

Kent immediately springs to mind and I have to squash my gag reflex. "They seem okay."

"They're quite brilliant. We found Connor and Jake last year. They enjoy cracking government encryptions and got a little . . . *careless*, shall we say? Kent is a former child prodigy. He specializes in malware. I'm assuming you see the connection?"

Of course, they're all hackers. They're all just like me.

"What about Alex?" I ask.

Norcut lifts one shoulder. "Basically, she's a thief—corporate espionage mostly. Alex needed help. We were happy to assist. Looking Glass is always *looking*"—Norcut smiles, amused by her own joke—"for talent. Our clients are Fortune 500 companies, major hospital networks, and a few select individuals who demand the very best in database controls, web securities, and antivirus applications. We stay ahead of our competition by hiring people who aren't just *on* the cutting edge. They *are* the cutting edge, and sometimes that gets them into trouble. Luckily, we're around to get them out."

"How did you find me? I'm not in trouble."

The smile slides into a full-fledged grin. "Your last job attracted quite a bit of interest. There's so much chatter on the networks now. And then there's the matter of every person connected with your father turning up dead. You're in danger. Your *family* is now in danger."

As if I needed the reminder. Thing is, I took my last job to keep my family safe. If I hadn't accepted Carson's offer, he would've blown my secrets and Bren's into the open. My adoptive mom had barely survived her husband, who was a pedophile *and* a rapist. Was I really supposed to let the detective reveal she might have bribed a corrupt judge to push through our adoption papers? That her company was failing? That she was crumbling?

And worst of all, that her older adopted daughter was breaking the law right under her nose.

I place both hands on the chair's armrests. "When do I get to talk to Bren again? I didn't get to say good-bye to Lily. I want to call them."

Norcut nods. "Totally understandable, but we think you need a little time before reconnecting with your family."

Heat creeps along my neck. "'We'?"

"Your mother and I. Bren will not take your phone calls until everyone's safe and you're doing better."

"And you'll be the one to judge 'better,' I guess?"

"I wish you wouldn't see it quite like that, but yes." Norcut crosses her legs and smoothes her skirt. "No one besides staff is allowed outside contact. No cell phones, no online chatting with friends, no distractions. Honestly, Wicket, you have a great deal more to worry about right now than keeping up with Lily's homework and Lauren's cheerleading schedule."

I grit my teeth and concentrate on the office. Aside from the massive mahogany desk, there's not much else to the room. In her other office, Norcut had couches, plants. I once spent two months pouring coffee into her orchids. If we're going to continue this freaking joke, it's kind of a shame I won't be able to keep up the tradition.

Norcut leans forward. "I want to help you reach your potential. This is what we do. Your education will continue—both in academics and computer science. I won't lie to you. It will be vigorous, but we wouldn't have extended the offer to your mother if we didn't think you were fully capable."

"How do I know this is the real deal?" I ask. "You played me before, remember? You were supposed to be the therapist and I was supposed to be the patient?"

"Is it really so hard to believe? Young hackers are in the news all the time. They have to go somewhere when they're picked up. Sometimes it's here. Sometimes it's not. I know we're not starting on the right foot here, Wick, so I'd like to offer you a bit of truth to make things right. I knew who you were—or should I say *what* you were?—the moment you walked into my office a year ago."

We stare at each other. I shouldn't ask. I shouldn't ask.

I shouldn't—"Oh yeah? How's that?"

"Because I worked with your father."

I swallow, swallow again. "Where?"

"Here. It was a few months before your mother's suicide. He was one of our first employees and probably our greatest failure. You have so much more to offer, Wick. It's just a matter of giving you the opportunities . . . and the right guidance."

"What happens after that?"

"It's different for everyone, but ideally, you take a position with one of our clients. Looking Glass is a full-service technology firm. We do everything from product testing to denial-of-service attacks. In exchange for your expertise, you will build a formidable résumé by working with some of the best in the business—a résumé we are always happy to pass on to our clients when you're ready to take a full-time position."

Norcut tilts back, considering me. "It's perfectly understandable for you to still be suspicious. But do you really think Bren would have sent you anywhere that's less than superb? This is *Bren* we're discussing." Her lips twist in a little half smile, a wordless joke shared between two people who know Bren keeps Norcut on speed-dial "just in case."

"I know you want to go home, Wick, but what's waiting for you there? Is that really your future?"

"I love them. I want to be with my mom and sister."

A muscle in Norcut's cheek spasms. She caught how I

called Bren my mom. No matter how smoothly I say it, the word sticks on my tongue. Not surprising. When your biological mother is murdered and your adoptive mother is afraid of you, "mom" is a complicated thing.

"You know, Wick, Bren says you're prone to shaking, panic attacks, and have severe intimacy issues." Norcut pauses, waiting for me to agree, and when I don't, she soldiers on. "I don't think you have any of those issues. You suffer from them, but not like other people suffer from them. Your anxiety is supposed to stem from stress, but you're under stress now, Wick, and look at you. You're not rattled at all."

My sweaty palms beg to differ. I keep my hands clasped tight between my knees to stop them from shaking, but it's funny because now . . . suddenly . . . I realize they're not shaking at all. Have I used up all my fear?

Did I leave it in the woods with Ian Bay when he tried to kill me? Or was it later, when Carson said "they" were coming for me? Or was it when Hart arrived?

I push myself a little straighter as something that might be dread wraps around my bones. Only, is it dread? Because it feels like truth.

Norcut and I have never talked like this before, but there's something so true, so honest . . . so *right* about what she's saying that, for an instant, it's lightning in the dark. I see a flash of myself, who I really am now, and I'm not sure I recognize her.

"You weren't scarred by chasing down Todd." Norcut tilts her head and a tendril of blond hair loosens from her slicked-down bun, brushes against the side of her neck. It makes her look soft. "I seriously doubt you're *that* damaged from what you did. You're broken, yes. But it's nothing that can't be healed."

I swallow. "Not 'scarred'? The night terrors kind of paint a different picture."

"Wick." Norcut leans forward and I get a whiff of perfume—roses and musk. It clogs my nose like it's going to burrow into my brain. "Out there, no one understands you. They think you're dangerous because computers and coding and viruses are magic they don't understand, but you do. That doesn't make you dangerous. That makes you special. Aren't you tired of feeling like you don't belong?"

I take so long to answer, Norcut should accuse me of stonewalling her. After all, that's happened before. I was never her favorite client, and honestly, the feeling was pretty mutual, but this . . . we've never ever talked about anything like this before.

Maybe we should have. I would have liked her more.

"What are you offering me?" I ask, careful not to lean forward too, because I can feel how much I want the answer she's going to give me and it scares me.

"I'm offering you the chance to fit in, to finally be safe. But most of all, I'm offering you the opportunity to belong to something. Isn't that what you've always wanted? For once, Wicket, be honest. What would happen if you were on the inside instead of always sitting on the outside and wishing it were different?"

My smile is lopsided. "And Looking Glass can provide all that? Impressive."

I sound like me and . . . not like me. Inside I'm struggling to hold up and Norcut smiles like she hears the wavering too.

It makes her tilt closer. "Forget the degree. Forget the job. Forget the safety we provide. I want you to think about the *real* opportunity I'm giving you. You'll be with your own kind of people. Haven't you always wanted to belong?"

I know my answer already and it isn't for Bren—even though I want to go home and I want to make her proud. And it isn't for Lily—even though I know she would want me to stay here until I'm safe. It's for me. I look at her and say, "Yes."

Norcut smiles. "Then let me show you how."

I leave Norcut's office with my own key card and a rough schedule for the next two weeks. I'll have work, work, more work—oh, and school. The class work binder is filled with color-coded handouts and homework, most of it picking up right where I left off at home. Norcut and Bren must've coordinated with my teachers.

In the meantime, I'm supposed to take over some of Alex's accounts until they see what I can do. I agreed, but it's a weird feeling. I've spent so much time hiding what I can do; I have no idea how to show it to someone.

I shut the office door behind me and lean against the frame, turning the key card around and around in my hand. There's a scuffing noise to my left and I jump. Alex. The Thief with Skills. Her hands are jammed in her hoodie again, but her eyes are watchful. Expectant.

"Well?" she prompts.

I don't have any idea what to say. I shrug. "It's not like I have a choice. If I want to go home—"

"You always have a choice."

I pass Alex and stop, realizing that even though I know I need to go down one floor to get to my room, I have no idea *which* room is actually mine.

Alex comes closer. We're practically toe to toe now, staring at each other. "She thinks I belong here," I say at last.

"Maybe you do. It wouldn't be the worst thing, would it? To be able to do what you love?"

I start to say something about how I don't love hacking. It wasn't born out of love. I didn't learn it out of love. It was survival. But that's not really the point anymore, is it? Somewhere along the line, what I did for my dad and Joe became part of me. And now I have to do something with it.

I'm just not sure what that means.

"You want to see our room?" Alex asks.

"Yeah." I rub my eyes. There's a dull, unrelenting thump behind them, just enough to make me grouchy. Well, grouchier. "That would be great."

We shuffle along in silence until we reach the elevator bank. The security cameras catch my attention again. I bump my chin toward the nearest one. "So the security camera thing . . . ?"

"Is to keep us safe." Alex swipes her card and watches the lights above the elevator doors. "They're on both floors and in all the common areas. Nothing near the work stations though and nothing in our rooms, of course."

Of course. It still seems weird. Paranoid.

Then again, if I stuffed my office full of people like me, I'd be paranoid too.

"So the elevator can only be accessed by key cards?" I ask. The doors ding open and we step inside. Alex presses the down button.

"Yeah, but key cards can be stolen. Ask me how I know." She turns to me, an enormous grin slung across her face. "No, really, ask me."

Now I'm grinning. Norcut made the whole situation seem kind of life-and-death, but Alex makes it sound like fun. We bump to a stop and the doors reopen. Alex points to the left and we trail down the hallway.

The sun's shifted in the sky, throwing light across the polished floor and along the walls. Funny how the white seemed so stark before. There's something awfully clean about it now.

"This is us," Alex says, stopping at a frosted glass door. There's a security pad here too. She swipes and the light on the box turns green, buzzing us in. "I know what you're thinking—it seems excessive—but seriously, would you *want* Kent going through our stuff?"

"God, no."

"Exactly. Also? I went through your stuff."

I stare at her.

Alex shrugs. If she's trying for sorry, she's missing it

by a mile. "I think it's important for us to be honest with each other."

"I honestly want you to stay out of my things."

She grins. "Fair enough. Also? I don't sleep in the dark. Not anymore. You cool with that?"

"Extremely."

"Awesome." Alex jumps onto the closest bed, kicking both legs in front of her and watching me. My bag is at the foot of the other bed. It's time to start unpacking, but I can't stop looking at the door. If they can lock us outside, they can also lock us inside.

"I know what you're thinking and it's not like that. I've been here over a year. I know." Alex props a pillow behind her and opens a *Wired* magazine. "Face it, Wick. You're with your people now. You can be who you really are here. It's going to be the best thing that ever happened to you."

The old Wick would've had a field day with that one, but I'm . . . trying. The whole thing does sort of, kind of feel like the best thing ever. But my brain keeps snagging on how the entire place seems too good to be true. If we're all one big happy family, what's with the security? Why are they watching us? Why can't we come and go as we please? I understand I'm in danger, but what about the others?

I pick at my lower lip. "Yeah, see the thing is . . . the bad stuff can't get in, but how do we get out?"

"We don't." Alex returns to her magazine and flips a page.

"How can you be okay with that?"

"Because I know what's on the other side of those walls."

I swallow around the sudden knot in my throat as Alex flips another page. She's trying to look busy and totally failing. Her eyes never move. She's not reading. She's stalling.

"And if I had to guess, you do too."

I open my mouth, close it. Alex is staring hard at her magazine, pretending the conversation's done. Maybe it is. In the end, does it matter? I told Norcut I'd play. I promised Bren I'd try.

"Don't you owe it to the people who love you to stay safe?" Alex's eyes still aren't moving, but she flips another page. "If I had anyone left, I'd stay put for their sake. Now, I stay put for mine."

I nod, turning my attention to unpacking. Bren has stuffed my bag with practically everything I own. On the one hand, it makes me smile because that's so her. She prepares for everything. On the other, it makes my stomach squeeze tight. I'm not going home anytime soon. I'm not here because I won the sleepaway-camp lottery. I'm here because I'm supposed to be improving myself. I'm here because I'm being hunted—and yet those aren't the only things filling my brain. It's all the other stuff: how I won't get to wake up to one of Bren's early conference calls blaring down the hallway. How I won't see Lauren at school or Lily at breakfast.

How I've never been away from my sister for longer than a week and now I don't know when I'll see her again.

I unfold two pairs of jeans and stare at them. It would

sound so trivial to say how much I miss them already and yet it's thumping in my head. There are things you lose that you will never get back, and right now I feel like they're all standing in front of me.

"It gets better, you know," Alex says. "Eventually, everything does."

We look at each other, the silence stretching between us. "How long did it take for you?" I ask at last.

"About two minutes. I never had what you do." She considers me, eyes so dark there's no transition from pupil to iris. They're just smudges of black. "So what's with the Kool-Aid packets?"

Kool-Aid? I glance down, realize Bren packed all my jeans, all my sweatshirts, enough underwear to open a store . . . and single-serve packets of Kool-Aid—cherry, grape, lime, even blue raspberry.

I clear my throat and it catches. "I used to dye my hair. These were all the colors I used to use."

"Oh." Alex's gaze lifts to the blond knot at the top of my head. "I thought parents hated it when their kids dyed their hair."

"She did." I put the packets on the table next to my bed, arranging them so the cherry flavor is on top. "She *does*. Bren likes my hair natural."

"I'll bet. You look like a poster child for the Aryan Nations. So why'd she send them?"

"No idea." A lie. I do. Or, at least, I think I do. The Kool-Aid packets feel like an apology, like an attempt to make things up to me. It's nowhere near enough, but still . . . she tried.

Alex snaps her magazine shut. "Security was increased before you arrived."

"Yeah?"

"Yeah. So who's hunting you?"

"I don't know." And there's something about Alex's question that stops me short. "And you? Are you being hunted or whatever too?"

"Pretty much."

"What'd you do?"

"Got sloppy. Almost got caught. Hart saved me." Alex smiles like it's funny, but we both catch how practiced she sounds. It makes chills push across my skin. This place is not what they say it is and yet . . .

My eyes snag on the Kool-Aid packets again. You can be who you really are here and I think I'm going to be a red-head again.

"Can we use the kitchen?" I ask.

"Duh." Alex sits up, eyes slitted. "Wait. Where are you going?"

I snag two towels from the bathroom and wiggle a Kool-Aid packet at her. "I'm going to dye my hair."

Because the boys are finishing some project, Alex and I eat breakfast alone the next morning. Mrs. Bascombe—a soft-spoken woman from South Africa who takes off as soon as we come in—has left us oatmeal, pancakes, and enough coffee to keep me going for days.

Which is probably just as well because the study guides for my upcoming classes are already waiting for me and they're crazy thick.

I heft the history guide onto the table next to my oatmeal. "I thought online studying was supposed to reduce paper waste."

Alex shrugs. "Wait until you see the homework assignments. If you're even a couple hours late, they email Norcut."

I groan and reach for the coffee, pour one for Alex and one for me. She dumps a metric ton of creamer into hers and downs half of it in a few swallows. I can't really blame her. I don't think either of us slept last night. From two a.m. to dawn, her breathing was as shallow as mine.

"Is it always this quiet?" I ask, and pop two of my pain pills.

"Nah. Most of the time it's noisy as hell, but no one's a huge fan of breakfast around here. We keep late hours."

Suits me. I pick at my oatmeal while Alex chugs more coffee and stares at the street below. I should say "tries to stare." The clouds curled closer during the night. I doubt she can see a thing, but it doesn't seem to stop her from trying.

"You ready?" Alex asks at last.

"Sure."

We go climb one floor and push through the glass doors just like we did yesterday, and just like yesterday, the boys are already there, leaning against their desks in a way that's probably supposed to look nonchalant, but fails miserably. Connor's eyes are too bright when we walk in. Something's up.

"She's kind of hot," Connor says, leaning down to study Kent's screen. I can't tell what they're looking at, but a few steps later, I see the video. Porn. Lovely.

"Looks like a girl I knew freshman year of college," Jake says. "She used to shake her can of pepper spray every time we passed."

"You went to college?" Kent tilts his chair from side to side. "That's so lame."

"Seriously?" Alex waves Jake and Connor to the side

and thumps Kent's chair. "*That's* what you're objecting to?"

The guys turn to glare at her and notice me. Kent studies my hair for a long moment, sucking on his lower lip. "What's with the hair?" he asks finally. "You think it makes you look like a superhero?"

"I dunno. Do those mirrors help you groom your Muppet eyebrows?" I motion to Kent's desk, where he has two mirrors on either side of his cubicle walls. Most people like to personalize their cubes. I mean, Connor and Jake have the typical crap lying around—action figures, candy wrappers, Mountain Dew cans—but Kent's cube is immaculate, just a sweating, plastic Big Gulp by the keyboard and the two mirrors hanging on either side of his monitors.

Odds are, they're for seeing whoever's walking around behind him, but judging from how many times he checks himself in the glass, Kent enjoys his reflection. He likes to watch himself work.

"Shut it, you guys," Alex says. "She has to do her skill assessment test this morning."

Kent snorts. "So?"

"So she doesn't need your crap too."

Kent takes his time looking me up and down. "If she can't cut it, we need to know."

The glass doors scrape open behind us and Kent minimizes his screen, replacing the window with an administrator dashboard instead.

"Gentlemen, ladies." Norcut passes Connor a tablet. "Your calculus teacher emailed me. He says your last homework assignment is late. I hope you have a very good reason."

Connor goes bright red and scurries to his computer station. Norcut turns to us. "You know what you're supposed to be doing, so let's get to it." She looks at me, looks at my hair, then points to the setup on my right. "We're going to put you here for now."

I nod and drop into the chair, scoping the system. It's way nice.

"This is a timed test," Norcut says, pulling another chair close. She sits and passes me a sheet of paper with a printed web address. "Log on to this laptop, and once you're in, use the laptop to scan for all wireless devices within the area."

Norcut leans closer and points to a twelve-digit alphanumeric serial number below the address. "When you find this device, tell me."

I take the paper and turn to my computer. "Then what?"

"Then you will turn it off and on at my command. Can you do that?"

Yeah . . . but *why*? What's the point? I want to ask. I bite my tongue instead. Then bite it harder.

They have to see what I can do, and I agreed to be honest. To do my best. To *try*.

To not ask questions.

Okay, maybe not so much the last one, but questions draw everything to the surface. They make you look like you aren't a team player and Looking Glass is all about the team and I'm all about graduating so—"Sure," I say. "I can do that."

Then I grin like I'm Susie Freaking Sunshine and get to work. The web address takes me to a password log-in page. Considering this is a timed test, I have to assume this computer has the same VNC password as the laptop and punch in "command: vncserver:1" followed by "vncpasswd" into the Linux box.

Wait for it . . . wait for—I'm in.

There are about three dozen devices within range of the remote laptop, and after a bit of hunting, I find one device that matches the serial number Norcut gave me. I hijack it and start running commands, looking for vulnerabilities in the device.

"Are you in?" Norcut asks.

I nod and she stands, takes a cell from her blazer's pocket, and punches in a number. She waits, eyes on me. "Are you ready?"

"One second." Something's a little weird here. Well, not weird. *Old*. There's an open port within the remote authentication, and immediately I start fuzzing—basically throwing variable inputs at the device until I can exploit a weakness. And it's that weakness that catches my attention. Whatever I'm accessing isn't properly secured. It's not a phone, tablet, or even a laptop because those would be better updated. This is something different.

"We're at the two-minute mark, Wick."

"I—" I've got it. There. There's an easily exploitable

heap overflow. Now I just need a quick script.

I start typing code from memory, praying I get it right. If I do, the exploit will run as a privileged service, giving me total control of the device.

"Wick?"

"Yeah . . . yeah, I'm ready." I fold both hands in my lap and take a deep breath, looking at Norcut.

"Do you have confirmation?" she asks into her phone. There's a pause, then Norcut nods to me. "Turn it off, Wick."

I blink, sudden nerves drying up my breath. Is there some other Looking Glass employee standing by the other computer? Is this how they're checking my work?

"It's okay, Wick." Norcut sounds softer than I have ever heard her. "Just turn it off."

I do. Nothing happens. I mean, on our end, nothing happens. On their end, obviously, everything's just ground to a total halt.

Seconds later, Norcut asks me to turn it back on, and I type the command prompts, nodding at her when I'm finished.

Norcut's eyes go a little blank as she listens to whoever's on the other end of her phone, then she looks at me. "Off."

It's easier the second time. The pause stretches much longer though. The boys are supposed to be working on their own thing, but I know Kent's watching us. I keep seeing his eyes following Norcut in those damn mirrors.

"On," Norcut says.

I do, and when I'm finished, I sneak a glance at Alex.

She grins and I give her a lopsided smile. I am trying. I am trying. I am trying.

Across from us, Norcut paces the length of the room, waiting, listening. The entire room is overstuffed with breathing and silence.

She stops. "Off."

We repeat the cycle four more times. Each time, the pause is longer, and each time, I get faster. Start. Stop. Start. Stop. Whoever's on the other end is getting a good idea of what I can do.

What I *will* do. Playing along is getting easier. At some point, Hart comes in. He leans against an empty desk, watching me, watching Norcut. Every time our gazes meet, his mouth twitches like we're in on the same joke.

"We're finished." Norcut eyes the phone, putting it in her pocket. "Good job. That was nicely done."

"She still took four minutes longer than I did." Kent thumps a fist against the top of his desk. "I still hold the record."

"Indeed you do," Norcut says, attention still on me.

"So did I pass or whatever?" I ask.

"Of course. Did you doubt you would? The test is only a formality, Wick. We know you belong."

Kent makes a disgusted noise like he disagrees. "I'm ready for you to look at this," he says to Norcut. She walks to Kent's side, stands next to his workstation to view his computer screen.

I'm glad for the space. I can't settle. There's something

really wonderful about being able to do this in the *open* and yet I can't make my smiles genuine. I can't bring myself to really laugh. It's like suspicion has tunneled through me—so deeply and for so long—that there's nothing left but hollows.

"Alex," Hart says. "Do you think you could show Wick those accounts you were working on?"

Alex gets up from her workstation and joins me at mine. Hart studies both of us as she walks me through the network, showing me the files I'll need.

"These are a few of our newer clients," Hart says. "I'd like you to take a closer look—"

"Mr. Hart?" Norcut lifts one slim hand, motioning to him. "Can you come here?"

"One second," he says to us and joins the huddle at Kent's computer.

"Alex." I nudge my knee against hers. "What did I just do?"

Her face scrunches. "Um, shouldn't you know this? You interrupted a wireless computer."

"But *why*?"

"Why not?"

I pause, trying to force my head around her answer. "That's not enough."

Alex shrugs. "Sometimes it is. Are you okay?"

I start to say yes. "No."

"You need to be okay, Wick." Alex flicks my knee, and for the first time I realize I was bouncing it. I press myself still. "You need to *look* okay with this."

Our eyes meet and a sickening pang reaches all the way to my toes. "You don't believe. You think there's something off here too."

Alex pauses. "I don't *not* believe. I've seen people graduate. I know they go on." Her voice drops to a whisper. "I know they go on and we can too. Hart and Norcut found us because we're special, and if we play by the rules, we're safe, and whatever's out there is way worse than whatever they're doing in here."

She's probably right. But I can't stop thinking about all the wiggle room you can fit into "special." Alex believes she's going to get a better life from this. I've been told I'll get a better life from this. But the best lies are the ones that people *want* to believe.

Is that what this is? Or am I searching for cracks again? It's happened so many times before. I have screwed up so many times. How can I trust myself to see what's right anymore?

I force a smile and Alex's grip tightens. "It's fine," she whispers.

Fine enough for me to get to call my sister? Somehow I doubt it. I smile wider, but over Alex's shoulder I see Hart. I'm not sure when he finished with Norcut and Kent, but he's done now and he's watching us.

I push that smile even wider and Hart instantly smiles back—not before his eyes narrow though.

I'm playing the game, but I don't believe.

And Hart knows it.

We eat lunch at our desks. This kind of bothers me because I don't like crumbs on my keyboard, but no one else seems to mind. Kent's pumping metal music through the overhead sound system and every time the bass thumps, Jake juts his chin forward, front teeth firmly clamped on his lower lip. Geek dancing. Gotta love it.

Or not, because Alex has noise-canceling headphones on, and every time Jake starts rocking out, she glares at him. It just makes him jam harder and then she laughs.

I half expect Hart to pull me aside, but he doesn't. He just watches me and smiles. I can't decide if it means anything.

Or if I'm just driving myself crazy.

In the end, Norcut announces she has client meetings and leaves all of us with homework, of sorts. Mine is disassembling and decrypting a series of viruses. Most of them aren't bad. One's definitely vicious—it wants to overwrite data on the host PC, rendering it inoperable. But the last one? The last one's just bloated code. More than I've ever seen on anything before and it does *nothing*. Whatever though. It makes my life easier. I delete it and move on, running checks against the others until the music suddenly cuts off.

I glance up and realize Alex is gone. Actually—I roll my chair around for a better look—everyone's gone except for Kent.

I roll back to my desk and check the time on the lower corner of my screen. It's after seven. I've been working for almost twelve hours now, but I don't feel exhausted . . . more like my head's finally evened out, like it's finally quieted. It's a weird relief, one I didn't know I needed.

Does that mean Norcut's right?

I push the idea around, poke at it until I realize it's mine. It's *me*. I just didn't know it was me. Apparently I do enjoy the work, and admitting it somehow feels like missing a step in the dark. There was a horrible breath where my insides scooped low.

And then I found my footing again. I'm okay.

Maybe this is who I am.

I log out of my system and push to my feet, spine popping. Something else I need? A hot shower and probably another cup of coffee. And I'm halfway to the double doors when Kent appears, rolling his chair almost onto my toes.

"What?" I ask.

"Ever since you got here, someone's been hitting my firewall."

"Your firewall?"

His lips thin. "Looking Glass's."

I shrug. "Isn't that kind of what happens around here?"

"Not like this. It's not just Looking Glass either. They're focused on hitting your personal computer's firewall too." The hacker's eyes crawl along my face like he can sense how my heart rate's suddenly quickened.

"You're checking my stuff?" I ask, and I sound good. I'm all light and unimpressed even though my insides are splintering. I was so careful. I was always looking over my shoulder.

"Hart told me to check on everything. You understand, of course?" Kent's smile is animal white. "Safety *is* a virtue."

"So's bathing. You should make a note."

I start to move around him and he kicks his chair in front of me again. "It's like they know where to look. You have a partner?"

"Nope."

"Liar. You have to. How else would they know where to look?"

"They're just lucky, I guess." There's a humming in my ears now and I have to push each breath through my nose. Regrettable since I can smell Kent even better now. "If you don't believe me, talk to Hart. I work alone. It's in my file. Whatever you're seeing . . . it has to be someone random.

Or maybe it's the people I'm hiding from. I'm popular. Ask anybody."

"I don't believe you. Whoever it is—they had to know what you were doing before Hart picked you up." Spit flicks past Kent's lips. He's getting more and more agitated, and strangely, it makes me calmer. He isn't rude to me because I'm a girl. He's rude to me because I'm a threat.

And maybe also because I'm a girl.

"You'll get in trouble for not being honest with Dr. Norcut." He's grinning now. "I'll make sure of it."

"Good to know. Are we done here?"

"You think you're so tough, but—"

"Yeah, we're done." I walk around him and shove through the doors like my legs aren't shaking. I want to stop, lean against the wall, and catch my breath and I can't.

I watch the security camera from the corner of my eye and wait for the elevator as my insides try to climb outside. Because it isn't a "they" at all. Someone who's familiar with my code? Someone who attacks firewalls?

It's Griff.

I can't concentrate during dinner. I can't stop thinking about everyone who might hunt me down—Milo, Carson, even some of my dad's thugs—but none of them know firewalls as well as Griff.

How does he even know I'm here? Did someone tell him? And why's he searching for me? Why now? We haven't spoken in weeks. The last thing he said to me was that he couldn't touch me. Not even once, because if he did, he'd have to touch me again.

And he wasn't going to let himself do that.

In Griff's defense, I deserved it. I lied. To him, to Bren, to Lily.

But mostly to myself.

I haven't spoken to Griff in two months now. It hurts and it has no right to hurt. It's not like I've been spending all my time away from him alone. I have Milo.

Had Milo. It's stupid for me to worry about him. He's way better at hiding than I am and yet I can't seem to shake the anxiety that he's going to get caught. Looking Glass and Hart and Norcut have cracked me and what-ifs are seeping through.

After dinner, we have group therapy in the common room. Norcut leads, Hart watches, and a woman in a wrinkled suit sits in the corner and takes notes.

"She's from some government agency," Alex whispers as we find seats in the semicircle. "She stops by every month or so to check on the program. I think it's for licensing or something."

Or something. The armchairs have been pulled away from the television and I pick the farthest one from the official. Thing is, out of everyone here, she seems the most legit. I've been around social workers enough to spot the type: bloodshot eyes from long hours, tote bag swollen with case files.

Group therapy is also familiar. I'm expected to share

more since I'm the newest arrival and I hit all the high notes: Mom died. Dad in jail. I enjoy computers, chocolate, and long walks on beaches.

Norcut's fingers tighten around her pen just like they used to. "And what do you want to work on during your time with us? What personal goal would you like to achieve?"

I'd like to stay alive. I'd like to know why Griff's searching for me. I'd like my old life back.

No, scratch that. I don't want to go back to that life. I want parts of it, but not all of it anymore. So that means . . . what?

I have no idea.

And by this time, I've taken so long to answer, Norcut gives me a little smile. "Is there anything you'd like to do over? Any mistakes you've made that you want to make sure you never make again?"

Thousands. I shrug. I get what she's doing, but this is why therapy can be so damn pointless: They think you can distill everything you do into one or two character flaws. I have way more faults than that.

And way more mistakes . . . still . . . "Trust," I say at last. "I need to work on trusting people."

Norcut beams and tells me what a good job I'm doing. Then she has the group tell me what a good job I'm doing. This is a therapist's version of passing out treats because I sat on command. Or rolled over. Take your pick.

Norcut wants to talk to all of us about boundaries now. People have them. We shouldn't cross them—especially when those boundaries are set by the government and are there for people's privacy.

I love this part, but for all the wrong reasons. Boundaries? Seriously? I just hijacked someone's wireless device. The irony is effing hilarious, but Norcut looks serious, Alex looks serious, the Bookends—Connor and Jake—look *very* serious, and Kent? Kent looks like he's sleeping with his eyes open.

"We haven't heard much from you, Kent," Norcut says, recrossing her legs and tugging down the hem of her navy skirt. "What do you enjoy most about working with systems and computers?"

"Computers are their own world and that world has no choice but to adore me."

The agency woman scribbles more in her notebook, but Norcut seems pleased. "You're living up to your potential here, aren't you?"

Kent nods, smiles.

Alex kicks my ankle and I almost giggle. The weird feeling from earlier is gone, replaced with something that . . . honestly? Something that feels *normal*. And it can't possibly *be* normal. None of this is remotely normal. We're a bunch of computer nerds locked in an office building. It's either the start of the world's geekiest horror flick or the world's geekiest X-Men movie.

But everyone else seems chill about it so that makes me . . . the crazy one?

After therapy, I follow Alex to our room. Once inside,

she kicks off her tennis shoes and climbs—fully clothed—into bed.

"Talk to me." I stand between Alex's bed and her dresser. "Please? You know there's more going on here than they're telling us."

She groans. "If you want to go off the deep end trying to figure this place out, go ahead, but you're not taking me."

"Give me some credit here," I say, watching Alex arrange her physics notes into neat, little piles. "I'm not planning a protest march. I just want to know what's going on."

"I already told you: Play the game and you're in. You'll have a degree. You'll have a new life."

"I've heard those lines before. It never works like you think it will. Or like you want it to." I played the game with my dad, with Joe, with Carson. I kept thinking if I did this one last thing, if I pushed just a little bit harder, it would all be okay.

It very rarely was, and in the end, it wasn't okay at all.

I take a step toward Alex. "Why would they let us go if we're doing what they want? What are they getting from this?"

The pause is so long I think she isn't going to answer.

"Don't care," Alex says at last and touches her fingertips to the first pile of notes and then the second. "I know I'm getting three meals a day and safety. You want the truth? You go get it. But I'm not helping. I know men like Hart. They all carry themselves the same way—that's how you spot them."

I study her. We really are alike. I know exactly what Alex means. "They do, don't they?"

She nods, eyes inching over me. If Alex is going along with this maybe I should too. Down the hallway, the elevator dings and both of us stiffen, turn toward our bedroom door.

"You hear that?" Alex asks. "Someone's coming up from the garage."

She pushes off the bed and cracks our door open, leaning close to the wall to see better. "That's weird."

"Oh good. Something else is weird."

Alex smiles. "You're really, *really* going to want to see this. He's *very* pretty."

Later, I'd tell myself it was the way her voice tilted low that told me who was in the hallway. I've heard it before after all. When it comes to him, girls can't help it.

I can't help it.

I nudge Alex to the side and peek through the crack between the glass door and the jamb. Hart's standing in the hallway, back to us. One hand pinned to a taller boy's shoulder. Hart's holding on to him like he's afraid he'll run.

Or bite.

"I thought they only caught you," Alex says, and I turn. Our eyes meet. "You know him?" she asks.

I don't answer. Actually, I'm not sure I can. Of course I know him.

It's Milo.

They "caught" him. Interesting word Alex used. I should ask her about it, but I can't take my eyes off him.

Milo.

I open our door a little wider and his shoulders straighten like he heard the whisper of glass on the carpet. Or like he feels my presence.

Slowly, *slowly*, he turns . . . and our eyes lock. His gaze is hot—hotter—and I can feel every space on me it touches.

I'm standing still, but everything in me is leaning toward him, and like Milo somehow knows, he shakes his head once.

It's so subtle Hart doesn't notice.

I do. It's a warning. He doesn't want me to say anything and the realization turns my insides cold and liquid. Why would he warn me? What's going on?

Hart's hand tightens on Milo's shoulder and Milo turns to him. The elevator doors open and both of them disappear inside. Are they going to see Norcut? I step into the hallway, watch the lights above the elevator illuminate and go dark.

"You *do* know him," Alex says.

"No." I swallow, feel my throat catch. "I thought I did."

A week ago, it wouldn't have bothered me to lie to her. Dishonesty is supposed to be bad, but lies are the only protection I've ever had. Only now that I know Alex sees the same things I do around here, my lie feeds on me. It's a betrayal now, and I hate it.

But look how well you're handling it. It's Norcut's voice in my head, like she dug a hole inside me and her words grew in the dark. It's true though. I'm not shaking. My voice doesn't break. I sound . . . fine. Even my stomach is unclenching.

"Interesting that they found another," Alex adds, leaning her head against the doorjamb. "I hadn't heard about him."

"Do you always know if there's a new person coming in?"

"Pretty much. Kent has to be prepared. You can't spring stuff on him or he gets hostile."

I laugh. "This is Kent on good behavior?"

"I know, right?" Alex retreats to her bed and gathers up all her homework, all her notes. She looks so young right now, closer to twelve than twenty. "Kent's some sort of a code whisperer genius. He's an utter asshole, but he does good work. And the *work* is what matters around here."

She sounds so final I don't bother pressing it any further. I take a T-shirt and shorts from my dresser, moving mechanically through my evening routine. I shouldn't push her. I shouldn't—"So, if that's a new guy, we'll meet him tomorrow, right?"

"Right."

Wrong. I spend the next three days doing schoolwork in the morning and puzzling through viruses in the afternoon. The bloated one keeps coming back. Every time I delete it, it returns. There are three versions waiting for me now, which is mildly interesting. Does it take over the host by flooding the server with so many requests it overloads them?

I run another check and wait for Milo, who never shows. I try not to look for him, but my eyes keep straying to the glass doors and the hallway beyond them. He should be walking in any moment now, right?

So why isn't he? What does that mean?

And where are they keeping him? Alex said we only have two floors, but the top floor is all work spaces and the bottom floor is bedrooms and common areas. You would hear him. Well, maybe not hear him, but you would see him.

Wouldn't you?

Kent rolls his chair into my line of vision. "Do I need to give you more work?"

My cheeks go nuclear, but I open my eyes very, very wide. "Why? Do you need help with yours?"

Someone behind me sniggers. I think it's Jake.

Kent scowls. "Get back to work, Tate."

I face my computer and rub my eyes until colors explode behind the lids. I need to concentrate and yet all my Milo questions are stuck on repeat.

I kick away from the desk and head for the bathrooms, ignoring Kent's grumbles as I pass. The hallway is drenched in late-afternoon light. The setting sun slants shadows across the opposite building and I'm almost to the bathroom door when I realize I can see into that office space again.

The Laser Microphone guy—the same one Alex and I saw in the opposite building a few days ago—is back.

I lean one shoulder against the door and pretend to admire the wedge of sunset I can see between the buildings. I count windows to double-check myself, and yeah, that's definitely the office I noticed on the night I arrived.

And that's definitely the same guy.

This time though he just seems to be watching—staring really. I know he can't see me, but as I turn for the bathroom his head tilts and I can't shake the feeling that he's studying me.

It's after dinner and after therapy and after probably everyone else has gone to bed and I can't sleep because I can feel my hair growing.

Six cups of coffee can do that to you.

"I can't lie here anymore." I sit up, shoving my blankets to the foot of the bed. "Am I allowed to go to work?"

"Don't you listen to anything?" Alex's voice is muffled by her comforter. I think she's trying for pissy, but it makes me want to laugh. And then annoy her even more. "It's not a prison. Do whatever you want, but do not bother me."

At the very end of Alex's bed, something twitches under the blankets. A foot. I ease forward, grab the edge of her comforter, and yank, sending the blanket flying. Alex shoots upright, but I'm already running for the door.

"You are so going to pay for that, Tate!"

A pillow hits the wall next to my head as I bolt into the hallway and run for the elevators. The guys are playing video games in the common room, and thankfully, none of them notices as I pass. One floor above, the workroom is quiet except for the low murmur of the air-conditioning, and I don't bother with the overhead lights before returning to my station. I power on my computer and drop into the chair, studying the illuminated buildings around us as it cycles through the system start-up.

I could get used to working like this: the darkness, the quiet. It's like being the last person in the world . . . until a shadow separates from the dark.

I turn, face it.

"I missed you."

I smile. He can't see it, but I know he feels my grin when his hands skim my face. Our mouths are almost brushing and my knees are already crumbling. Milo touches me like I'm perfect and he's in awe.

"You missed me?" I whisper. His laugh is a silent ghost and turns my joints liquid.

Molten.

Now I'm laughing. "Prove it."

Milo's lips catch mine and it's everything I remember: soft, teasing. And then insistent. He presses me into the chair, pinning me underneath him as my hands dig into him, dragging him closer.

Always closer.

"Where have you been?" I murmur against the angle of his jaw.

"Looking for you."

I start to pull back and Milo cuts me off, covering my lips with his. He's on his knees now, and I am disintegrating.

Where *has* he been? What happened? I splay both palms against Milo's chest and push. He doesn't budge.

"Milo!" I rip my mouth away from his, hear him panting. "Seriously. Where have you been? We can't get caught doing—"

"It's okay. I told them about us."

"You *what*?" I kick both feet into the floor and wrench my chair away, putting space between us.

"Ashamed of me?" Milo's still on his knees, the tips of his fingers grazing the floor. The half-light from the windows has caught his eyes, turning them plastic bright.

"Don't be stupid," I whisper, feeling my stomach go cold and oily. "It's just . . . just . . ."

"Just what?"

"You don't give people stuff like that." In the dark, it's easier to say what I mean. My voice is climbing and I'm struggling to make it stop. "You don't volunteer info on yourself—or someone you care about."

Milo stiffens, watching me for a silent moment before pushing to his feet. "Just say it, Wick. You think I gave them leverage on you. You think I sold you out."

I do . . . sort of. I didn't tell Hart anything about Milo. I withheld. I protected him. And now . . . I square my shoulders. "You *did* sell me out. I didn't tell them anything about you."

"Maybe you should have." Milo shrugs. "It's not like we have anything to hide. Not anymore."

He's right of course—all the lies and all the sneaking around. It's finally caught up to me. I'm paying for it.

But by now the silence between us has stretched too long. I take Milo's hand in both of mine. "How did they . . . catch you or whatever?"

"Catch me?" His smile is equal parts cocky and

amused and perfect. "No one catches me. You should know that."

I wait, brows raised, until Milo looks away, dipping his face into the shadows.

"Fine. I think one of my customers sourced me originally, but after I figured out you were here, I wanted to come."

"How . . . ?"

"Circled the block and caught the license plate of the town car. You're acting like they dragged me here; is that what happened to you? When I saw you walking out of your house with Hart, I thought . . ."

I grimace. "It was a surprise, but only to me. Apparently, Bren had been planning it for a while."

"Damn. That's cold."

"Pretty much." I chew my tingling lower lip and taste the mint from Milo's ChapStick. "So what's the deal? Are you stuck here like I am?"

Another soft laugh. "You mean, can I leave if I want to? Yeah, I can leave." Milo drops his chin, considering my mouth, my eyes, my ragged Kool Aid—red ponytail. I try to smooth it down as he leans into me.

"However," Milo breathes, making the words feel liquid against my lips. "I have a fairly compelling reason to stay."

I grin. "And that is?"

Milo smirks. "I might've accidentally blown up the restaurant. Like sky-high."

"How do you 'accidentally' blow—" I stop myself. No, it could totally happen. Milo lives—*lived*—in a run-down restaurant and had that place rigged with explosives from top to bottom. "You're lucky you weren't killed."

"Luck has nothing to do with me."

"Ass." I give him a shove and Milo gives me a single step back. "What about your dad? Where's he?"

The mention of his father passes through Milo in a shudder. It's so quick I'm not even sure I saw it.

"Haven't seen him," Milo says. "He hasn't been at any of the shelters. He isn't at any of his usual haunts so . . . I don't know. He could be anywhere."

Or he could be under an overpass. Or floating facedown in the Chattahoochee. Or in the ground. All the horrible possibilities hang between us and I want to tell him how sorry I am, but that's never something Milo wants to hear. Ever.

"Anyway," he continues. "They've had me on lockdown while they ran a background check. Now that I'm clear, they're offering me a place to work—until I get on my feet again."

I stare at him. Of all the things I've ever expected from Milo . . . "Well, that's big of them."

"Isn't it though?" He cocks his head. "I know what you're thinking. It sounds convenient because it *is* convenient. I'll get to crash with you and they'll get some hardware upgrades. Hart and Norcut do have their uses—for me and for you."

Now *that's* more like the Milo I know. "I don't know . . ."

"Give it a chance, okay?" he asks. "Before you completely blow them off, give it a chance. It's good to get your skills in the open. You hide them too much."

"Yeah, because I don't want to go to jail."

"In the right company, you won't." He pauses. "In the right company, you can make a lot of money. You could make a whole new life."

And pretend everything that happened before . . . didn't. Milo doesn't say that, of course, but that's the tone. He's waiting for an answer and I don't know what to give him. Milo's always wanted me to embrace hacking, make things happen on my own terms.

But even if I get on board with Looking Glass, I'm still not doing that. I'm not rewriting *my* world.

I'm rewriting *theirs*.

"Wick," Milo says finally. "I'd be the first to break you out of here if I really thought they were bad news. You know that."

The look he gives me is meaningful and funny at the same time. It's supposed to remind me of the bombs he's made for me and the lies he's told and the things he's helped me with—and it does.

"You trust me?" Milo asks.

"I don't trust anyone," I say, but I do it with a smile so he'll know I'm joking. Sort of.

Milo rolls his eyes. "How many times have I saved your

ass? You think I wouldn't tell you if these people were a problem?"

"No."

"We can control this." His hand closes around mine, and when he squeezes his thumb against my palm, I squeeze back.

"It's crazy being with you, you know that?" His words are stuffed with wonder and disbelief. "I can't be this close. I can't touch you just once. I've never been like this with other girls."

My mouth goes dry. Seconds pass. A minute. Time goes right on and I'm stuck, jammed on a moonless night two months ago, blood running down my face as Griff said, "If I touch you once, I'll have to touch you again."

And then he left me.

"Wick?" Milo palms my cheek. His thumb skims over and over my skin. Testing for cracks? I'm so full of them I nearly laugh. Or sob. "Come back to me."

I lean into him. "I haven't gone anywhere. I'm not going anywhere."

"Good, because I want to be where you are."

We consider each other for a long moment until Milo puts both hands on my chair and drags me to him. I tilt my face for another kiss, but he holds back, fingertips touching the half-healed cut by my hairline. "I'm sorry. Really. How're you doing?"

Tears—hot and unexpected—prick my eyes. That's the

thing about Milo. There's all this swaggering and attitude and then he suddenly turns around and focuses on me like there's nothing else in his world. "Sometimes I'm good. Sometimes I'm not."

"How do you like it in the ivory tower?"

A smile. "Too soon to tell," I say. "I'm trying to give it a chance, but . . . something feels off to me."

He nods. "I get it. People like us, everything feels off." Milo touches his fingertips to my jaw, tracing the bone. "But I've worked with some of their people before. I'm telling you they're legit—"

"It doesn't *feel* legit. They're always checking for bugs and you can see people watching the building—"

"You know how much money is in securities. It's probably competitors trying to get an edge."

"My second day here they had me breaking into some wireless device while Norcut was on the phone. She would cue me to start and stop based on"—I pan my hands—"whatever was going on at the other end."

Milo lifts one shoulder. "So they were testing you."

"On *what*?"

"Does it matter?"

"It does to me."

"Then you should ask."

I jerk back. "Ask Norcut?"

"Why not? It's the only way you'll get an answer. You think she's been honest so far?"

"Yeah, pretty much. Maybe." I study Milo, feeling stupid. He's right of course. I should ask. It's just that, I'm not used to getting answers, and I'm damn sure not used to asking questions.

I take a shaky breath. "If they're so trustworthy, why didn't you say something to me the night you arrived?"

"I wanted it to be on my terms." Milo pauses. His thumb finds my lower lip and traces it carefully. "I've worked with them before and I wanted to be the one to break the news about us."

Us. We both take a breath around the word.

One corner of Milo's mouth lifts in a smile. "I can't trust you to tell the truth, and I needed to tell the truth. If this is going to work . . ."

He trails off, and in the silence I can fit in everything I can't say. "I'm trying to be better with that. It's hard to change old habits."

"I think it's hard for you to accept you have a future."

I laugh. "You sound like Norcut."

Now Milo's laughing. "And you sound different. Better."

"Do I?" I hate how hope wings my voice higher, but I've lost a lot and if Looking Glass is my ticket home and Milo trusts them . . .

"Definitely. You sound lighter." He brushes a strand of hair away from my cheek. "I like the new color. It's about time. I've been waiting for you to get better. When we met, you were so broken."

"I ruined everything."

"No, you didn't."

My fingers curl into his shirt. "How can you be sure?"

Milo doesn't answer. He just pulls me closer.

The next morning, I sit at my computer station, chewing the skin next to my thumbnail and watching the hallway. All I need to do is just ask Norcut what she had me working on that first day. I should've just asked her when we started. It would've been natural.

Normal.

I am not normal. I have a laundry list of reasons I will never *be* normal. I bite down hard and wince. I can fix this. I just have to remember Norcut isn't my dad. She isn't Joe. She damn sure isn't Carson.

There's a flash of shadow in the hallway and Hart appears—suit and smile, just like always.

Milo's with him.

Our eyes meet through the glass. He grins and I grin,

and somehow, this feels so much easier because Milo's going to be here.

Hart bumps open one door and motions for Milo to go ahead of him. Everyone stops, stares. It's pretty much a repeat of my first day, but it's also Milo. He's a little over six feet with a lean build, dark skin, and darker eyes—black eyes, honestly. Milo has a grin that can drop jaws . . . and panties.

He's sexy as hell.

And he knows it.

"Can I have your attention?" Hart asks. It's totally unnecessary because everyone's already staring, but Hart's pretending not to notice our lack of manners. "This is our newest addition: Milo Gray. He's a hardware expert and I hope you'll take advantage of his expertise."

There's a soft murmuring to my left. Connor and Jake.

"I *also* hope," Hart continues, "that I can count on you to make him comfortable and feel welcome."

Hart's staring at Kent. Kent's staring at Milo. And Milo? Milo's staring at me. It's like no one else exists.

Maybe for us they don't.

Milo was the first person to see me, *really* see me, for what I am. He wasn't shy then. He's not being shy now. I kind of want to cringe. I'm still not used to the attention, but then I remember that I don't have to hide anymore and I grin at him, daring him to laugh.

Kent clears his throat. "Oh, you can count on us to make him feel at home, Hart."

Milo's mouth twitches. He's chewing down that laugh and, suddenly, so am I. If Kent thinks he's going to bully Milo, he can think again. The jolt of happiness is furious and hot and entirely Milo.

Entirely *us*.

Sometimes I think most of our relationship is based on how we look at each other and then, together, how we look at everyone else. It's a constant shared joke, a song we can't get out of our heads. Like we're alone, even though everyone else is in the room too.

I used to think it made us dangerous. Maybe it's actually what makes relationships—real relationships—work.

Maybe that's something else I'm learning.

"I'm glad to hear you're eager to help, Kent." Hart's iPhone beeps and he checks the screen. "You all know what to do, right? Dr. Norcut won't be in until later."

Our cue to get back to work. Everyone shifts around in their seats and the sound of tapping fills the room. Hart's striding toward me to get to the door. It's now or never.

"Hart?" I ask as he passes me. "Can we talk?"

Hart stops. "Of course. How are you liking it here?"

"It's good. It's fine."

"Is everything okay?" He sounds like a talk show host again and I try not to squirm. Calling Hart a talk show host isn't exactly fair. He's more like a Boy Scout. Which is a nicer description, but makes me feel worse because it reminds me of Todd.

I force my chin up and push my foster father under.

"Yeah, I just . . . I wanted to ask you about my second day," I say. "About what I was doing."

Hart's laugh is a soft burst. "From what I understand, you took a skills assessment test—something about accessing a remote device."

"I know *that*. I don't know *why*. It makes me . . . nervous that I was turning it on and off. It seemed weird."

"Weird?"

I try not to grimace. Yes, weird. Just like how I'm acting now.

Hart leans against my desk. "You were running tests for a new client of ours, BioFutures. They do medical devices—pacemakers, insulin pumps, and other implantable devices. Our job is to test the devices' security. Follow me?"

Absolutely, and *that's* why the whole thing looked off. It wasn't one of my usual targets. Medical devices have been found to be vulnerable to attack. It's scary to think how someone can switch you off. Terrifying. But honestly there's better money, better *returns*, with other types of hacking. Credit cards or bank accounts or whatever.

I nod. "Oh. Okay. That makes sense."

"We should've told you. The others never care. I guess Dr. Norcut didn't think you would either. Sorry."

I study Hart. No one ever apologizes to people like me. It's such a small thing and it means so much. *I'm sorry* means I regret betraying you. *I'm sorry* means you exist to someone, that you mean enough for someone to regret hurting you.

"But why wouldn't we test the device here?" I ask at last. "You could test the software from a location on-site."

"True, but our customers are rarely here. We don't want them bothering you guys. Besides, BioFutures wanted to see if the device could be accessed remotely. Since medical devices are under such scrutiny, they want to be first to the market with a hacker-proof device. Wandering through a coffee shop and having someone hijack your pacemaker would be bad for business, you know?"

He laughs at his own joke and I force a smile. It's a perfectly good explanation. It makes sense and yet I'm still trying to pry it apart, dig for any inconsistency. I mentally shake myself. Hart's being helpful. If I would just stop being so suspicious . . .

Hart studies my face, my hands. They're wrapped tight around the chair's armrests. "I'll be sure to tell you more in the future, okay? You'll know exactly what you're doing and why."

I nod, knowing I should say something, but I have . . . nothing. Zero. My conversations with my dad and Joe never went like this and I'm not sure what to do. This is how normal people behave. It's stupid easy for something that was so damn hard to say.

"We're the good guys, remember?" Hart's grin is as wide as his face. Wider. "That means you too. You're doing the right thing." He laughs and scratches his thumb across his eyebrow, ducking his head closer to me. "We're fighting the good fight, yeah?"

He says it like it's dorky and he knows and it *is* dorky, but now I'm laughing too.

And honestly? I kind of might possibly like the idea.

I used to hack to catch cheaters and abusers and deadbeat boyfriends and I believed in it. I saved other women from what my mom went through, but I was never proud of it because I hacked for money—to save myself, to save my sister. And some days, those were absolutely the right reasons.

Until they weren't.

I spent so much time looking for monsters, I saw them everywhere.

Hart's grin fades and he crouches down so our eyes can meet. "Look, Wick. I know what you had to do."

It's the soft voice again, so soft I know the others can't hear, but I still stiffen. I don't talk about who I am. I'm too used to burying it. I am my family's undertaker. I bury all the bad memories, all our lies, putting everything in little coffins so we can go to bed. And then we all get up and do it again.

Or is that just what I tell myself? *Told* myself?

"I know what happened," Hart continues. "I know what you had to do and I *understand*. But it's not like that anymore."

Milo rocks to one side of his chair, watching us. I can see the edge of his face around Hart's shoulder. He looks so relaxed, I start to relax.

"I know," I say, forcing myself to take a deep breath.

"We're going to make sure people with these medical devices can't ever be hurt by hackers." Hart's voice drops a little more. "It's not so different from what you used to do, right?"

I'm nodding again—or still; I'm not sure.

"Good." Hart stands and brushes away nonexistent wrinkles from his pants. "I'm glad we talked. You can come to me anytime."

"Okay."

"Promise you will if you get concerned again?"

"Promise."

Hart beams at me and then glances down at his iPhone, which just buzzed. "Sorry. Gotta take this."

He steps away and I turn to my desk, sneak a glance at Milo.

"See?" he mouths, but he's grinning too. It's an *I told you so* smile, a *you owe me* smile.

A makes-everything-in-me-go-bright smile.

I face my computer so he can't see how I'm turning ten shades of red.

"Milo? The boss wants to see you." Hart opens one of the glass doors and motions for Milo to follow him, leaving the rest of us to our work. We spend the next few hours in silence—a good thing for me because that bloated virus is back and I'm no closer to identifying the purpose. I know it's a worm—a type of virus that can easily replicate and carry a variety of payloads—but this worm still isn't carrying anything. There are no malicious or encrypted files . . . in fact, the payload just seems to be replicating itself.

Seventy-four characters over and over again: 596F752 0646F6E2774207265616C6C792062656C6965766520686 96D3F20446F20796F753F

I don't get it. On top of the worm being obsolete and a low security risk, it was written in assembly code. If the author wanted the virus to avoid detection, it would've been written in a modern polymorphic code.

And yet it keeps coming back again and again, getting detected, getting deleted. What's the point?

I sit back, stare at the screen. What if . . . what if I'm looking at it wrong? What if I'm seeing what it *can't* be instead of what it *is*?

I punch "hexcat" into my Linux workstation and watch the lines of hexadecimal code scroll past. My breath catches.

The virus doesn't make any sense because it's not a virus. It's a message.

You don't really trust them, do you?

All the hairs on my arms go rigid. I sit a little straighter, pretend to stretch as my eyes cut across the room. Everyone's at work. It's a relief until I realize I'm being stupid. What am I looking for? A gigantic sign above someone's head saying "I sent that!"?

I scowl, look at the message again.

You don't really trust them, do you?

Well, I did. I *do*.

No, I *need* to. The word is a small but incredibly crucial difference. I need this to be the real deal because if it isn't . . .

There's a link below the question, but it's a link to what? Proof? Pictures? A cheap Viagra prescription?

Odds are, it'll give my computer some virus I'll have to fix and Kent will flip out because I should know better than to dig into this. I drum my fingertips against the edge of my desk because I *do* know better.

I click the link anyway. It opens another page in my web browser, taking me to an article published yesterday about a dead man.

A dead former judge, Alan Bay.

My hands go cold, clammy.

No. It couldn't be. It *couldn't*. I skim the top paragraph, hitting all the high notes: Apparently, Alan Bay was at home when his pacemaker malfunctioned—at least they're speculating that it was malfunctioning. Full details won't be known until after the autopsy, but an "insider" maintains it kept turning on and off—multiple times, according to the data history—until he died.

In agony.

I suck air. Suck more air. I cannot get enough breath.

It kept turning on and off. It kept turning on and off.

Because *I* kept turning it on and off. Bile tips into the back of my mouth and I scroll to the top, read the website name: Datajunkie. It's like a forum, but this is the only post. That's good. It makes the whole thing feel made-up.

I need it to be made-up.

I scroll down, check the time stamp. The article was published late yesterday, but was posted to the forum this morning. An hour ago. I take a breath and hold it, keep holding it. Think this through. I've been getting these viruses since the first day I arrived. It couldn't be the same link, though, because I hadn't hijacked Bay's pacemaker yet. Which means the previous viruses were what? Other messages? Junk?

I've permanently deleted them so I'll never know, but this message comes so close on the heels of my conversation with Hart—plus there's only one article posted.

Maybe it's a prank.

Or maybe that's just the nausea talking. It's simmering under my tongue. If this is true . . . *I* was the person turning the pacemaker on and off.

I tortured Bay, the man who denied my mother's restraining order and pushed through Bren's adoption paperwork. I exposed his sons as murderers. He was my last job for Carson and this *has* to be a coincidence because if it's not . . .

I take two sharp breaths. How many times did Norcut tell me to do it? Four times? Five?

No. Leave it. Don't go there. I open another window in my browser—keystroke logging programs be damned—and search Alan Bay's name. Out of the thousands of results, only the top four are about his death and they basically all say the same thing: Bay fell from political grace, his pacemaker failed, and now he's dead. Everything else is about his sons and their murder spree.

Because I'm a minor, my name's never appeared in any of the news articles, but people who were involved with the case knew I was there the night they caught Ian and Jason. Does this person know too? Is that why they sent me the link?

No, better question: Why would Norcut want me to kill Bay?

There's a wordless roar in my brain again. I rub my forehead, feel the scab by my hairline, and wonder if I shouldn't take another couple painkillers. I need to *think*.

No good, the only thing I can think of is tracking down who sent this to me, and maybe for the first time in my life, my hand stops. I don't reach for the mouse.

Used to be, I would've done an investigation. I would've bargained, snooped, spied. I would've found whoever sent it.

Only, I'm not supposed to be that girl. To borrow a phrase from Hart: It's not like that anymore.

Which means I can't make the same choices I used to make.

I have to tell someone.

But telling Hart means trusting him, *believing* him. Just as the message implied I shouldn't. The reminder is frantic, a hysterical voice buried alive in my head and clawing for the surface.

I swallow. This was supposed to be different. Milo *said* it was different, and Milo doesn't believe in anything or anyone.

Except for me.

Well, he believes in my abilities, which might as well be the same thing. This is who I am now, right? I have to tell someone.

I put both hands on my desk, force myself to stand. My legs tremble and I push them straight, straighter. I'm almost to the door before I stop shaking and I feel a little more like myself when I see Hart in the hallway. He's waiting for the main elevator—off to meet a client?—and talking on his cell. At the sound of my footsteps, he turns and I stop.

I clear my throat. "I need to show you something."

Hart's eyes narrow. "I'll call you later," he says and punches a button on the iPhone. "Are you okay?"

I shake my head and motion for him to follow me, trailing back to my workstation on spongy joints. I jam my thumb toward the computer screen. "Take a look."

He bends down, inhales hard. "When did you get this?"

"I've been getting them since I arrived, but I just now figured out the message portion." I chew the skin next to my thumb again and study the white tile under my feet. I don't know how they keep it so spotless here. "The link . . . the link says he had a BioFutures pacemaker. That it kept malfunctioning."

Hart goes still. "You followed the link? You know better than that."

"Like I'm going to ignore that message."

Hart shoots me an annoyed look and I glare right back. I know what he's getting at. I'm supposed to trust him and Looking Glass, and two seconds after our little heart-to-heart, I'm clicking links designed to freak me out or infect my computer with a virus.

Or tell me the truth.

"It's okay." Hart sighs like it isn't though. "Trust takes

time," he says quietly, eyes going from geek to geek, checking to see if anyone's paying attention. "I can see why you'd follow the link."

"What do we do now?"

"Nothing. I'll take care of it." Hart puts one hand on my shoulder. "You did great, Wick. Thanks for showing me this."

"That's all you're going to say?" I whisper. "I have history with that man. You know that."

Hart stares at me. "You actually think you were involved in Bay's death?"

"Why would someone send me that message? How do I know that—"

"You weren't behind the malfunction. Look, I'm not going to lie. We don't work for BioFutures because we're being generous. They pay us and they pay us well. We're a business. We fill a need and that's how we *stay* in business, but just because we're contracted to them doesn't mean we're responsible for every malfunction, and deep down, I know you understand this."

"But . . ." I want to say, *But how do I know you're telling me the truth?* I can't say, *But what if you're a liar?*

I'm not supposed to think like that anymore.

"Malfunctions happen, Wick. BioFutures is an enormous company. I'm sure there are plenty of people you know who have benefited from their technologies. The fact that you knew this man . . ." Hart stops, considers me and considers the screen, and when he speaks again, his voice has lost all the used-car-salesman shine: "What would we gain from having you do such a thing? Think about it logically, Wick. Weigh the benefits for me. We have no connection to this man. Where's the angle?"

I like this Hart better. He's using terms that actually mean something to me, and judging from how focused he's gone, Hart knows it. "That's the way you think, Wick. That's why we wanted you. So I'm going to ask you to apply the same logic here: What do we stand to gain?"

"Nothing." Bay has no connection to them. He has no connection to anyone besides me—not anymore.

"We can't help malfunctions," Hart continues. "We *can* help keep people from manipulating the devices' other weaknesses. We're helping BioFutures stay proactive—not much different from what you used to do. Bay could've been close to a microwave or some other electromagnetic device. He was probably a victim of an engineering flaw and that's terrible, but it isn't our problem. You're on the right side."

Hart's looking at his phone again, tapping a text message. "I'll need to look into the link and sender. If we have a security breach, we need to take measures."

"I want to know *why* I got the message."

Hart's eyes meet mine, pausing for a beat before he nods. "I don't know why you got the message, but I promise I will find out." He takes another long look at my screen. "I also promise I'll take care of it."

I nod, tell him thanks even though my stomach's twisting. He'll take care of it. That's what he's supposed to do, right?

So why doesn't it feel more reassuring to be saved?

"What was that about?"

I jump, slamming my hip into the desk's corner. "Jeez, Alex! I'm going to get you a bell."

"Yeah, yeah. So I noticed you and Gray are a thing? Why'd you say you didn't know him?"

"Sorry." I pause. "I should've told you."

"Whatever. It's what people like us do, isn't it?"

I don't answer and Alex doesn't seem to care. She rocks back and forth on the balls of her feet, trying to see my computer screen. "Seriously, what's going on?"

I hesitate. Hart didn't say *not* to discuss it, but the message—and what it implies—doesn't seem like something I should just blab to anyone. Only . . . only if anyone would know more about this stuff, Alex would and I kind of can't help myself when I say, "Any idea who might send me this?"

I move to the side so she can lean closer. I click on the virus first and watch Alex's brows draw together.

"That's not even . . . it's *gibberish*," she says at last. "Why are you all worked up?"

I run the hex dump, then show her the article, deliberately skipping my eyes over Bay's name. It surfaces too many memories I want to forget.

Alex's expression never changes, but for a very brief beat, she stops breathing and the skin along her neck slides as she swallows.

"Whoa," Alex says at last. She straightens and looks around. "Kent! C'mere."

"No."

"Now."

Kent heaves himself to his feet with the grace of a water buffalo and stomps toward us. "What? I'm busy."

"Who could've sent her this?" Alex points a finger at my screen, and unwillingly, Kent's eyes drag to the message. He waves one hand when he's ready for me to switch to the other window. "You have a problem," Alex says.

"What is it?" Milo. I didn't realize he was back until suddenly he was. The heat from his skin pushes chills across mine.

"Nothing." Kent pulls himself a little straight and a little taller. "Just something stupid."

"It doesn't look stupid." Milo's eyes flick from my computer screen to Kent's face. "It looks like something you need to fix. No one's supposed to be able to reach her here."

"And I'll *fix it*."

"I thought you were supposed to be good, man."

Kent exhales hard and he steps into Milo's space. Milo has an inch or two on him, but Kent has an easy hundred pounds on Milo. If it were me, I'd be backing down, but this is Milo and I don't think Milo's backed down from anything in his life.

"I *am* good."

"Prove it," Milo says with a smile so full of teeth it makes Kent wince.

"Don't put this shit on me," Kent says. "We're supposed to catch viruses and this one's caught. Maybe she just knew to check it."

I go still. "What are you trying to say?"

"That the virus hasn't done anything to the system. It's just a message. For *you*. Maybe because someone knew you would be checking it."

I gape at him. "That's stupid. Why would anyone want me to know this, Kent?"

"The hell should I know? You think I have time for your shit? Do you have any idea what's going on with our firewall? I'm plugging holes as fast as I can and they're still able to make inroads. I have way bigger issues to deal with."

"Look," I say. "Odds are, there are two kinds of hackers trying to get in. The first? Some kid who wants to look around. The second? Someone you should be more worried about."

Kent tenses. "Like who? Someone you know?"

I blow out a long sigh and rub my eyes. It's no good though. Griff's face blooms in the dark. "I don't know, Kent. Trust me, if I knew, I'd tell you." I drop my hand and keep my face plastic smooth. "Michael—my dad—used other hackers. What if he hired one to find me? I'm here kind of because of him."

I mean, it's possible. I guess. It might not be Griff. If it is though—I smother the idea.

"Wick?" Everyone pivots. Hart's at the double doors, smiling. "Norcut wants to see you. *Now*."

I'm half expecting small talk, but Hart doesn't say a word as we walk to Norcut's office. He knocks twice on the door, watching me like he did that first day, like he's afraid I'm going to run.

"Come in." Norcut's voice is muffled. "Wick?"

"Yeah." I'm barely through the door before Hart shuts it behind me. Norcut's at her desk, and as I walk closer, she slides paperwork from the blotter into a folder and locks it away in a drawer.

"How are you feeling?" she asks.

"Fine."

"And the arrangements? Rooming with Alex?"

"Fine."

"And if I were to tell your mother how you're doing?" The question jerks me straight and Norcut meets my eyes as she asks, "What would you want me to tell Bren? That you're doing fine?"

"Yes. I'd also want to know how she's doing, how my sister's doing, and when I'm going to get to go home." I pause, hoping Norcut will volunteer what I want. She doesn't. "Did Bren say I can call yet?"

"They're still adjusting, Wick. I don't think it's wise. Give it some time, okay? You haven't been gone a week yet." Norcut sounds so reasonable and yet the smile is still the same. Always the same. "This isn't just about them. It's about you and I don't think you can decide who you want to be when you're still mired in who you were."

Who I want to be. I'm not even sure what that is.

Norcut waits, watches. "Mr. Hart tells me you received a message this morning about your work and implying you were behind Alan Bay's death. Why do you think someone would have done that? Think it through. Who would gain by scaring you?"

"I have no idea."

"I do. Your father's escaped from prison, Wick."

My hands . . . my feet . . . my face go numb. Cold. "That's impossible!"

"That's what I thought too, but it's not and he did."

"My sister—"

"Is safe," Norcut finishes. "We're keeping your family under watch, but you have to realize Lily was never as . . . useful to him as you are. I would be surprised—very, very surprised—if he attempts to engage her. It simply isn't in his nature."

"You don't know that."

"True. He could surprise me." Norcut's attention switches from my face to my hands. She catches how they're trembling. "But I don't think he will. I do think he's behind that message."

"That's a little sophisticated for Michael."

"Is it? He was extremely manipulative when I knew him. What about the car accident? What if he's coming for you? Do you have something he wants? Maybe he's trying to rattle you."

I laugh. It's so sudden we both jump. "Michael doesn't 'rattle' people," I say. "It's not his style. If he wants to make a point, he'll make it in person—or *through* a person. He has people still. They do what he wants, when he wants, without question. If he wants to make a point, he'll do it."

My father has always been more physical than psychological. When he retaliates, it usually involves your body and blood. He doesn't tolerate disobedience. He doesn't tolerate betrayal.

My stomach drops a sickening inch. "Griff."

"What?"

"Griff. He's in danger. If my dad's loose, Griff's in danger. He provided testimony incriminating Michael."

And in the process erased every one of my digital fingerprints from my father's credit card scams. Griff saved me and now he's in danger. I know what happens to snitches.

I brace both hands on Norcut's desk. "You have to do something for him. You have to keep him safe."

"I'm not interested in trailer park boys, Wick, and your father wouldn't have time for revenge."

"He would *make* the time." I pause and pull up straight. "How did Michael escape?"

Norcut's smile is a straight line. "Forged paperwork. Someone went in with legitimate—well, they *appeared* legitimate—release papers and walked him straight through the front doors. From what I understand, the forgery was excellent."

"When?"

"Three days ago. Do you have any ideas who could help him with something like this?"

Bay could. I try to brush the thought away, but it lingers. "Alan Bay seemed . . . sort of friendly with Michael when I was growing up—got him out of a lot of restraining order requests, that sort of thing. What if Bay helped Michael before he died?"

Norcut's eyes go bright. "That's exactly what I was wondering. I treated Judge Bay's sons years ago. I know how Alan can be motivated. If Michael had the right amount of money, anything Bay had would be for sale."

I shake my head. "Trust me on this: Michael doesn't have any money."

"He does though. He stole eleven million from us."

My stomach goes oily. "What?"

"I'll level with you, Wick. Your father accessed Looking Glass's corporate account and wiped it. We're missing eleven million in cash and we need it back."

"Eleven. Million?"

Norcut rubs her thumb against the blotter. Her computer beeps and Norcut's gaze cuts to the screen, reading something. "Two eyewitnesses placed Michael close to your old home," she continues. "And Kent just emailed me the virus sender's location—it's Joe Bender's former address. Why do you think that is? What would he want badly enough to make him stay?"

"No idea."

"But how could you *not* know? You worked at his right hand for years."

"I worked a lot with Joe too. It doesn't mean I knew everything that was going on. Neither of them trusted me."

Norcut goes quiet, considering this. Or maybe just considering why Michael would stick around. It's not a smart play. He has to need someone. Or something.

"I think Michael's looking for *you*," Norcut says at last. "Why not find him first?"

"I'm sorry . . . *what*?"

"We could help you. We have aligned interests, Wick. We want our money and your father has it. You want your freedom and your father stands in the way. Why not finish this? Michael could have killed you in that accident and we both know he'll try to take you again."

She pauses, waiting for my answer, and I can't give her one. There's a droning in my ears now, a whine I can't shake.

"We both know you don't flinch from eliminating problems, Wick."

Problems like Joe Bender. Problems like Todd. I'm nodding now, but my stomach's still clenched.

Norcut's eyes inch across my face. "Your family, your future—they're all within your grasp if we eliminate the one thing that stands in your way. We want our money and you want your freedom. Will you help us?"

I start to ask if I have a choice and stop. There's always a choice. That's what I didn't get before. By reacting or not reacting to Todd and Joe and Michael, I was still making a decision.

Sometimes you make the choice and sometimes the choice makes you and everything I chose until this point has made me. I caught Joe and Todd before they could hurt me. I could catch Michael too.

I smile, smile wider. "I'm in."

Just like that first day, I leave Norcut's office with instructions. She wants whatever computer equipment we can recover from Joe's, so I'm to go as soon as she can coordinate security. Hart will take me. Milo will come help.

I agree to everything. Maybe that's why Norcut smiles and smiles. "Do you like him?" she asks as I stand to leave.

"Who?" I know who—what—she's talking about, but I'm stalling and we both know it. Milo. "Yeah, I do like him. A lot."

"He's a good match for you."

"'Match'? You do arranged marriages too?"

"Hardly, but for someone of your talents, you could do worse."

"Wow. What a glowing recommendation."

More smiling. "He understands you."

Does he? Milo gets what I can do, but I don't know if he gets who I want to be. Then again, I'm not sure I know who I want to be. There's who Looking Glass wants me to be. There's who Bren wants me to be. So why don't I know who I want to be?

Norcut's still staring at me. "Love is for other people, Wick. Lesser people. From now on, everything you do is about power—who has it, who doesn't. Do you understand?"

I nod. "Are we done?"

"Yes."

I'm almost to the door when she clears her throat. I stop. "Yeah?"

"Keep this to yourself, okay? Obviously, Milo will know and you'll have to tell Alex you're leaving Looking Glass but there's no need for the other boys to know what we have planned for you."

I close the door and shuffle up the hallway, Norcut's question on loop in my head: What's the one thing that stands in the way of becoming who you want to be?

Is it only Michael?

"There you are."

My feet stutter. Milo.

"Hey. I didn't see you." I lean into him and he kisses the top of my head. "Aren't you supposed to be working?"

"Probably. I wanted to check on you. Everything okay?"

"Yeah . . . yeah . . ." I can't stop staring at the windows. The sky's gone dark and the overhead lights have brightened. They're on timers, I guess. I'm not sure I like it, turns the windows into shadowy mirrors. I'm staring at myself, staring at Milo, who's supposed to be such a good match and understands me.

"You okay?" he asks.

"Sorry. Yeah. My dad's out. Norcut wanted to tell me." It's so matter-of-fact it might as well be someone else's life I'm talking about, someone else's problems. "She thinks he's trying to contact me."

Milo tilts his head. "What's the plan?"

"Norcut wants me to catch him. She's going to have you and Hart help."

Milo tugs me around to face him. "Are you going to do it?"

"Of course."

"Good. You can hurt him before he can hurt you. Think of the look on Kent's face when he hears too."

"I'm not supposed to say anything yet."

"When you do, you'll rule this place." Milo tugs me forward and I refuse to move.

I tip my head back to look at him. "Why does it matter so much to you that I fit in, that I make it here?" The question surfaces too quickly, like it's been holding its breath the whole time, like it's been waiting.

"Because this is where you belong. You're not made for the stuff out there. It was wasting your talent. And . . ." Milo pauses. "Because you matter to me."

I matter. Not what I can do. Not what I can provide. Just

me. I've wanted to hear that from him. It's another realization that I didn't know I'd buried.

"Why would someone like me ever matter to someone like you?" I've asked him variations of this before and always gotten some glib answer. I could use glib right now. Maybe it's the windows, maybe it's my dad, but it feels like darkness is closing in all around me.

Milo sucks in his lower lip, releases it slowly. "Because you're broken."

"That's not any reason to want someone."

"It is though. Because I'm broken too." He angles closer. "Maybe my scars recognized yours. Maybe pain is like a magnet and it pulled us together."

I smile and Milo sees it, bends to me. One hand cradles the back of my head. One hand touches the edge of my jaw. It's so gentle . . . it makes me grab him harder.

Milo kisses me like he's missed me, and I hold on to him like I'm lost.

It takes Hart two days to coordinate the security side. Norcut doesn't loop me in, and I'm half expecting a team of super-conspicuous rent-a-cops to meet me in the elevator lobby, but it's just Hart. For the first time, his suit's gone, replaced by pressed jeans and a tucked-in polo shirt.

"What?" he asks as I come closer. "I wanted to fit in."

"Oh yeah, totally." I'm nodding like that makes sense, but I can't stop staring at the tiny monogram on his right pocket. A monogram. That's fitting in.

Hart punches the down button. "Do you need anything else?"

"Me." Milo appears at the hallway turn. Sunlight slants behind him, turning his body into a shadow. Milo's walk is long and loose and doesn't stop until we're toe to toe. "She needs me."

I cock one eyebrow, but Milo only leans closer. The elevator dings. "After you," I say as Hart swears under his breath. When we reach the parking deck, there's another black town car waiting for us, running. The driver tosses Hart the keys, ducking his head lower as he passes us.

It feels weird, like all the support staff isn't supposed to acknowledge our existence. I can't figure out why that would be a rule.

"You go in the front with me," Hart says, hiking a thumb in my direction. "You're in the rear, Milo. I can trust you to watch for a tail, right?"

"A what?"

"You're not funny."

Milo smirks. "*She* thinks I'm funny."

And it's sad, but I do. I hop into the front seat before either of them can see my smile though. Hart flips on a pair of sunglasses and floors it across the parking garage. The gate's barely up before he's rolling the car through.

We're doing sixty on the side street. By the time he reaches the interstate, we're clipping along at seventy . . .

and then eighty. It's hard to gauge Hart's mood, but judging from the way he glances from rearview mirror to side-view mirror, he's expecting company.

"Are you worried something's going to happen again?" I ask, and it's a little softer, a little more scared than the way I'd planned it in my head.

Hart glances at me, tries for a smile. "I'm always worried something's going to happen again. I don't think you should be doing this."

"Why?"

Hart's fingers flex. "It could set you off," he says at last, and there's something about the way his tone tips lower that catches me.

He sounds honestly concerned.

"I promised you we would move forward, Wick. This is going backward. This is *stupid* if Michael's trying to draw you into the open."

I nod. "But you're doing it anyway."

"She's the boss," Hart says, lifting his eyes to the rearview mirror. Is he looking behind us? Or at Milo? I can't tell.

"Dr. Norcut said Looking Glass was providing security to my family. Do you know anything about it?"

"Yeah, I handled it."

"So . . . could you tell me what you organized?"

"Worried I don't know what I'm doing?"

Yes and it's unfair of me. He probably knows way more

than I do. He damn sure has better resources. But it's my family, my *sister*, and I need to say something and I have nothing.

Hart sighs. "It's fine, Wick. I promise. If we have time after this, I'll drive you by, okay?"

I nod.

"Good. I want this to be fast. You know where you want to look, right?"

"Not really." And I hate admitting it. "I figure we could just scope the whole place together. I know it's pretty broad, but there are three of us and we know how people hide stuff. If the message was sent from Joe's, maybe the equipment will still be there."

One corner of Hart's mouth tilts in a smile. "Isn't that the truth."

"Hey, Hart." I push against the seat and keep my eyes trained on the passing buildings. "If this goes well, can I call my sister?"

I can't tell if Hart looks at me, but judging from the silence, I'm guessing he does.

"Find something good for Norcut, Wick, and there's no telling what you'll get in return."

Joe Bender lives—lived—in a neighborhood on the edge of Peachtree City, a bedroom community mostly known for golf courses and BMWs. The subdivision has cheap houses, cheaper trailers, and plenty of kids desperate for work, which made it pretty much perfect for Michael and Joe to set up shop. The newspapers called us "a blight." Everyone else called us "trashy." For Lily and Griff and me? It was home.

Joe lived in one of the few proper houses, a leftover from when the builder thought the neighborhood would grow into more than trailers. I spent a fair amount of time there—sometimes working for my dad, sometimes working for Joe. He lived there for as long as I can remember.

And now the house is empty.

Hart parks the town car one street over and we walk

the rest of the way, plenty of time for me to reexamine the cracked sidewalks and abandoned trailers. I haven't been outside in days. It feels good. Better than good. The air smells like freshly mowed grass and sunshine heats my skin.

"This is it," I say, nodding my head toward the faded blue house on our left. Hart's hands go to his sides—adjusting a sports coat that isn't there?—before trudging up the walk. After a deep breath, I follow.

In some ways, it's the best the house has ever looked. When Joe lived here, the yard was orange dirt and dead cars. Now . . . well, it's still orange dirt, but the cars are gone and you can see the front better. The windows are boarded and there's a "No Trespassing" sign hanging off the sloped front porch.

Hart takes the porch steps two at a time and checks the door. Locked. His hand goes to his pocket, retrieves a palm-sized lock pick. The slender metal arm slides seamlessly into the keyhole and Hart adjusts it with flicks of his wrist until we all hear that unmistakable click.

"Awfully good at that," Milo says.

Hart shrugs. "Setups like these are easy."

Except, when he turns the knob, the door won't budge.

"You have to put your shoulder to it," I say, stepping closer. "It sticks—"

Hart shoves the door once and it pops open, yawning dusty, hot air over us.

Milo groans. "Don't you just love field trips?"

I follow Hart over the threshold and into the foyer. Milo tests the light switches, and after a beat, the electricity clicks on. Not that it makes much difference. Even with the overhead lights, the whole place is awash in grays and browns, and somehow this feels even more familiar. Joe used to keep the lights low to conserve energy for the computers and servers.

I shift, swallow. I used to stand right here to get my orders.

It feels like a lifetime ago.

"I'll check this side," Milo says and looks at Hart. "You do the bedrooms?"

"No." I push between them. "I'll get the bedrooms. You guys take the other side of the house. We did almost all our work in the kitchen and living room. I'll meet you there after I do my sweep."

Milo shrugs and follows Hart. The house's two bedrooms and one bathroom line a narrow hallway to my left. I pick the first door and spend several minutes going through the room, finding nothing. Same deal with the bathroom.

Surprisingly, and thankfully, I've never been in the last bedroom until now. It was Joe's. It even still smells a little like him: old pizza and sweat and a touch of some cologne that always made me gag. I'm so busy thinking about the stench, I don't even notice the balled-up sleeping bag until

I'm already through the door.

My stomach squeezes. Squatter? It's possible. I toe the edge and the navy-blue bag unravels a bit, revealing the plaid lining. Looks awfully clean for a homeless person, which could mean it belongs to whoever sent me those viruses. Could the same person be hitting Looking Glass's firewalls as well?

Cold sweat pops up between my shoulder blades and my next thoughts leap to Michael and cling, but that's stupid. No matter what Hart or Norcut think, my father wouldn't hang around here for long—definitely not long enough to hit the firewalls. It's too risky, too obvious.

But *someone's* been here. I drag the sleeping bag away from the wall and uncover a box of PowerBars and an empty bottle of water. Someone's definitely been here and they've been staying for a while. The question is why.

I stand, study the single window at the back of the bedroom. It's next to the folding door closet, and the closer I get, the more I realize something's hissing.

No, that's not quite right; something's whistling. The window. From this side of the house, I'm facing the backyard now and there's a breeze squeezing in from outside. I brush my hands off and check the sill. Sure enough, there's a hole in one corner of the glass pane, just large enough to fit my thumb into. The wind sweeps higher, a reedy whine that instinctively makes me jam one finger in the hole.

The screech stops. If I rented this place that would be the first thing I'd fix. And that's when I realize the window's not just loose. It's open.

I curl my finger and lift; the frame follows me easily. Soundlessly. Warm spring air pours into the room. I take a deep breath . . . hold it, eyes traveling past the grass-pocked backyard.

You know, between the shielded yard and the open window, someone could slip in and out of here with very little notice. If you wanted to hide something . . . if *you* wanted to hide . . . chills scatter across my skin.

I cock my head, listening. I'm not the only thing breathing in here.

Slowly—too slowly—I turn. The bedroom's empty, but the closed closet to my right? I watch it, wait, and the silence stretches. Everything's exactly as it should be, but this doesn't feel right. I retreat one step and then another, my hand extending behind me, groping for the door.

Another exhale. It *is* coming from the closet. I didn't imagine it.

I'm not alone.

"Who's—"

Something heavy drops behind me. The breathing wasn't coming from the closet. It was coming from *above*.

One arm snakes around my waist; a hand covers my mouth—and presses down.

No gloves this time.

I pry my teeth apart to bite him and there's a hiss in my ear.

"It's *me*."

I register the words the same time I register the smell: grass and the faintest scent of gasoline.

It's Griff.

He releases me and I spin around, face him. For three whole seconds, I stare . . . he stares . . . and then Griff swallows, eyes still speared to me. I take a step forward. He takes a step back. We both stop.

"How did you find me?" I breathe and he retreats again. "Wicked . . ."

The nickname forks lightning across my skin and I shiver. He looks rough. Griff's always been thin, wiry, but there's a hardness to his muscles now. There are smudges under his eyes and his T-shirt is worn through in two places, revealing slivers of skin across his lower abs.

"He's out," Griff whispers, the words escaping on a hard exhale. "Michael."

"I know."

"He's still here. He's *close*."

"I know."

Griff shifts from foot to foot. Is he hesitating to come closer? Or is he holding himself back? "Your handle popped up. I know you're working. What's going on?"

"It's complicated." I swallow. "What are you *doing* here? Are you sending me those viruses?"

Griff's face screws up in confusion. "What?"

"Wick?"

Blood thumps in my temples. Milo.

"Wick?"

Closer now. Oh shit, he's headed this way. I whip toward Griff.

"I'm sorry, Wicked. For everything."

I blink. There's white all around Griff's eyes now, but he doesn't look away from me and I can't look away from him. If he doesn't go, they'll catch him. They'll know there's more to him than just a guy I was dating. Milo's sneakers scuff closer and I wave one hand toward the closet.

"Go," I snarl under my breath.

Another beat of hesitation and Griff steps to the side, disappearing into the closet. There's a faint thump—his sneakers hitting the wall?—and then nothing.

Until Milo swings through the bedroom door.

"Hey, are you okay?" Milo saunters in, gaze catching on the window, on the closet. Does it linger? No. No, he's looking at the open attic door above my head now. "Anything up there?" he asks.

Not anymore. I shake my head. "I pulled the door down just to look."

We both stare into the darkened opening. The ladder's still pulled up, no sign that Griff was ever there. I shrug, glance at Milo, and realize he's studying me.

"You okay?" he asks again.

"Yeah, fine. Look what I found." I nudge my chin toward the sleeping bag and Milo's eyes go bright. He pulls the sleeping bag apart again and checks the Power-Bar box.

"Whoever it is, they're planning on returning."

"Unless we were spotted coming inside."

"True." Milo scowls, and somehow it makes him look prettier. His attention drifts past me to the closet. He stands and his hands flex once. "Did you check in there?"

"Yes, it's empty. Let's go."

"You're sure?"

I force a cocky smile, but my chest stays two sizes too small and my fingers still ache for a boy that isn't mine. "What's the opposite of full?"

"Empty."

"Then, yeah, I'm sure." Okay, that's probably closer to bitchy than cocky but I can't seem to stop. Griff is hiding in the closet, I'm no closer to finding Michael, and my phone call to Lily is slipping away. "This place is worse than I remember," I add, concentrating on rerolling the sleeping bag for the second time.

"No joke." Milo grins. "I can't believe you lived around here."

"Says the boy who stayed in the world's most disgusting restaurant."

"Well, I made up for it in other ways." I stand and Milo's in my space now, my breasts brushing his chest. "Want me to remind you?" he asks.

Yes. *No.* I want to go. Get out of here. It would take so little for Milo to catch Griff. And Milo . . . poor Milo. I'm looking at him and my brain is brimming with all the possibilities of who's been here.

And who's here now. What the hell is Griff doing?

I grab Milo's hand, tug him toward the door, but Milo shakes me loose, cups both hands around my face, and tilts my mouth toward his. "I'm very, very good at reminding you."

His lips brush mine and I shiver.

"Sorry," I manage as Milo lets me go. "I'm sorry." My hand connects with the wall and I shrink into it. "Sorry, it's just this place. I hated it here. Still do."

"Then I'm sorry we had to come."

Milo actually sounds like he's sorry too and it cracks something in my chest. I don't meet his eyes. The regret in his voice makes me feel worse.

"This is what we agreed, wasn't it?" I ask. "I'm supposed to play along."

"I want what's best for you."

Now he's got me. My eyes swing to his. Stick.

Milo smiles. "And we're clear here? Are you sure you looked around enough?"

"Yeah." I grab Milo's hand and pull him with me into the hall, away from the bedroom, away from Griff. "There's nothing here for us."

We find the computer setup in the kitchen and load everything into Hart's car. I don't know how much good it's going to do us—the tower case is rigged with trip switches to destroy the hard drive if we tamper with it—but Hart keeps his promise anyway and drives us past my house. I don't know what I was hoping for. To see Lily in the yard? To pass Bren driving by? I don't get either of those things. The house looks like it always does: nicely mowed yard, closed-up garage. There's a new flower wreath on the door and I can't help wondering if Bren noticed the equally new nail hole in the mahogany wood. It was courtesy of Jason Baines, a hammer, and a dead rat.

The gesture was meant for me, a reminder of what happens to snitches, and now all I can think about is Griff and what Michael will do if he catches him.

Hart doesn't slow as we drive past, but when our car reaches the corner, he nods toward a telephone repair truck parked at the curb. "Those are our guys."

Our guys. Like I'm one of the team.

"It doesn't look like much." I twist in my seat, studying the panel van as we pass. "How do I know anyone's in there?"

Not a team player comment, but it's out there now and I'm not taking it back.

Hart's teeth grind briefly together. "The same way you know if we get sideswiped again, I'll haul your ass out of there."

I turn around and tuck both hands under my legs. "Sorry."

"I'll get over it."

"Stop worrying, Hart." Milo's voice is almost singsong. "No one knows she's out—unless you haven't been doing your job."

Hart makes a right, turning us away from the neighborhood and toward the interstate. "We'll switch the van before it gets too obvious. The security system has been upgraded and we have someone shadowing your sister at activities. We know what we're doing."

I slump a little lower, feeling stupid. "Right."

"Better?"

"Yes." But there's a pang beneath my ribs and I can't pry it apart. Is it from homesickness? Worry?

Or something else?

As Hart eases the town car onto the interstate, he outlines the plan for Joe's house. Long story short? Now that they have the computer setup, they're going to watch for anyone to return. It's reasonable. In his place, I'd do the same thing, but honestly? It's a waste of time.

"You won't catch him," I say at last. "That neighborhood has eyes even when it looks empty. There's no way your car wasn't noticed. There's no way we weren't spotted. It would be stupid for whoever was staying there to return."

And somehow it doesn't feel stupid. Why use Joe's house to send the viruses? Why not some Wi-Fi hot spot? Why not somewhere less conspicuous? Honestly, the whole thing feels calculated.

Except the part with Griff. That part feels . . . off. Wrong. He didn't know what I was talking about. He didn't have a clue.

"Well," Hart says, changing lanes. "It would also be stupid not to have someone there."

I nod. "Yeah. True."

It's just after four when we reach the parking garage again. Hart swings into the space nearest the elevator and we all pile out, Milo following close on my heels.

"You seem off, Wick." His fingers climb across my arm and I string up a smile.

"Sorry. Just tired." I lean against the elevator wall and close my eyes. It's kind of to prove my point and kind of because I can't look at Milo for a second longer.

Too bad I see Griff in the dark. The last time I saw him was supposed to be the end. Why does this feel like a beginning?

Why does this feel like the start of something *worse*? And because my brain's already on overdrive it kicks into all the things worse could look like: What if he returns to the house? What if Hart's people catch him?

What was he *doing* there?

I clench my teeth together. He won't get caught. He won't. Griff would never be that stupid. He knows the house is compromised now.

Right?

"You don't look okay." Milo again.

I open my eyes. "Headache."

Now they're both watching me. I look away—look at the elevator buttons, the floor, the wall. The wall. That'll work. There's a glossy steel handrail and Hart's palm is wrapped around one corner. But as I watch, his fingers begin to drum.

Is he irritated? Or thinking hard?

I don't wait to find out. The elevator stops, the doors drag open, and I bolt, heading for my bedroom. I swipe my key card, and inside, it's blissfully quiet and totally empty. Alex must still be upstairs. Technically, I should be upstairs too. After today's field trip, I'm behind in schoolwork and in computer work. I should try to get on top of things before dinner and group therapy, but I can't quite bring myself to do it. Too many nights of insomnia plus seeing Griff and not finding Michael equals . . . yeah, it's all a bit much.

I kick off one sneaker, reach for the other, and stop. Listen. What was that? I turn and—*there*. There it is again. Whispering? Or is it hissing? Whatever it is, it's so soft I take a step toward our window, stare into the air vent. Nothing.

Except there's another hiss. This time, it's louder, closer to a murmur. It *is* someone whispering, and for the first time, I notice our bathroom door is closed and there's a shadow behind the frosted glass.

Alex is in there and it sounds like she's talking to someone. One of our teachers? I stand on the other side of the bathroom door and study her outline. Maybe she's doing some sort of Skype session. But why would she do it in the bathroom? And why would she be so quiet?

Alex's shadow moves, twists, and we both freeze. Damn. If I can see her shadow, she can see mine.

"Wick?"

"Yeah." I clear my throat. "I just got back. Are you okay?"

Alex's arm arcs toward the handle and there's a click as she opens the door. "Course." She braces one shoulder against the frame, looking like this is any other day: same hoodie, same bored expression. "Why wouldn't I be okay?"

"Just being nice."

Her eyes narrow like I am anything but and I ignore her, drag off my other shoe, and collapse onto my bed. She's still watching me and I'm still thinking about who she was talking to. Herself? God?

Or someone else?

"Where were you?" Alex asks and I hesitate. Alex was already upstairs when we left. She probably waited for me all morning and I feel bad. Thing is, Norcut wanted this kept private—but how private can you keep anything when we all live practically on top of each other?

"My dad escaped."

There is the slightest, almost imperceptible beat of hesitation before Alex says, "No shit?"

My mouth goes dry. Slight hesitation. Almost imperceptible, but still there. I push myself up, bracing on my elbow. "You already knew."

"How would I know?"

"You can't lie to a liar, Alex."

"So tell her the truth." The voice is tinny, far away, and definitely not one of us. Alex and I stare at each other and seconds pass before she tugs an iPhone from her hoodie pocket, tilts it so I can see the dark-haired woman on the screen.

"This was going to happen sooner or later," she says, and I shoot to my feet. The words are slow, deliberate, like she's talking to an animal she's spooked or an addict on the edge. "Alex has told me all about you, Wick, and I really like what I've heard. We want to make you an offer."

"Who the hell are you?" I back up and my legs hit the bed. My brain's stuck on ridiculous loops about how Norcut said we're not allowed to have contact with the outside world, how we're not allowed to have cell phones.

How this is bad. This is really, really bad. Has to be.

And yet . . . I could call Lily with that phone. I could call my best friend, Lauren. I could check my bank and email accounts without Looking Glass tracing my keystrokes.

"She's one of my contacts," Alex says softly. "I'm not here because I got myself in a bind—well, I mean, I did get caught, but it was on purpose. I needed a way into Looking Glass."

"You were hired for a job," I say softly, watching for Alex's flinch. She doesn't. "And here I thought you were Looking Glass's biggest fan. You told me I was being ridiculous."

"I had a job to do. You know what that's like. What would you have done?"

Same thing and we both know it. That's what makes this whole thing so very sad.

"I want out," Alex continues softly. "I want you to help me. The payout for this job is *serious*—plenty for us to split. All we have to do is pull files from the main system and get them to my client. It's a victimless crime. We get paid and no one gets hurt."

Except, possibly, for me. And then my sister. And Bren. Looking Glass is funding their protection. If we were to steal from them, what happens to my family?

My head goes light and I swallow.

"Wick," the other woman begins, but there's a faraway shout. Her side of the phone drops, showing us a terrific view of her feet and the pavement. Another shout.

"I have to go." Her voice is still hushed. It's a bit hard to separate the words through the sound of her sneakers scuffing against the ground. She's running, fast. "Alex, you have to tell her. Tell her about the cameras and tell her about *him*."

Alex flips the phone around before I can see the disconnect. It's the same old Alex looking down at the screen and yet she's different too. It's in the way she lingers on the final image and pulls at her lower lip. She's worried. Scared.

That makes two of us.

"What kind of job takes over a year?" I breathe.

"The kind where you have to navigate Kent."

"Who else knows about this?"

"Just the three of us."

Just the three of us? Can I believe her? "Alex, all those promises, all that *stuff*—"

"Yeah, yeah. College degrees. Job futures. You can do all of that or you can take your share of the payout and do whatever you want for the rest of your life."

Escape, freedom. The words squirm under my skin and grow.

I force myself to inhale. "You're crazy. Even if we did get away with it, they'll hunt us. Forever."

"So? Not like they'll find us. You know how this works, Wick. With enough money, anyone can disappear."

Absolutely, and the idea fills every inch of me. For

years, I did computer work for clients and banked the money in offshore accounts. I was always ready to run. Until Bren, the foster homes never lasted. I had to be prepared, and if you have enough money, you can be prepared for almost anything.

"My people know about their clients, their technology," Alex continues softly. "We just need the right help to get through Kent. You're that person. You could do this."

I stare. I don't even know where to begin.

"Hart and Norcut engineered your arrival, Wick. You don't owe them anything. They used your mom. They used *her* to get to you."

"There's more to it than just my mom."

"Oh, you mean that accident? Those people who are after you?" Alex's picking up speed now. "How do you know that accident wasn't arranged? How do you know it wasn't created so you would trust them? Face it, Wick. You're nothing more than a tool."

I stiffen. "And what's that woman to you? How do you know you're not a tool to her? How can you trust her?"

A pause. "You don't have to be related to someone to make them family. So. Are you in?"

"I don't . . . I can't . . ."

"You can. In fact, I think you're already in." Alex fiddles with her phone screen. I can't tell if she's actually doing something or pretending so we don't have to look at each other. "I think if you weren't, you wouldn't be whispering. You'd be yelling. By now, everyone would hear us."

Alex's eyes flick to mine, and I know she can tell she hit bone with that one.

She's right. I am still whispering.

"Face it, Wick, there's more to Hart and Norcut and you *know* it. You're like us. You've felt it from the beginning."

"I feel that about everyone." I half mean it to be funny. Too bad, it surfaces sounding serious. Worse, my legs suddenly give out. I collapse on the bed in a heap. Everything is sinking in now. Maybe that's how it works. First comes the burn, then comes the pain, but there's always a space in between.

I cannot afford to be involved in this. Not when I have so much to lose. There's Milo, my future . . . forgiveness. The path back to my family is *through* Looking Glass. I promised Bren I would try.

"Tell me if you're in. With or without you, this is happening." Alex is going for hard, but her eyes are baby-animal soft and round. My answer means something to her. *I* mean something to her.

It makes the whole thing hurt that much more. We will never be the same after this. Whatever friendship we have won't survive, and in some ways, now I wish I had never found her because this one's going to hurt.

"I'm not," I manage and scrub one hand across my face. "I can't be. I can't take down the one thing that stands between my family and my father. He should be running and he isn't. That scares me. Seriously. I don't know if that means he's looking for me or for my sister or for something else, but Norcut says she'll help me catch him."

"And you believe her?" Alex is pissy, edgy now, and I get it. Of all people, I so get that and telling her no hurts more than I ever expected. I've drawn a line now. She's on one side and I'm on the other. It won't be the same anymore.

"That's where we were today. Thanks to Looking Glass's resources, they're safer." Possibly. Maybe. I close my eyes and take a deep breath. There's so much you can fit into a *maybe*. More than I like.

"Those resources include all the cameras in your house?"

My eyes pop open. "What are you talking about?"

"You heard. She wanted me to tell you about the cameras." Alex jerks her head, making her ponytail bounce. "Explain to me how Hart and Norcut are protecting your family if they have more cameras on the inside of the house than the outside."

I don't say anything, but then again, I don't have to. We both heard my exhale. It was hard, sharp, like I'd been punched.

"That's right," Alex continues and there's something round and satisfied leaking into her voice. "There are at least six different camera angles and I don't think Bren and Lily have looked at any of them. Ever. Do you think that's because they don't know they're there?"

My skin goes cold. "How do you know that?"

"Because I helped order the cameras."

"And you're telling me now? Why? Because I'm finally useful?"

"It's not like that. I didn't know if I could trust you."

I'm shaking now and I can't decide where to begin—where Alex didn't tell me this until now or where my family's being spied on. Unless they're just being protected. Maybe Looking Glass is covering all their bases. I would.

Still, I have to force a noncommittal shrug. "You and I both know indoor surveillance isn't that unusual."

"Don't try that on me. If you're going to make excuses at least come up with something decent. Why would they need to watch your sister and mom?" Alex brightens, points at my chest with the cell. "Think it's because they're perverts like your stepdad?"

Nausea slithers through me. "No, I don't."

If Hart and Norcut are watching Bren and Lily, it's for another reason. Because they think my dad will contact Lily? Another twinge of nausea. Could be, but there are better ways of tracking that. So that leaves . . . no idea. I don't know what they're hoping to gain here.

I do know that, without my family, Norcut and Hart don't have leverage on me.

Stop it. I lift my chin, glare. *Don't think like that. Stop letting her goad you.*

"I'm sorry, Alex. Truly. I wish I could help."

"You can, you just *won't*."

I start to argue and stop. She's right. I do know some-thing about Looking Glass feels off. I do know it's weird for them to have more cameras inside than outside, but they're also standing between Michael and my family. I'm not jumping into this on just Alex's word—and I'm damn sure not going to be someone's teammate or weapon with-out knowing her angle. "Why are you doing this?"

"We all have our reasons, Wick. You should know that better than anyone."

Yeah and that's the thing: I do. I also know how it can be used against me and maybe she's doing that now and everything before was just a lead-up to this: getting me on their side.

There is something seriously wrong with my life that I have to consider each person's angle before agreeing to help. And suddenly, it's like Griff is right there with me, a whisper rushing down my ear as he says, "Once you prove yourself useful to the wrong kind of person, you're never free."

Is this just another round of it?

"Did you send me those messages? The viruses?" I ask.

She shakes her head. "No, but it's great luck for us. Kent's so busy chasing his tail and Hart's so worried about you, it's the perfect distraction."

I glance down at Alex's hand, and watch how her fin-gers tighten. "That cell secure?"

"Of course."

I dig my feet into the carpet, press until my legs hurt. I

can't believe I'm going to do this, but I will. "I'll keep quiet about whatever you're doing as long as you let me use it."

There is no coming back from this and the knowledge makes my joints so heavy I feel like I'll get dragged through the floor.

Alex's shoulders slowly straighten. "Why do you want it? To check my sources? Make sure I'm not lying to you? I don't have to lie about Hart and Norcut—"

"I need to look for someone." My heart double thumps. A mistake. A horrible, horrible mistake, and as soon as I say it, I know I should've said something—*anything*—else.

Alex goes very still. "Someone like who? Your sister?" She pauses. "Or maybe a partner?"

"No." But it's half-assed and we both know it. In another life, I would've had a better lie. But in this moment, Griff is so close to the surface, my surface, and I need to know he's safe. "I just need to do a little work off record. There's no partner."

Alex's eyes go flat, dull. "Maybe not a partner like Kent thinks, but there's definitely someone." She waits and I say nothing.

"Fine," Alex says at last. "Be like that. You ready for the other secret?"

"I don't want to know." I press both hands into the mattress, struggle to my feet. I want a shower. Or maybe just a break from this, from all of it. "I don't want to know anything else you two are doing."

"Oh, you'll want to know this one. Trust me, it's good."

I start for the bathroom and Alex follows me. "Has your pretty boy been honest with you?"

I grab a towel from the rack and turn, ready to shut the door in her face. "I'm guessing you don't think so."

"Still not interested?"

"Nope." Yes.

"Has Milo told you the deal with his mom yet?"

No, actually. We talk about a lot of things—mostly computer related, yes, but I know about his dad. I know all about Milo's fascination with explosives, the run-down restaurant his uncle left him. And he knows all about my biological mom. He even helped me find the real truth about her.

But *his* mom? We never really talked about it.

Alex smiles. "That's what I thought." She puts one hand on the door handle and the other on the frame, leaning closer and closer. "That's because he doesn't want you to know."

Another pause. Another waiting game. I don't rise for the bait, but I have to stuff myself down to do it.

"And you know why that is?" Alex asks. "Because his mom is Dr. Norcut."

I stand under the hot water for ages and it never goes cold. I almost wish it would. I'd be forced to get out.

I face the shower spray and let the hot water burn the top of my head. Maybe Alex is lying? She's mad at me. Could she be desperate enough to lie? Maybe. Probably.

But somehow, I can't brush it off. My brain keeps circling something Milo said to me once, when we were outside the courthouse and he'd saved me by cutting Carson's video feed.

"I understand you better than you know," he'd said. "This is survival. We all do things we aren't proud of."

What if I'm one of those things?

It isn't so much that his mother is my therapist that bothers me. It's that he didn't tell me. It's why *wouldn't* he tell me?

I grab the metal dial and crank the water off, stand there, dripping. Milo's mother runs Looking Glass. Which means he wasn't just "picked up." He wasn't hired on for some work. This isn't casual.

Which also means all his interest in getting me to do as I'm told isn't casual. It isn't about me finding where I belong. It's about getting me to play along. And I have played along—because they're protecting Lily and Bren, because they're protecting me. *Think about Michael being loose. Think about how I was almost kidnapped.*

Only . . . now I'm wondering how much of *that* could've been manufactured too. Chills ripple across my skin and when I close my eyes all I see is the grille of that SUV ramming into us. What if the whole almost-kidnapping was really just to gain my trust? To make me think there was a problem?

No. No way. Looking Glass had nothing to do with Michael's release or Jason Baines's death—two other reasons I'm here. I still don't understand why I'm so special to them though. There are better hackers in the world. Is it because I was convenient? Because I was already caught? It's possible, I guess.

And the pacemaker? It's a cold, little voice whispering in my head. There were all of those excuses and all of it was so convenient and I so, so, *so* wanted to believe it.

Still do, because if I don't . . . if I *did*—

My stomach heaves into my mouth and I yank the shower curtain aside and wrap the towel around me.

Don't think about it. Think about Lily. Bren. Think about how Norcut and Hart are protecting them. I don't like my therapist and I'm pretty sure she's not a fan of me either, but we are *useful* to each other and that's something . . . right?

And I'm all the way finished drying my hair before I realize that if Norcut and I are useful to each other, what does that make Milo and me?

My stomach makes another drunken lurch and I force myself into a clean T-shirt and jeans. It's not the same thing.

Is it?

I sit down, hard, on the tub's edge. In this light, Milo coming to work for Looking Glass seems awfully convenient. His excuse about the restaurant seems manufactured. Except . . . except, Milo and I get each other. You can't fake that. We're too alike for this to be just about usefulness or whatever. He took down Carson for me. Hell, he blew away a chunk of Judge Bay's house for me too. He gave me the chance to get away *and* alerted the police. Milo specializes in stuff like that, creating wiggle room, spaces in between. We both escaped that night.

He even apologized for leaving me and he didn't need to because I understood. I would've done the same.

Wrong thing to remember, though, because it leads me to Griff again. Griff, who heard about the explosion over the radio and came to the site.

Who had eyes only for my injuries.

Who walked away.

I stand, wrench open the bathroom door, and stop dead. Alex is sitting on her bed, legs stretched long. They're crossed tight at the ankles and it almost hides how she's vibrating.

"They need you upstairs," she says and there's a *gotcha* tone to her voice that makes my feet drag. "Someone's sent you another message."

Hart, Milo, and the rest of the guys are crowded around Kent's computer station. I don't think any of them even notice Alex and me until Milo steps away.

"Hey." He comes so close there's maybe an inch between us. If one of us takes a breath, we'll touch. "How're you feeling?"

"I'm . . . I'm . . ." I'm noticing for the very first time how Milo shares Norcut's cheekbones and jawline. How did I not see this before?

"I'm okay," I finish. "I took meds. Hopefully, it'll head off the migraine."

Milo smiles. I smile. And I have just enough time to realize we have the same smile before both of us turn toward the group.

Kent rolls his chair maybe an inch to the side to give me room. "What is this? It came to your email."

I lean around him. There's a Hushmail message on the screen—no greeting, just a string of numbers. "It's an IP address," I tell him. "See, every computer device has a numeric label assigned to it—"

"No shit. This one connects to some unsecured nanny cam in Connecticut. What are you doing?"

I pause, shake myself. "Nothing."

"Then why would someone send you this?"

"I have no idea."

"Wick." Hart nudges Connor aside. "I need you to be honest about this."

"I *am*. I don't know anyone in Connecticut." And I don't. I have zero clue why anyone would send me that address unless . . . "Can you open it for me?"

Kent grunts but does it. The camera shot reveals a nice-looking living room. Lots of white slipcovers, beige walls, and jewel-toned modern art. Bren would like it.

But aside from that? Nothing looks like it should mean anything to me. It's not familiar.

Hart crosses his arms. "Maybe it's from one of your past clients?"

"I didn't really work like that. My stuff was more background related—finances, job histories." I chew my lower lip. There's something here. I can feel it. "What's the physical address?"

Kent minimizes the window and opens another tab in the browser. The IP address tracks to a Chris and Julian Moore. The names are just as unfamiliar as the living room.

In fact, the only thing familiar about any of this is the actual IP address. Or at least, the first part, and the realization makes my chest funnel tight. It couldn't be . . . could it?

I lift my gaze to Hart's and realize Milo's drawn closer. He's close enough to touch me now and I have to fight not to lean away. I focus on Hart instead, try not to fidget under the way his eyes cling to my face.

"Are you sure you don't know them?" Hart presses.

"I'm pretty sure. I mean, I guess either of them could've used someone else to pose as my client, but why? It makes the whole thing complicated, cumbersome. He'd have to give his personal information to one more person and my people get nervous. They don't like to do that."

"What about the targets?" Hart's arms tighten around his chest. "Maybe they're one of the guys you looked into?"

"No." I shake my head and study the names again. "No. I can go through my records, but I remember almost everyone I research. I spend too much time in their lives not to remember who they are."

"Check anyway."

I glance at Hart. The ever-present smile is gone, like it never, ever existed. His lips are bloodless.

"Of course." I tap Kent's shoulder. "Can you flip to the IP address again?"

He returns to the window and I trace my eyes over each number until I reach the end and my chest is even tighter than before. There's no getting around it. I definitely know the beginning of the IP address. It's Griff's, belongs to the laptop he loaned me to catch Todd.

But it *isn't* Griff's because the last two digits don't match. That's why we're in Connecticut, staring at two guys' living room instead of staring at Griff's bedroom. It's got to be a coincidence.

So why doesn't it feel like it?

"Whoever sent you this *knows* you." Hart's teeth snap as he speaks. "They knew to send it to this location. It *has* to be someone you know."

"Maybe she's supposed to see something," Jake says.

Hart rounds on him. "How's that work? She just sits around until someone shows up?"

"I don't know." Jake raises his long-fingered hands in surrender. "It was just a thought. I mean, that's why you have nanny cams, right? So you can see whatever's going on in your house?"

And just like that, my insides free-fall. No. Of course not. I *am* supposed to see something, but not here and not right now. That address looks like Griff's IP because it's *almost* Griff's IP.

He contacted me.

He wants to talk and the realization unhinges me.

He changed the last two digits to tell me what time. 0-2. Two o'clock. I'm not sure whether that's a.m. or p.m., but considering the message was sent at 2:53, I'm guessing it's a.m. *Tonight.*

For three whole seconds, I'm not at Looking Glass. I'm not staring at a computer screen. I'm with Griff. I'm standing in the days after Todd, but in the weeks before I was blackmailed by Carson, when Griff's touch felt like he was drawing a poem on my skin.

Why does every memory of him taste like hope?

"Wick?" Hart. His tone turns my name blunt and bloody. "Everything okay?"

Hart's turned his back to Kent and the computer to focus on me. Actually, everyone's focused on me.

I shiver. "Yeah, I'm fine. It's just weird."

Hart nods, waiting for me to add something else. I definitely want to, but I shrug like I don't. My shoulders are strung so tight they pop. I want to ask about the cameras at Bren's, but how do I do it without giving away Alex? Maybe I shouldn't care. Maybe this is every girl for herself.

"Continue watching her email accounts," Hart says, still focused on me. If he's searching for a reaction, he doesn't get it. I'm good at the glazed-eye look.

Then again, Hart's good at it too. There's nothing in his expression now. His eyes are shiny as marbles. He doesn't believe me. Another line's been crossed and I need to fix it, make it look like I'm on their side still.

Hell, I *am* on their side still.

"Hey, I've been thinking." Kent snorts and I ignore him. "Do you think you could get copies of the security footage from my dad's release?"

"You want to watch him leaving?"

"Yeah, I want to see who was with him."

Hart perks up. "You think you'd recognize the guy?"

I pause, turning the question in my mind until it clicks. "You've already seen it."

A single nod. "I can get the video clips to you immediately. We still have them on file."

"Since when?"

"Since the day after it happened." Hart faces me fully now. "We had to know, Wick. We're keeping you—and your family—safe."

He sounds so reasonable. Unease shouldn't be trickling through me. It's the same Hart from Bren's living room. The same guy who worried searching for my dad was dangerous.

That it was backtracking.

He's been looking out for me. So why am I feeling light-footed, like I'm seconds away from bolting? Because there's something wrong here? Or because I can't see straight? Because I've *never* been able to see straight when it comes to trust. I always pick the wrong person. I feel sorry for dangerous people and I don't realize my mistake until it's too late.

I've been a really great target over the years, which is hilarious since it's the one thing I never wanted to be.

"I'll make sure the files are in your Looking Glass account after dinner," Hart says. "You can review them tonight or tomorrow."

"Thanks." I start to turn and Milo reaches for my arm.

"Wick—" he says.

I freeze and Hart steps between us. "I need a few more minutes with you, Milo." He flicks his gaze to Alex. "Both of you can go. Remember there's therapy tonight—and bring your completed homework. Don't forget."

It would be a little hard to, but both of us nod like we totally appreciate the reminder and shuffle for the door. Alex doesn't say a word as we head toward the elevator. Once we're inside though she faces me and waits.

And waits.

I grind my teeth to keep from snapping at her.

"Isn't that interesting?" she asks at last. The doors open on our floor and we step off, Alex trailing so closely our sleeves brush. "You think he would've ever told you if you hadn't asked?"

"Who cares? Point is, I did ask and I'm getting the files." I sound so light; I almost believe it doesn't needle me. I face her. "I need to borrow your phone."

"Phone?"

"Don't start."

"Or what?"

"Don't make me tell Hart."

"Then neither of us will have a line to the outside." She shrugs and swipes her key card through our room's security pad. Inside, I lean against the frosted glass door as she rifles through her stuff.

"They're protecting my family, Alex. I can't lose that."

She turns. "Are you convincing me? Or yourself?"

I don't have an answer, but I don't think I'm supposed to. She passes me the cell and the battery's hot to the touch.

"Use it," Alex says. "But only because I'm generous and because you're going to need me, and I prefer it when people owe me favors."

The rest of the evening drags. We have dinner. We have therapy. We turn in homework and Milo never shows.

When I ask about him, Hart shrugs and says, "Maybe he had something to finish up."

Maybe, but if that were true, Hart wouldn't be watching me like he's waiting for a reaction. I smile like there isn't something festering inside me and follow Alex back to our room. We don't say much. We've both been assigned more homework and I'm nowhere near finished with my chemistry notes when I quit. Milo's in my head, but the cell is calling me. I want to use the phone's internet.

I want to search for Griff's name.

I stuff my hand between the bed and the dresser, wiggling my fingers until I can tug the cell from its hiding spot. It's kind of stupid how much I've missed my own phone. Holding this one makes me feel more like myself.

"Just can't wait to make that call, huh?" Alex doesn't look up from her math homework, but I like to think she can feel me giving her the bird. I jump off the bed and shut myself in the bathroom.

"What?" she calls. "You shy now?"

I prefer to think of it as being practical. I can't afford to give her leverage.

But yeah, there might be some shyness too. Griff is mine. Not mine in the sense that I own him. More like . . . it's personal. What we had was something that belonged to me. Just me. And the loss of it sinks me to the floor.

I press my shoulders to the tiled wall and search Griff's name. Top two results are local newspaper articles about his art school scholarship. He'll be attending Savannah College of Art and Design in the fall, and even though both columns are basically the same thing, I reread them and I can't stop my grin.

Griff always wanted to go to SCAD. It was part of his master plan, part of that happily ever after he wanted more than anything. And I want to concentrate on how this is wonderful and amazing and "a great example of a disadvantaged youth conquering adversity."

But my brain keeps circling how close Griff came to losing it all.

Carson would've ruined that. Gladly. I traded myself for Griff. My future for his future. He will never know how close he came and I'm glad for that. Truly.

I think once you realize that safety is just an illusion, that family is just a word, and that everything is always on the edge of disappearing, nothing ever looks the same again. Because once you lose that belief, you don't lose it just a little. You sink it ten thousand miles below your surface. In the muck. In the mire. And even if you resurrect those beliefs, they don't look the same. They will *never* look the same.

Griff does though. As I'm scrolling through pictures of his drawings and articles about his art show wins, he looks exactly the same. Beautiful. Untouched. Not damaged. Damn sure not broken.

I close the cell's browser and lie on the cold tile floor, stare at the ceiling until the minutes smear past and I'm chilled through. Alex turns the bedroom light off around one thirty, but I doubt she's sleeping. She's waiting, listening. We're both watching each other now, hunting for cracks. If I were in her position, I wouldn't lose this opportunity either.

The quieter she is, the better chance she can hear me.

Good luck with that, Alex, because there won't be anything *to* hear. I downloaded an iCam app to the phone. The upside is I'll be able to see Griff. The downside? He won't be able to see me. I won't be able to communicate any answers and the only way he'll know I'm even there is when the cam goes live and the light turns on.

I check the phone's screen: 1:55. Still a little more time.

I could so do without that. My heart's already stuttering in my chest. If I get caught . . . best not to think about it.

1:59.

I sit up and open the app, plug in the address. The screen goes black, then gray, then fills with Griff and I can't breathe.

His eyes flick to the top of his screen—probably noticing the web cam light—and Griff bites his lower lip once before his gaze drops. I can't tell where he is. The surroundings are dim and people are passing by. It's definitely not his bedroom, so . . . internet café? It's awfully late for a Starbucks.

Griff scoots lower in his seat, passing one hand over his jaw. It's the same T-shirt, same scruff, but he looks . . . strained. Exhausted.

I tell myself it has to be the lighting.

His attention dips, and briefly, I'm confused; then he lifts a pad of paper. There are a few lines scribbled across the page:

I only have a few minutes. This was the safest way to talk I could think of.

I nod and immediately feel stupid. He can't see me, but I agree with him. Video feeds aren't as easily monitored as calls. This is smart for both of us. Griff flips the pad again and dashes off a few more lines:

Michael's looking for something. Rumor says it's money.

I tense. That . . . doesn't make any sense. Why would Michael be looking for money? He already has the eleven million he stole from Looking Glass.

Doesn't he?

Griff's eyes track over and over the screen. I want to call him, but even if I could, I'm not sure I could find my voice. I feel suddenly buried.

He turns the pad, tears off the top page, and scrawls another line:

Rumor also says you stole it from him.

Stole it? I slump forward. I didn't even know about it until this week. And furthermore, rumor from who? Rumor from around the neighborhood? From one of Michael's guys? The first doesn't worry me. The second does. A lot.

Griff waits, studying the screen before flipping the pad around once again. This time, he takes a little longer, hesitates before turning it to me.

That means he's looking for you.

My heart stutters and I have to force myself to breathe. Breathe again. It's fine. It is. I knew Michael was looking for me. Aside from the searching-for-money thing, Griff isn't telling me anything I didn't already know.

Too bad no matter how many times I repeat this to myself, my stomach is still sloshing around my feet. Michael thinks I stole money from him? This is bad. This is very, very bad.

Griff's eyes return to the top of the screen, lingering. He flips the pad around, jots another line, and holds it up:

I hope you're safe.

"I hope you're safe too," I whisper, and once again, my fingers itch to dial his cell, to take the risk. I could stuff towels underneath the door and crank the shower full blast. Maybe I could get away with it. I want to ask him about the viruses again, see if he has any idea who would be trying to warn me.

Griff turns the pad to him and makes a quick slash across it, then turns it to me:

I wish I'd told you how much I miss you.

He hesitates again, opening his mouth like there's something else to say, and I lean toward the screen because I'm ready for it, but he shakes his head once. Twice. He grabs the top of his laptop and closes it. My screen goes black and he's gone.

The smart thing to do would be to go to bed, but even if I did, it's not like I'm going to sleep. I push to my feet, and once I'm standing, all I can feel is how my legs are shaking.

I clear the phone's history and unlock the bathroom door, grab my Chucks from the floor, and toss the cell onto Alex's bed.

She catches it. "Where are you going?"

"To work. You want to follow me there too?"

"Nah." Alex settles deeper into bed. She's just a shadow now. "If you're going to work for them, I don't need to see it."

She pitches the cell at me and I have to put up both hands to avoid being clipped in the face.

"Keep it," Alex says. "You know you want to."

"Not enough to risk getting caught."

"Who's going to tell?"

I can't bring myself to say she would, but my silence does it for me.

Alex's laugh is smoke in the dark. "Call your sister. It'll only prove me right. I dare you."

I jam the cell into the waistband of my jeans and pad down the hall, stuff my feet into my shoes as I wait for the elevator. Upstairs, the workstations are under low lights, but Kent's still working away, one hand on his keyboard and the other wrapped around a plastic Big Gulp. A gift from Hart? I would've thought Kent's standards would be higher.

"What're you doing?" he asks around a mouthful of crushed ice.

I shrug. "What're *you* doing?"

"I have important things going on."

"Yeah. Clearly." I drop into my seat, rub the back of my neck as I wait for my computer to boot. As promised, the video file is in my email, and at first I'm slightly confused because there should be more files—different angles from different cameras—and then I realize everything's been edited into one clip.

There's my dad emerging from some holding cell . . . another few seconds of him coming down one hallway . . . and then another hallway . . . and then to a processing area. There's a desk and some guy manning the desk.

Michael waits as they go through his paperwork. From this angle, I can really see him. He's dropped weight and there's a smudge of darkness near his collar. A new tattoo?

Clipboards pass between two guards, and ever so briefly, my dad's eyes lift to the camera and hold. His gaze flicks left then right, counting the cams probably. I squirm. It's another habit we share.

Whatever was on the clipboard apparently made the second guard happy because he waves Michael through. The video jumps to my dad going down another hallway . . . through another secured door . . . and into an open receiving area. A blond guy is waiting for him and they walk out. There's maybe another forty-five seconds of the two of them leaving the parking lot. Walking.

Whoever this guy is, he was smart enough not to leave his car where the plate would be picked up by the security cams. Which probably means he left it down the road a bit. Risky. There isn't a cop alive who wouldn't check an abandoned vehicle that close to the jail.

Maybe somebody else met them?

I watch the whole thing again. And then once more. Hart's right. It's not particularly useful. Yeah, Michael doesn't look surprised, so you could assume he knew what was coming, but the biggest problem is not knowing Blondie's real identity. He had the release papers. He walked both of them straight through the doors. That means purpose; he needs Michael for something.

The money? That can't be it—not if my dad thinks I have it. Unless . . . unless Blondie is supposed to help Michael get it back.

I skim two fingers over my still scabby forearm. Did Blondie pull me from Hart's car in the accident? If so, who was waiting in the SUV?

My stomach threatens to swoop into my mouth and I swallow. Get a grip. There's no point in speculating. I need to stick to what I *do* know: There are some serious connections at work here. You don't get those kinds of papers at Walmart or whatever. This took thought, planning, and the right kind of forger.

I don't know anyone capable of pulling it off and I know—knew—most of my father's contacts. I rewind a few frames to watch the two men walk out like it's no big deal. Maybe Michael's expanded his circle of friends since landing in jail? I mean I guess it's possible, but wouldn't that sort of thing take money?

Which Michael doesn't have. He's never had.

Except maybe he did and now he thinks I have it.

I pause the video and rewind it until I'm at the receiving area again. They don't shake hands. I can't see Michael's expression since the camera's behind him, but the blond guy seems relaxed enough. This could be any other day. Like he does it all the time.

And that worrisome feeling I'd had earlier breathes up from the grave I put it in.

It couldn't be.

Or is it because I don't want it to be?

I rewind frame by frame until I'm dead on Blondie. The angle's perfect and I need to know this, but I still have to take a deep, deep breath before I open the editing program. It takes me a few minutes to manipulate the images. I have to enlarge his face and smooth some of the pixilation.

I don't know a ton of cops. I know the faces of the few who came to our house for domestic disturbances. I could probably pick out the one or two who worked security at our school. And then, of course, there was Carson.

Blondie is definitely not Carson.

But he *is* one of Carson's guys.

I twist my chair from side to side and glare at my reflection in the windows. Every minute or so, Kent looks my way and our eyes meet. His narrow. Mine narrow. I give him the finger and he turns completely around and focuses on his computer again.

I don't know what to do. I still don't know Blondie's name, but I do recognize him. He was riding shotgun in Carson's car one day when I left the jail. I didn't think too much of it after the detective disappeared, but Carson had a team that worked for him back when he was a rising star in the police department. I assumed they were reassigned once he was put under investigation.

What if this one is still working for him? Maybe he thinks Carson's innocent? The detective's been running for over a month now. What if they're trying to clear Carson's name?

I mentally kick myself. There's no connection between Carson and Michael other than Carson hunted and arrested my father. Why would he get Michael out of jail?

Or better yet: What would Carson *gain* by Michael getting out of jail?

Of course, that's assuming Blondie still works for him—unless Blondie works for my dad.

Now that's a disturbing thought. I keep my eyes on Kent, but he doesn't turn around. I twist my chair some more, still thinking. Michael's been in jail for months. Why wait until now to escape? Why not do it sooner? What *changed*?

I sigh, rub my forehead. Because he thinks I stole the money from whatever super-secret account he put it in? That's stupid. I haven't been around the neighborhood in months—not since Griff and I were still dating. And it would *have* to be somewhere in the neighborhood, somewhere physical. The Feds knew about his bank accounts. If it had been deposited, they would've found it and confiscated it, right?

Maybe. I'm having a hard time thinking past my fear. My father's loose and I'm afraid. It's filling every corner of me and I am so ready to be done with being scared.

Beyond our windows, pink and gray light leaks past the neighboring building. It's almost seven thirty and my thoughts leap—and cling—to Lily. I have the cell. I could call. No one would know . . . unless Lily's phone is tapped too. But if it's not . . . if I had a shot at talking to her . . .

Hope tiptoes along my spine on spider legs. I'm not supposed to contact them. Those are the rules. Bren even told Norcut she didn't want me to, but surely—*surely*—Lily doesn't agree. I just need to know they're okay. I just need . . . my sister. She's worth the risk.

I stand, stretch. There's still no reaction from Kent so I wander to the door, down the hall.

The girls' bathroom is to my left and I never once look at the security camera. I am my father's daughter right now. I'm pretending everything is fine. Inside, I turn on all the faucets, sit in the first stall, and stare at the phone.

Problem is, if the house really is wired, there are probably bugs as well. Hart and Norcut will hear everything. Which means my best shot at reaching Lily is right now—before school, but after she's left the house.

They haven't wanted to talk to me. What if she hangs up? I'm not sure I could handle that.

Then again, I definitely can't handle not knowing. I want to hear her voice. I want someone I can trust telling me they're okay.

Even so, my fingers are slick on the keypad. I hold the phone to my ear, listen to it ring. Ring again. What if it goes to voice mail?

I switch ears. I can't decide whether to leave a message. Leaving one would be as bad as having a conversation around the bugs and cameras. It would leave a trace and totally compromise this phone. And if Lily really doesn't want to talk to me and she shows the message to Bren, I'm beyond hosed.

On the other hand, I may *have* to leave a voice mail. Lily might not pick up if she doesn't recognize the number. Crap. Crapcrapcrapcrap—

"Hello?"

I sit straight. I want to yell and I'm having to whisper. "Lily!"

"Wick! Oh my God, Wick!" There's a bubble in my sister's voice. It's either tears or laughter and I can't decide which, but I feel the same way. "Are you okay? Is everything all right?"

"I'm fine! I'm fine!" I pause, jerking her words around until they make sense. "Why wouldn't everything be okay?"

"Because Mom's been trying to reach you!" Lily holds the mouthpiece so close I can hear each breath. "They keep saying you're not taking our calls."

"Are you there?" Lily asks. "Wick? Mom feels really bad about what happened. Please don't shut us out anymore."

Shut them out? My brain is tingly, fuzzy, and I sound so very far away when I answer, "Lil, I haven't refused your calls. I was told I wasn't allowed to call."

She hiccups. "Mom would never do that!"

I take a deep breath and then another. Either Bren's lying about the phone situation . . . or Norcut is.

"Mom *wants* to talk to you, Wick." Again, the mouthpiece is tucked close. Her breathing's ragged and shallow as mine now. "I miss you. I miss you so much. It's not the same without you. We're not the same family. Please come home."

Now I *am* crying.

"I'm scared, Wick."

I grip the phone tighter. "Why?"

"There are men watching the house. I've seen them. Mom—Bren won't admit it, but I know she sees them too."

I rub one fist against my breastbone, but the knot in my chest refuses to loosen. "She probably thinks it would scare you worse to know the truth. The house is being watched for your protection. Michael escaped and those men are there to make sure he doesn't bother you."

"Why would he?" Lily's words skew up an octave. "Why would he even stay around here? Isn't he worried about being caught again?"

"I don't know." I waver. My gut's telling me not to say anything further, but I kept Lily in the dark for so long. Maybe it's time I trust her? She's not the girl she used to be. Honestly, neither am I.

I pinch the skin between my eyes and force the words. "They think . . . they think there's something around here he wants." I pause, listening to her breathing. It hitched once, but she's still there.

"You need to come home, Wick. We need to fix this. Promise?"

"I promise." It escapes before I realize I even said it, before I realize I even *thought* it. That's the thing with Lily and me, she asks and I answer. Always. And for several seconds, all I can think about is how Hart and Norcut took this away from us. If they lied about the phone stuff, it's very possible they lied about the security too, and in my head, Alex's smile slithers wider and wider.

Explain to me, Alex said, how Hart and Norcut are protecting your family if they have more cameras on the inside of the house than the outside. Something's going on. I just don't know what.

I tuck one arm around my middle and stare at the tile under my shoes. "Look, Lily. I don't have much time. I just need to ask you a couple questions, okay?"

"Okay."

"Have you noticed any cameras inside the house?"

"Cameras? No. Are we being watched inside too?"

"That's what I was told. Has Bren mentioned anything? You know how she gets. Is she being weird?"

"Definitely, especially since . . . I think I know when the cameras were installed." Lily's tone slows and flattens. "We had exterminators. You know the ones that come every month?"

"Yeah." Bren can't stand bugs. She gets the house sprayed every month.

"Well," Lily continues. "I came home early and they were still working. I surprised one of them. He was in your room. I think he was looking for something."

There's a humming in my ears now. A droning. I grope for the wall with one hand, feeling like the floor just tilted. "Did you . . . you didn't happen to check . . ."

Lily makes a huffing noise. "I moved your stuff the night you left. Don't worry."

Easy for her to say. I'm sweating through my clothes now. I was hauled off so quickly I didn't have time to stash my jump drives. They store all my work: viruses, accounts, client information. I kept them pinned behind my bed's headboard. Not a genius hiding spot, but I hadn't exactly anticipated forced rehab.

"And wherever you put my thumb drives," I say slowly, "they're safe, right?"

"Of course they're safe. You're not the only one who can do this."

I think she means for it to be funny, but it's not. Lily has always wanted a normal life, a good life, one that doesn't involve sneaking around and breaking the law and hiding. It's what I want for her too. I don't want my sister to know the things I do. Then again, maybe she always has.

Maybe she's just been better at hiding them.

"Thanks for looking out for me," I say.

"Always." And Lily seems so happy to say it, happier still that I noticed how she looks out for me. On her end, there's another murmur of voices and we both go quiet as they pass.

Why would anyone want my drives? I mean, there's enough stuff—viruses, client information, usernames—on them to build a bridge into me, but none of it is as good as what Hart has on me.

The realization makes my breath go shallow. If those are Hart's people, there's no way they're looking for my thumb drives. Looking Glass already has everything—or at least enough to warrant a police investigation.

So what else is there?

Chills spread across my arms and I stand. No, that's not the right question. It isn't about what I have. The real question is what else do they *think* I have? The money? They know Michael took it. Do they think I helped?

"So," Lily says as soon as it's quiet on her end. "Do you think your stuff is what Dad's looking for?"

"No ide—" I stop. My sister's tone. It's so . . . hopeful. "What do *you* think he was looking for?"

There's nothing but Lily's breathing now. Too light. Too fast.

I grip the phone tighter. "Lil?"

"I think they were looking for some money."

"Why?"

"Because I took it."

"I don't . . ." I switch the phone to my other ear, switch it back. "How did you . . . ?"

"Know?"

I can barely hear Lily now. She's whispering softer than I am, probably close to tears, and I should try for comforting, but I'm barely holding down a scream.

"Tell me everything." I grit my teeth as she pauses. I grit until my jaw hurts. "Lily!"

"Dad used to talk about it in front of me—he and Joe would talk about it. Dad was part of some partnership and it was doing really well and Joe was helping him, working for him or whatever."

I shake my head. "I never heard anything about that. They never said anything to me."

Lily sniffles, but her voice goes flat and even. "Of

course not. They were worried about you. They were afraid of *you*. Not me. I'm the stupid one, remember? It was safe to say anything in front of me."

"You're not stupid."

"But I wasn't useful either."

I hesitate. "Why didn't you ever tell me?"

"What was I supposed to say?" Lily sniffles. "Our dad might have access to eleven million dollars and we can't keep the power on?"

My stomach free-falls. "Eleven million? That's what you took?"

"Yes." My sister stops, waiting for my next question, and honestly, I don't have one. I don't have anything. I can't stop staring at the bathroom door.

"Dad didn't discuss the money until after she died," Lily continues. "I mean, if I had known, I would've told . . . *her*."

Her. Our other mother. The one who jumped. The one who was murdered. If it were another time and another place, I'd ask Lily why she can't say *Mom*. Right now though? I think I might get it. Sometimes you can't name your pain, but it lives with you anyway.

"Trust me," Lily continues. "If I had known then, I would've happily raided whatever stash he had to buy groceries or keep the lights on."

"I believe you. I just . . ." I scrub one hand over my numb face. "Why now?"

"We needed the money. Mom needed the money. And

it was there. I didn't think anyone even knew about it. I mean, Dad was in jail and Joe was dead and then you were gone . . ."

"I still don't understand why you wouldn't have said something *before*. All that time, all that work I did trying to raise money in case we had to run—"

"I didn't believe it would work!" Lily huffs into the phone as a bell rings. Homeroom must be close to starting. "After Detective Carson arrested Dad, everything was supposed to be gone. Detective Carson *said* everything was gone, and what did it matter? We had a new life. We had money. We had Mom. We didn't need any of our dad's stuff. I didn't even really believe him."

Because she didn't need to. I force myself to take a deep breath. "How bad is Bren—Mom?"

"I don't know. She cries a lot. Not when I'm around, but I can tell. I notice."

I wrap one arm around my middle and still feel like I'm crumbling in half. "So you took care of it."

"Yeah."

"How? Tell me how you got the money."

"I accessed the account he talked about and then just . . . transferred the balance."

Nausea sweeps through me. "Lil, where'd you transfer the money to?"

"Your account. The offshore one."

The one I told my sister about in case something ever happened to me. The one I created to safeguard the money

I earned from my hacking. The one I guarded in case we ever needed to run.

My head goes helium light and fuzzy. This is why Michael's chasing me. My sister accidentally made it look like I stole from him.

"Lil, you have to transfer the money back. All of it."

"I can't." My sister sniffles again, louder this time. "I mean, I can transfer almost all of it, but I already paid some of our bills. The mortgage statement was on the table so I used Mom's log-in and paid everything through the end of the year."

"How are you going to explain that? She's going to notice someone paid the mortgage."

"I don't *know*! What was I supposed to do, Wick? You're not here and she won't talk to me and everything is ruined! I don't know what to do and I don't know how to help!"

"It isn't your job to help. Bren has to take care of this."

"And she can't so I did."

"Lily—"

"You took care of me."

I pause. "It's not the same."

"No, it's not." Lily's voice ratchets into something smaller again, more like my little sister and less like the girl from seconds before. "But it feels kinda like it. I don't know who I'm supposed to be anymore, Wick. When we were with dad, I knew what my role was."

I wet my lips, swallow. "What's that?"

"Leverage. He kept me around to keep you in line."

"That's not true."

"Yes, it is. I don't know which was worse: getting hit to keep you going or watching you watch me get hit to keep you going."

I open my mouth and can't say a word. All this time, all this worry, everything I've done to *protect* her and it didn't matter. I couldn't erase what she saw. I can't erase what we went through.

"Wick, you did what you had to do so we could survive and that's what I'm doing too."

My eyes sting with tears and I dash my hand against them. She learned that from me. It's another relic from our past. How many times have I thought that? How many times have I behaved that way? I wanted to spare her, and instead, I taught her how to be just like me. "I'm sorry, Lily. I'm so sorry."

She hiccups and I wince. Crying. My sister's crying now and I'm miles away. I can't save her. I never could.

"Wick, I looked at other stuff too—just like you used to. I searched Looking Glass's name and I get why our therapist is down as a company owner, but I don't understand why Alan Bay is."

I go still. "What?"

"When I searched the company information, the state site said Allison Norcut and Alan Bay are owners and Alan Bay is *Judge* Bay, right? The one that handled our cases?"

I swallow. "Right."

Another bell on Lily's end and she groans. "Crap. I have

to go. That's the late bell. I don't want to get in trouble."

"No . . . of course not."

"I won't tell Bren you called. It'll be our secret. I love you. All this stuff muddies everything, but they can't take that."

I sink onto the toilet seat again. "No."

Lily disconnects, and for several long seconds, I just hang my head in my hands. Michael worked with Looking Glass, with Norcut. All those scams, all those jobs we did . . . was I always working for her? And what about Judge Bay? Why was he involved in Looking Glass? I can't figure out the angle. Bay dealt with politics and criminals. I don't understand how he could've been useful.

Norcut made such a pretty speech about taking down Michael. Was it just because he stole from her? Or is it because she's eliminating everyone attached to the company? Because Bay was an owner and now he's gone, and Michael was an employee and now she wants him gone.

I open the stall door and turn off both faucets, brace my sweaty palms on the counter. My sister stole from Looking Glass. How long until they discover the money went to my account?

What if they already know?

Lily and I talked for too long. I'm sure my absence has been noted. Maybe someone even heard the running water. I need excuses, good ones. I need to fix this and I have no idea how, but I do know where I stand with Bren and Lily.

Looking Glass wants to be my only light in the world and it's not.

I tuck the phone into the waistband of my jeans, flip my T-shirt over it, and examine myself in the mirror. Not bad. You can't see it and—unless someone goes in for a hug—it's not like anyone will feel it.

Milo might.

I grimace, shake myself. Alex owes me an "I told you so" for the cameras. She'll think it changes things.

Has it?

Hidden cameras or not, Hart and Norcut are still protecting my family, right? I mean, I saw the van.

Or did I just see what they wanted me to see?

The best lies are the ones you want to believe. Is that what happened with Milo too? He just had to whisper the things I always wanted and I fell for it? Maybe he was just doing what his mommy told him to do.

The idea hits me low, almost taking me to my knees as something very close to tears crowds my eyes.

Stop it. Get moving. Get to work and pretend nothing happened.

I can hide in the open. I've been doing it for years. I can do it a little longer. And somehow, the reminder really helps. I can do this. I can.

Or, I think I can until I open the bathroom door.

Hart's waiting for me, and this time, there is no smile. "Hello, Wick. Been making some phone calls?"

I stagger back a step. Stupid, really. Even if I ran, there's nowhere to go.

I press one hand to my chest, feel my heart slam against my palm. "Jeez, Hart, you always lurk outside the girls' bathroom?"

"Don't play dumb. You heard me." He pushes off the wall, one hand extended. "Give it to me."

I swallow. I can't think of how to play this. I can't think of anything past the humming in my head. My brain feels filled with ginger ale.

"Now."

I slide the phone from under my shirt and pass it to him. Hart punches two buttons and then looks at me. "That's your sister's number, isn't it?"

I don't bother answering. If he wants to know, he can

look it up. The silence is starting to help me now. I'm breathing through my panic. Hart knows I have a cell and he knows I've been making calls. That's it.

I won't give him anything more. I'm done giving.

His eyes flick up and down me. "You know what this means, right?"

"No TV for a month?"

Hart makes a disgusted noise low in his throat and grabs my arm, hauls me down the hallway. We're almost to the elevator when the doors open.

Milo steps off. He stops, stares.

"Not now," Hart says and Milo retreats into the elevator without a word. Without ever meeting my eyes. The force of it—of what it means—makes me stumble. Is this how it's going to end?

Hart keeps going, dragging me with him. I'm glad for it actually. My legs are numb through. He's heading for Norcut's office and it's almost a relief. Let's do this. Why not?

This time, Hart doesn't bother knocking.

"Found her." Hart pushes me forward and shuts the door. The cell arches above my head as he tosses it to Norcut. She catches it with one hand and there's a long, long moment of silence as she examines the cell, scrolls through all the functions.

Norcut's eyes lift to mine. "Sit."

I do and we consider each other for several seconds. "So where does this leave us now?" she asks at last.

I lift one shoulder. "You lied to me. To them. You said

they didn't want to talk to me and they did. Why would you do that?"

"Because you needed some space."

"No, you could have just *said* that and you didn't. You said they didn't want to talk to me. You told Bren I didn't want to talk to them. You made me think I had *no one*. Why would you do that?"

"Because if I made you afraid, I could control you."

The honesty is sharp as a slap. She's right, and even though she's grinning like this is some brilliant move, it's not. Norcut isn't the first person to do that. There was my dad and then there was Carson. There were other fears wedged between them too. Fear of losing my sister. Fear of losing Griff. Fear of being discovered.

I'm nothing more than a coward. I spent my entire life in knee-jerk reactions, devising plans to get away when, in reality, there was no escape. Because everywhere I go, I am still what I am. The coward. The accomplice. The right hand for more powerful people.

People like you were meant to be used, Joe once said, and the idea enraged me. I thought about it after he died.

Correction: after I had him killed.

I thought about it a lot. But until now, I never thought he was right.

"Is it really that terrible?" Norcut leans forward. "We can give you money, power, all the technology you could ever want. We can give you protection. *Family*. You don't want to be alone anymore. You want a family and we can be that family. We want more for you."

"That's a lot of promises coming from someone who uses her son as bait. What promises did you make him?"

Norcut goes still. We both do. I wasn't planning on saying that. I've given up my hand because I got mad. That was a mistake.

Then again, now I'm the one who's leaning forward. "Why *would* you do that anyway? Isn't he useful to you anymore?"

No reaction. Norcut doesn't flinch. She doesn't blink. There's no shudder and damn sure there's no regret in those pale eyes. Not really surprising, I guess. She is a shrink. They probably teach them how to stay professionally blank. How very useful.

I wonder if she taught her son, Milo, the same?

I smother the thought and force myself to keep staring down Norcut. "What happens to me when I'm not useful anymore?"

"What do you think?" Norcut studies me, then glances at Hart. Judging from the way her eyes waver, he's doing *something* and she's watching it, but I can't tell without turning around. My skin crawls.

"How did you get the phone?" Norcut asks at last.

"Found it."

"Did *she* help you?"

She. Alex. I shake my head and Norcut goes blank again, kicking into therapist mode. "It bores me when you play games."

"Then let's stop playing." I place both hands on the armrests and sit straight—straighter. "Forget finding Michael, what if I could get back the money he stole from you *right now*?"

From the corner of my eye, I watch Hart draw closer. The air is straitjacket tight, a breath held before the plunge.

"I'm listening," Norcut whispers.

"Let me use your computer. He moved the money to another account—one I can get into. I'll transfer the money wherever you want it to go, and in return, I get to leave."

"Why do you think we'd let you go?"

"How do you know I haven't planned for that?"

And there it is. There's the flicker. For all her power over her merry band of hackers, Norcut still doesn't understand what we do. She's afraid of it. Of us.

Of the damage we could do.

"You don't let me go," I continue, lifting my palms to indicate the office, "you won't keep your money—or any of this—for long. I know exactly how I'll burn you." The biggest lie I have ever told and it sounds so logical, so believable, and she's buying it.

But she won't for long. If I'm going to bluff, I need to be fast.

I want out of here. I want to be the farthest thing from Norcut's mind and the farthest I can get from Looking Glass.

I watch her carefully. "Besides," I add. "Why would you want me anymore? You could get someone new, someone who's more . . . your type."

She doesn't answer, and in the silence, I realize why: "I never was your type, was I? I was just bait for Michael."

Norcut shrugs. "Who were you talking to?"

Lily. Lily. Lily. I shrug. "Michael, who else?" Norcut's gaze slides to the cell, lingers on my sister's number. "Surely you know he'd spoof his real number," I say.

"Then why's Michael looking for you?"

"Maybe he loves me? I am his *daughter*."

"He didn't come for you when I sent you to Bender's house."

I take an unsteady breath. "Maybe that wasn't part of the plan."

Norcut pauses, considering me for a beat, before rolling her chair to the side and rising. She smoothes down her dark gray pencil skirt. "You have ten minutes."

"I only need five."

We trade places and I try not to flinch as we pass each other. Hart and Norcut both stay within easy reach and it doesn't escape me how Hart's hand goes to his pocket and lingers. Too small for a gun, so that leaves a Taser? Something else?

I grit my teeth against the shiver and open Norcut's internet browser, go straight to my online bank, and select the log-in. The account number was unwieldy to remember so I had switched to a username years ago.

It opens a home screen. There are options for transfers and payments, a quick overview of the account contents.

And the overview . . . that can't be right.

My mouth goes dry. I click another link, drilling down to the details page. Unsurprisingly, it matches the overview. The account is empty.

All the money's gone.

I refresh the screen.

Same result: no money. All the funds were swept from the account in a single transfer. Even everything I'd earned on my own is gone. I stare at the page. Now would probably be a good time for some tears. Too bad all I want to do is vomit.

"Well, well." Norcut's voice is slippery and smooth. And *satisfied*.

"Isn't this interesting," she says.

"I can get it." The words shoot from me so fast, I'm barely aware I'm saying them until they register with Norcut. She raises one brow.

"I can get it," I repeat.

"How? You clearly thought you had it and you don't."

"Yes, but I did have it." I tilt the screen toward her

and point to the transfer. "I can track down whoever did this. There are only so many people who know about the account."

"And they are?"

I press my lips together, but the names are a heartbeat in my brain: Lily. Lily. Lily.

Griff. Griff. Griff.

He knew about my offshore account. He knew why I had it, how I funded it. When my computer was confiscated by Carson, Griff actually loaned me his laptop for a while. I used it to access my banking. If there was a keystroke tracker on it, he'd have my usernames, my passwords, my . . . everything.

No. No way. I tuck both hands under my legs and grip. I *trust* Griff. He would never use that against me. He warned me about the money, about my dad, about Carson.

The thought makes something else climb to the front of my mind: what *about* Detective Carson? He had my computer at his house. Just because it didn't look tampered with doesn't mean it hadn't been. If he had me working for him, who's to say there wasn't some other computer kid too? Maybe he had someone else go through the files, comb for keystrokes. It would take forever. He'd have to go deep . . . or I would have had to make just one mistake.

Like Alex said, if you have enough money, they can hunt you all they want, but they'll never find you, and Detective Carson has been missing since that night I took down Ian and Jason. No one's been able to locate him.

What if it was because he had enough money to run?

I give myself a mental shake. No, impossible. Lily took the money while I was in here and Carson was gone before then.

Unless he accessed the account after going into hiding. Once he saw the sudden deposit of eleven million dollars.

"Tell me who else, Wick." Norcut takes another step toward me and I flinch.

"Detective Carson," I say, flicking my attention from the therapist to Hart and back again. They were interested in him before. Are they still now? *I* know the timeline doesn't work, but will they?

"He could've accessed the account," I continue. "Transferred the funds. You said yourself you haven't been able to find him. This is probably why."

"That's quite a suggestion," Norcut says. "Are you sure it couldn't be someone else? Someone *closer* to you?"

Chills crawl up my spine. They're thinking Griff. Have to be.

I start to deny it because it *can't* be. But the thing is . . . if they stop looking at Griff and start looking at the other people around me . . . how long until they suspect Lily? Just because I was blind to her doesn't mean Norcut will be. She treated my sister as well. She knows her.

But will she *suspect* her?

"I keep telling you I work alone."

Norcut scoffs. "Clearly, someone knew about you."

"Someone like your son?" I regret the words as soon as I say them but it is possible. Milo was Griff's builder long before he was mine, and I used Griff's laptop for months. If Milo had installed something on the computer, it's very possible he knew my log-ins . . . I just don't think he did.

Or is that just my hope talking?

I sigh and try to look bored. "Again, I work *alone*. The closest I ever came to having bosses was Michael and Carson."

"So wiping your account is what? The detective's revenge?"

She might have a point. I did help expose his blackmailing habit. Milo may have planted the bomb evidence on Carson, but I motivated him to do it.

"I dunno," I say. "I think eleven million is pretty good motivation all by itself."

I don't bother asking Norcut if she agrees. Judging by the single muscle spasm in her jaw, I'd say she does.

"I want the money," Norcut says at last.

My smile feels stapled on. "And you'll get it."

"You're right, because otherwise I'm going to burn *you*, Wick. Do you understand? I'm not talking about how you broke privacy laws or how you helped run credit scams. I'm talking about premeditated murder. I'm talking about how you took revenge on Alan Bay for refusing to grant your mother those restraining orders. I will give the police everything and then I'll start on your family."

Cold trickles into my veins and spreads. "You'll get your money," I whisper.

I just have no idea how.

Norcut doesn't bother telling me to keep my mouth shut—I'm sure she knows she doesn't have to—and I spend the next two days in a blur, pretending to track down money I have zero idea how to find. Hart never says anything, but the others keep their distance like they've been warned, and Milo doesn't show. It's probably just as well. I don't think I could take Alex's questions or face Milo's smile. I need time to collect myself, think of a way out.

But the longer I think about killing Alan Bay? The longer I think about having to find the money? The worse I shake. I sit on my bed and rub my sweaty palms against the comforter, trying to decide where to begin. Whoever took the money logged in as me so I should be able to track the outgoing transfer. The date, time, and amount are no problem. The real issue will be getting into the receiving account. That sort of stuff takes time.

Which I don't have.

The other problem . . . it may be impossible. If the money was transferred from the receiving account, if I can't find a way in—because, let's face it, my usual Trojan viruses are *not* going to work here—if I can't fix this . . . I take a deep breath. Still feels like there's a brick behind my heart, but whatever. I *have* to find a way in.

I rinse my clammy hands in the bathroom, take a

thumb drive and notebook from my bedside table, and return to my computer station. I start with the receiving account—another bank in the Caymans—and I'm so absorbed I almost don't hear the whisper of the glass doors.

Almost.

I've kept the overhead lights low and it makes his shadow sweep across my desk. We both pause, and for a very long moment, there's nothing but our breathing.

"I know, Milo." I keep everything I am focused on the computer screen, but my hands have gone to my lap. My fingers keep twisting each other. "I know she's your mom."

"Yeah. That's why I came." Milo pulls a chair close to me. We're near enough to touch now, but we don't. "You said once that we were the same," he says at last. "Do you remember that?"

I turn, force myself to look at him. Milo's eyes are hazy and far away like he's pretending to be somewhere else, like he'd rather be *anywhere* else.

That makes two of us.

"I remember." We were arguing about whether we should be together. I told him I thought we were dangerous together, that we were too much alike. Milo said that's why we were perfect for each other.

I said that's what made it scary. Who was going to be the voice of reason? Or, worse, guilt? I engineered Joe's murder. Milo destroyed Detective Carson. We both know what it's like to lash out because it's our first instinct.

"You were right," Milo continues, studying his palms.

His hands are shaking. "We are the same. We're the children of criminals. You didn't realize what you were saying at the time, but you were totally right."

I turn away, train my eyes on the wide windows. It's another gorgeous day, but behind the tinted glass and without the overhead lights, we're sitting in a pocket of shadows.

"You're simplifying this a bit, don't you think?" I ask.

"No, not really. We are what we are. I think that made us right for each other—who could understand me better than you? But that's not what you want. You want to be better. You're looking for a hero. Hell, you *are* a hero. I'm not."

"You saved me." And in spite of the anger and in spite of the fear, I know this is true. I turn and almost touch him. I curl my hands into fists instead. "Who knows what would've happened at Judge Bay's if you hadn't rigged that explosion—"

"I didn't do it to save the others. I did it to save you. I'm not interested in sticking my neck out to save other people. I don't have that instinct." His smile is thin and pained and nothing like the boy I know. This isn't Milo looking at me now. There's nothing swaggering or cocky or confident. "Considering my genetics, I probably wouldn't have understood self-sacrifice even if they'd tried to teach it to me."

My laugh is a single sputter. "Are you trying to say you're the bad guy? Because that's stupid, Milo. I know you're not."

He considers me, those gorgeous eyes nothing but smudges of dark now. "I am though . . . and I'm okay with that. Or I was. Until you. That's the thing, Wick. You're going to want honesty from me, and *hell*, I'm going to want to give it to you, but if I do, you'll never forgive me."

My stomach twists hard. "Forgive you for what?"

"I sourced you to Looking Glass."

I blink, stare. "I know. You told me you told them we were dating—"

"You're not getting it," he says and I can feel his eyes traveling over my face in spite of the fact that I can't see them. "I *sourced* you. Not your dad. They never would've been able to put a face on you without me. I even made money on it. Wasn't until later that I regretted it. Well. I sort of regretted it because then we were together. That was because of me too."

I try to swallow and can't. "Milo, you took away my life. You made my secrets theirs."

"Yeah, I did." He leans forward and I shy away, press my spine into the chair. "But what if you're better because of it? What if you used Looking Glass as an opportunity?"

If there was regret in his voice before, it's gone now. Excitement's piling up the sentences and I know what's coming next.

Maybe because I always did.

"I was never kidding when I said you could rule the world," Milo says. "Why play by the rules when you can make your own?"

"Because it's wrong. I know you know what my dad did. He broke all the rules and look what happened."

"Your mother followed all the rules and look what happened."

My breath hitches like Milo punched me. He might as well have. "Don't you *dare* use my mother to prove your point."

Milo shrugs, sits back, and watches me.

"Do you work for them?" I ask. "Is that why you came here?"

"Yeah, they knew you weren't buying into the program." Milo takes a deep breath in, holds it, and when his head twitches, I know he's looked away from me. "They knew if I came in and told you to trust Hart and Norcut, you would—because you trust me. Or you did."

I'm suddenly falling. I'm falling and I'm falling and I'm sitting so still he won't be able to tell.

But I can. I can feel every crack and fissure as I break.

"Then all of the kissing and . . . and—" And I can't say it. I'm Bren now. I'm a coward now. I'm too scared to say the words I need because once I say them, they'll be real. He faked everything. None of what we had was real.

It was engineered. Just like when they used my mom. Just like Alex said.

I study Milo, try to cram my thoughts into something useful, but all I can think is *What do you do when you find out everything you are is made-up?*

"No. What we had wasn't a lie." Milo looks away and there's a soft breath of movement by my knees. His hands press together and separate, go to his knees, and move to his lap. "What I had with you might have been the truest thing even if it is the truth that will end us."

"How am I supposed to believe you?"

"Because I'm being honest enough to tell you." Milo laughs. It's so sudden I jump, maybe even recoil. Everything feels so different and so entirely the same.

Milo watches me. "And that's the most hilarious part, isn't it? Before you, I would never have told the girl I wanted—I *loved*—the truth. Not if it meant losing her. But now . . . now I know that when you love someone they deserve nothing less than the truth."

"I . . . I . . ." I can't breathe. He can though. Easily. Milo's chest rises and falls. He's relaxed. Unburdened.

Because now I am. He gave his lies to me to carry, to hold, to *know*.

Tears smear the room and blur his face. I inhale hard. There's a choice that has to be made now. I have to decide what we're going to be and somehow, some way, I know if I cry now it's over. If I lose control, I will lose him.

I hate that. I might hate him. Or I might just hate me. For believing him.

I clear my throat. "Why are you telling me now?"

"Because I need you to run."

"Why?" I ask. The word is high and reedy and nudging dangerously close to tears again.

"Because I know you're in trouble." Milo leans closer, bracing both forearms on his knees. "My mother lied to me too. I really wanted to believe her and she lied. You're not safe."

No shit, I want to say. *You think?* I want to add.

"How can I believe you?" is all I say. I scoot my chair back another inch and he does not follow me. "This could be another lie."

Milo winces, then nods, like he deserved that and he did. He *did*.

So why do I feel like I just wounded myself?

"It's not a lie," Milo says finally. "I know you've seen the guys watching the building. They're not competitors. They're *government*—FBI, CIA, something. They're onto Looking Glass, which is bad for you because now Hart and my mother need that money. Fast. They can't disappear without it."

"How do I know this isn't another one of your games?"

"You were never a game."

"Don't."

Milo's sigh is harsh, ragged. "Even when I told *her* about you, it was never a game. It was survival. It's what I did to keep going. You get that. I know you do."

I do.

"Where would I go?" I ask, sounding light, amused. It *is* amusing. "They'll hunt me. You've given them what they *need* to hunt me. My cover's blown. I can't go home. I can't even access what I need to escape."

"Bren knows something's wrong."

My head snakes toward him. "What do you know about that? Did they do something to her?"

"No. They'll stall her for as long as they can, but considering you spoke with Lily and now Bren's asking to see you . . . they know they don't have much time." Milo pauses, but we both know what's coming next: "That's going to make things difficult for them and they'll make it difficult on you."

"I know."

"You don't. Otherwise, you wouldn't sound so confident. They will kill you, Wick. Trust me. Everyone here is expendable—that's why they knew it would work. No family. No histories. No one to come looking if the hackers disappear. It's one of the reasons Looking Glass works so well."

"And the other reasons?"

"My mother sourced the talent and Bay found the clients. It was great. They were racking up millions, then Michael raided the account." Milo waits until I look at him. "You didn't kill an innocent man, Wick. What you did . . . you had no way of knowing."

"Is that supposed to help me sleep at night?"

Now it's his turn to look away. Milo studies everything—*anything*—that isn't me. "Hart and my mother know what Alex is doing."

My heart jams into my throat. "Why haven't they done something then?"

He lifts one shoulder. "Not the right time? She has

something else in mind? No idea, but you might want to pass that along."

"*How?* On my way out the door? There's no escape from Looking Glass."

Milo's laugh is soft this time. "I didn't think you were capable of playing stupid."

"I have no idea what you're talking about." Except I do. Of course I do. He's talking about the security system. I know how to scam the cameras—they're fixed, they're vulnerable—and he knows I know it. They're Looking Glass's sole weakness and he didn't tell them.

Which means he's on my side.

Or that he was always leaving himself an escape hatch.

Or that this was planned all along and they'll be waiting for me.

Milo leans forward, presses something small and hard into my hands. His cell phone. I shove to my feet and thump into the corner of my desk. "What are you doing?" I manage.

"A good builder always leaves a back door into his system, right? That's my back door and your way out."

I force myself to move. "Why are you telling me everything now?"

No answer. I didn't figure there would be. Somehow, I've blundered all the way to the door without realizing it and Milo hasn't followed me. It's a relief.

So why am I lingering?

My hand fists around the door handle and Milo's voice snakes from the dark.

"When you run, promise you'll be fast, Wick. Disappear. Use every trick you have. Because when they come for you, it will be with everything they have. There will be no mercy, no pity. You'll only have one chance."

I slide my card through the elevator's reader with shaky, sausage fingers. Everything's gone numb. Clumsy. I lean one hip against the polished metal wall and focus on my feet.

On my anger.

Like an idiot, I believed in Milo. I wanted this fairy tale to work. I ignored my gut. Oh my God, I've been so *stupid*.

Kind of amazing how the realization makes everything go hard inside me. My legs straighten. My brain starts to click past the panic and into my next move. First I'll need to override the camera feeds. Then I'll need to override the elevator. Would it be better to go out the front? Or through the parking deck?

My instinct says parking deck because there will be fewer witnesses, but there's a gate at the exit and I'm not sure if I could climb it. The elevator doors open and I turn for my room. I don't look at the security cameras I pass, but I feel them. Everything that keeps us safe also keeps us in place.

I swipe my key card and push through the bedroom door. Alex is still at her desk. Her fingers pause over the laptop keys. She doesn't say a word though. She's still mad at me and I should let it go, but Norcut knows about Alex.

Alex, who just wants to be safe for a little while.

Alex, who had to pick between the monsters out there and the monsters in here.

We are so alike. Can I live with myself if I leave her?

God, no.

"We have a problem," I say softly, putting the cell on my bed. She starts typing again and I take a step toward her. "We have to run. They know what you're doing."

She stops typing and slowly—too slowly—pivots to face me. "What?"

"You heard me."

Her eyes narrow. "You told them."

"I wouldn't. I'm getting the hell out of here, Alex. Come with me."

She jumps to her feet, stands next to me as I grope under my bed for my bag. "How?"

My fingers snag the nylon strap. "I'm not sure yet."

"Oh, that's brilliant. What are we going to do, genius?" Alex backs up a step as I drag my bag onto the bed. "Just let ourselves out? Even if you could, they'll see you in the cameras."

I look at Alex. "I don't think so."

Her dark eyes gleam. "What are you talking about?"

I grab the cell, hold it up. "Milo gave it to me. He says he sourced me to Looking Glass and I'm in danger—that you're in danger too. I don't know what's on here, but I'm pretty sure it'll get us out."

"You trust him?"

"On this . . . yeah, I do."

"And why should I believe you?"

"Because I didn't have to tell you, I could've just left and I didn't. Alex, you didn't have to be so nice when I arrived, but you *were*. We get each other. We know what it's like on the other side of those walls, remember?"

She doesn't answer. She stares at me, saying nothing.

"I won't leave you here," I add.

Alex exhales hard. "What do you need?"

"I'm not sure yet." Milo's phone is already unlocked and connected to the Looking Glass private network. I check his apps . . . his browser history . . .

The most recent hit? Milo's private server. I recognize the IP address. I click on the page and my stomach sinks. I need a username and password.

"What's wrong?" Alex asks.

"I don't know the—" I type "m" into the field. Nothing. I type "w" and a dropdown box suggests *wick*. I select it and a password autofills. "Nothing," I say. "It's fine."

It's fine because Milo planned this all along. He's making it stupid easy.

I scroll through his project list and find a folder labeled "Looking Glass." Inside, there's information on the networks, on the users, and on the security cameras. I open the first spreadsheet and find columns of camera locations, their corresponding IP addresses, and DUBS.

DUBS being *duplicates*.

I click the first dupe and it shows the hallway just outside our door.

"Hey." I look at Alex. "Can you open our door?"

"You're weird, you know that?"

"Just do it."

Alex drags herself to our bedroom door and opens it as I watch the feed. Nothing. My heart double thumps. Milo's given me camouflage. All these dupe links? They're recorded loops of Looking Glass's various hallways—and they're all *empty*, no customers, no staff, and especially no hackers. Now I just have to tell the security cameras' DVR to look at the duplicate IP address and not the live feed. We could do cartwheels down the hall and no one would ever be the wiser.

I lift my eyes to Alex. "If I can get us out undetected, can you override the elevator?"

One corner of her mouth walks up. "I can't believe you even have to ask."

———◆———

Turns out, Alex has more than contraband cell phones. She also has an elevator override key—the kind firefighters use.

"The building owners have to keep a copy in the maintenance office," Alex says as she watches me access the security cameras' DVR settings. "I kind of helped myself. I knew I'd need it when I finally ran."

"Won't that set off an alarm?"

"I don't think so. The elevator repair people would have to use the same key and they check the elevators monthly."

"Let's hope you're right because we're going to have to move *fast*." Milo's list covered every hallway in Looking Glass, but he didn't cover the parking garage or the main lobby, which means as soon as we step off the elevator, they'll see us.

And we'll have to run for it.

"How much longer?" Alex asks.

"Right about . . . now." I pause, staring at my screen. There's the slightest blip in the video before Milo's video takes effect. I wait, listen. Nothing. No alarms, but maybe they're silent?

I tilt my head toward the bedroom door. "Try it again. See if I triggered a lockdown."

Alex crosses the room and tries the handle. It glides open just like normal and Alex lets out a long breath. She peeks into the hallway, waits for a beat, then turns to face me. "In another life, we would've been great partners, you know that?"

My laugh is a single, short bark. "Don't thank me yet."

I leave the cell and take my bag from the bed, glancing around our room once more. Is there anything here that can help me once we're on the outside?

There isn't of course. Looking Glass is excellent at providing everything we need as long as it's on their terms.

I look at Alex. "You're not bringing anything?"

She shrugs. "Why would I? Are you ready?"

It's the same old Alex staring at me—hands in hoodie, expression bored—but her words shiver on a shudder. She's afraid.

That makes two of us.

I hoist my bag onto one shoulder. "Ready as I'll ever be," I say and brush past her like my blood isn't thumping in my ears.

Alex follows close behind, head swiveling from side to side. We're both listening for something and there's nothing. Surely we couldn't be that lucky?

Please let us be that lucky. I swipe my badge into the elevator panel and the metal doors part. We get in and Alex goes to the keypad on the right-hand side, drops to one knee.

"Close the doors," she says, unlocking the service panel to reveal the override. I mash one finger into the close button and hold my breath.

"Hit 'ground.'"

I do and the elevator *moves*. We shift downward and I lean one hand against the wall, watching as the floor buttons light up. Down . . . down . . . down.

"No alarms!" There's a giddy grin in Alex's voice, but I feel like my chest's full of sand. I can barely breathe around it. "They have no idea what we're doing! We're going to get out!"

I almost can't believe either. I definitely can't take my eyes from the floor lights. Every new flash twists my stomach sideways.

I wet my lips, force myself to think. "When we reach the parking lot, we have to run. They *will* see us. We need to hit the gate fast, climb it, and head for the train stop. We'll split, go separate ways, blend in, okay?"

No answer. I look at Alex and she nods, still grinning.

Actually, we're both grinning now. This is really happening and the thrill makes my heart hammer harder. The elevator's lowering and lowering. We're past the twentieth floor now, past the tenth. We're one floor above the parking garage. We're—the elevator wrenches to a stop.

Alex staggers into me, digs her fingers into my arm. "Wick?"

"I—" The elevator jerks again, dropping a few feet and tossing my stomach into my mouth. "Alex," I say, and the lights go out.

I shove Alex toward the doors, claw my fingers into the seam between them. "Pull them open!"

The emergency lights cut on and the elevator shifts hard. Both of us stagger.

"Pull!" I scream.

"I am!"

"Then pull harder!"

The doors grind open an inch, then another. We work our hands around the edges and yank and yank until I can wedge my shoulder into the gap. I brace my foot against the other door, pushing with my whole body. It scrapes open another few inches.

Enough to see we have another problem.

We're between floors. There's maybe an eighteen-inch space between the bottom of the elevator and the ceiling of the parking deck.

"You can fit," I say to Alex. "Here, hurry. I'll push you through."

"No, you're smaller. You should go."

"I can *push* you easier than *pull* you. Come on."

Alex looks at me, looks at the gap. "No . . . no way . . . what if it goes up?"

If it goes up, she'll get crushed. If she stays . . . tears prick my eyes. "If they catch you, you'll never get out. No one will come looking."

The elevator shudders and drops. We have another six inches.

"You know I'm right," I whisper to her.

"Shit," Alex breathes and kneels, eases both legs through the space until she's shimmying on her belly. I hold on to her shoulders, then her upper arms, and she drops and drops . . .

And the elevator starts to rise.

"Wick!"

"Jump! You have to jump!"

"I *can't*!"

She's wedged, shoulders pinched between the floor of the elevator and the roof of the parking garage. If the elevator keeps going—

"Kick! Wiggle!" I shove both her shoulders with all my weight, my sneakers skidding on the elevator's polished floor. Above us, there's a heavy click. The elevator shudders once more and the regular lights flicker, flicker, *return*.

We drop two inches and Alex screams, falls. I'm holding only her wrists now and she's scrambling.

"Come on!" She yanks at me. "Come with me!"

Another shudder from the elevator. Our eyes meet. I won't make it and we both know it.

"Run," I whisper and release her wrists. Alex drops, disappearing into the dark.

The elevator takes forever returning me to Looking Glass. I lie on the floor and stare at the shiny metal ceiling, feel my stomach pull against my spine as we go up, up, up.

Closer and closer to them.

It wasn't supposed to be like this.

I need a plan. I need some leverage. I need *something*.

I can't think of anything.

The elevator bumps to a stop and the doors open.

"Well, that was cute." Kent fills the opening, watching me with a shit-eating grin. "Caught you."

I don't bother answering. There's no point. For him, this was payback.

"Mr. Kent." Norcut now. I roll over as she moves around him, not stopping until the pointy toes of her pumps are touching my rib cage. I'm expecting a kick, at minimum. But she leans down, kneels next to me with the saddest expression.

"This is going to go badly for you." Norcut brushes hair away from my face and I shudder. "You know that, don't you?"

I nod, the side of my head sliding against the polished floor.

"Good," she says and stands. "Get up."

I do. Norcut grips my sleeve as I sway, steadying myself.

"We will find her," she says.

Her. Alex. "No you won't."

Norcut's fingernails dig into my bad arm—finding exactly where Todd rammed in his knife—and I hiss, squeeze my eyes shut against the pain. She presses harder and I force myself to grin.

"We both know it's true," I say. "What made Alex the perfect victim will also make her perfect for disappearing. What makes us weak also makes us strong. Didn't we talk about that once? In therapy?"

I sound really good for someone whose stomach is close to spewing everywhere. The harder Norcut presses my arm, the more my knees want to crumble and the higher my voice swings. The money's gone. Carson's gone. These are the kinds of people who will track every lead.

And what will I do when it leads them to Lily?

I won't be able to do anything.

I'll have to watch.

"I'm immune to tears," Norcut breathes, the words curling down my ear canal.

She's not the reason I'm crying, but I let her think it is. Who cares? At this point, I can barely stay upright. I've never been so tired.

So completely and utterly done.

Hart appears at the elevator opening. "We have a problem."

A wordless something snakes between them and Norcut hauls me forward. I can't tell what's going on.

Two seconds later, I'm pretty sure I can guess. Someone's here. There's a female voice—high and pissed—coming from farther down the hallway. Norcut stares toward the sound, fingers digging deeper and deeper into my arm as we all try to place the voice.

It doesn't sound like Mrs. Bascombe and it's not the caseworker.

It's *Bren* and my knees drive toward the floor. I open my mouth, but Norcut yanks me around, puts her face so close to mine we are breathing the same air.

"You owe me eleven million dollars."

I nod.

"If you don't deliver, I'll go to the authorities about Bay. I'll tell them you did it on purpose. And then I'll go after your sister and Bren. Do you understand?"

Another nod. It should be exactly the response Norcut wants, but she presses her nails into my scar like she's digging for bone. I grit my teeth, but a whimper escapes.

"Do not keep me waiting," she says and releases me. I sag against the wall, tasting bile. I need a moment, but they're not interested in waiting. Hart and Norcut push me forward, flanking me. We're all headed for Bren now.

"Smile," Hart hisses.

I can't. Because when Bren hears our footsteps, she whirls to face us and I've never seen her look so bad. Her hair's coming loose from its chignon. Her clothes hang so limply on her frame, they look like they're borrowed from someone else.

Norcut's hand goes to the small of my back and a single finger touches my spine. Another reminder to behave. Unnecessary. Looking at Bren is an excellent reminder. Thinking of my sister is even better.

All Norcut has to do is count all the things I have to lose.

"Why, Mrs. Callaway," the therapist says, releasing me and stepping forward to shake Bren's hand. "It's so good to see you. I didn't realize you had an appointment."

"I don't." Bren's gaze skips along my face, my clothes, my sneakers. Does she see the oil smear on my shirt? I got it all over me when I leaned into the elevator doors. "I wanted to see my daughter."

"And here she is," Norcut says, motioning me forward. "Mr. Hart, could you give us a moment?"

Hart hesitates, then nods, following Kent down the hallway. Bren watches him before switching her attention to me. Her eyes spear mine and hold. "Get your things, Wick. You're leaving."

Norcut stiffens. "I don't think that's really wise, Mrs. Callaway."

"I don't care what you think."

"Mrs. Callaway—"

"I don't care."

The hallway goes quiet and Bren takes a wobbly step toward me . . . and then another. She's shaking, but holding it together. "I need you to get your things, Wick. *Now.*"

Norcut touches one hand to her chin, eyes switching between Bren and me. She's angry, but not surprised.

"Mrs. Callaway," Norcut says, edging around me. "Have you thought this through? Wick's father is still loose and you cannot guarantee her safety."

Bren's smile is a slash of teeth. "I have already spoken with my attorney. He's on his way. Don't make me call him again."

"I have no idea why you would think that's necessary," Norcut says, suddenly beaming at Bren like they're besties. "We've always been open with you about her progress."

"Don't start. I don't want to hear another word from you. Ever."

There's a pause before Norcut's hand slides between my shoulder blades. She gives me the gentlest push. "Go on, dear. Don't make your mother wait."

I hesitate. Norcut sounds ever so mild. Like what just happened between us didn't.

It scares me.

I spin and power walk to my room. Before, I had only brought the absolute bare necessities. Now, I throw the rest of my stuff into the bag and make a dive for the bathroom. Only a few things there. More clothes. My class notes and homework. I grab everything I can and drag the bag's strap over my shoulder.

"*Now*, Wick!" Bren's voice is close. Just on the other side of the door.

In the hallway, Norcut and Bren are squared off in front of each other. "Ready?" Bren asks, eyes never wavering from the psychiatrist's smile.

"Yes," I whisper.

"I know what you're doing," Bren says, still focused on Norcut.

The therapist's laugh is light and tinkly. "And what exactly am I 'doing'? Rehabilitating children who would otherwise be in jail?"

"You're not a hero."

Norcut's mouth snaps shut. "And you're lying about your attorney being on the way. You can't do anything against me, not without giving up *her*."

Bren pales.

"If you take her," Norcut continues, "I'll withdraw our security teams. You'll be on your own—alone—against *him*. Is that what you really want?"

"I don't want anything at the expense of my daughter," Bren breathes.

"I'll need your key card, Wick." Norcut turns her attention to me and I have to stab both feet into the carpet to keep from running. "Do you have it?"

I nod, tug the card from my pocket, and pass it to her. Norcut's fingertips touch mine and they've gone completely cold. "I'll give you a call soon, okay, dear?"

I reposition my bag to hide my sudden shaking. Norcut

raises her brows, expecting an answer, but Bren wraps one arm around my shoulders and pins me to her side. She steers me toward the elevator and swears under her breath when we have to wait. The doors finally open and she hauls me inside, punching the down button again and again. It doesn't move.

"One moment." Norcut glides into the elevator, swipes her badge through the reader, and presses the lobby button. "Now you can go," she says to Bren.

But Norcut watches me until the doors close.

We hurtle downward. Neither of us says a word. There's just our breathing—shallow and harsh—between us.

The elevator doors grind open, revealing a spacious lobby and lots of people. I'm ever so briefly confused—I thought we were going to the parking deck?—and then I realize we're in the main lobby, the one customers would come through. A few guys in dark suits watch as Bren hustles me along, but no one says anything. We pass through heavy glass doors and onto the street. Bren's sedan is still running, parked just a few steps away. There's someone leaning against the passenger door, and for two whole heartbeats, I don't recognize him.

His face is too bruised . . . both hands are bandaged . . . but then I see the eyes. They're bottle green and they make my feet stutter against the pavement.

"Griff?"

Griff doesn't respond. He retreats to the sedan's backseat and I'm grateful for it because he doesn't see my sudden stumble. My hands reach for him as Bren's hands reach for me. She pushes me toward the car.

"Bren—"

"Get in." She shoves me again, only releasing my arm to go around the other side.

"What's going—"

"Now!"

I haul open the passenger door, throw my bag on the floorboard, and drop into the seat on wobbly legs. I'm barely buckled in before Bren pops the car in drive and floors it. Behind me, there's the click of Griff's seat belt and the slide of his jeans against the leather seat. I can't believe it's him. I can't believe—

I turn to prove it to myself and I'm right: It *is* Griff and his hands are *bandaged*. We stare at each other and he touches one wrapped-up hand to his wrist like it hurts. I remember the thin skin there, how his heartbeat felt that night he met me at the ambulance. Who hurt him? What happened? I have too many questions and I'm too stunned to ask any of them.

"Are you okay?" Bren asks, making a right at the corner.

I turn to her, try to find an answer. "No . . . are you?"

"No." Bren yanks the car around another turn and slams on the brakes to wait for a traffic light to change. "I'm sorry I sent you there. I didn't know what to do."

"I didn't exactly make it easy on you."

Her head jerks toward me, but then the light goes green and Bren guns it. We turn onto another side street and Bren makes a left and then a right, hands holding the steering wheel hard even as the rest of her shakes. Adrenaline? Or something worse?

"I don't understand." I tense through another jerky turn. My own adrenaline is wearing off, leaving me numb. Tingly. "What's going on?"

"I had to get you out of there."

"Why?" I watch a shadow flash across Bren's expression. She knows something, but she isn't saying. "What changed?"

"Your sister told me what was happening, how they were keeping you from talking to us—*lying* to us about you. I know your father's escape is another reason for you to stay, but I disagree. Michael's people have been spotted in Tennessee. They're moving north. They're running, and Dr. Norcut never said a *word*."

"How do you know that?"

"Because I found out for her." It's the first time Griff's spoken and it squeezes my chest even tighter.

"It makes sense," Bren continues. "Michael can't risk sticking around here."

"Are you sure?"

"No." Bren makes a small huffing noise. "Yes. *He* thinks so too."

Bren's eyes cut to the rearview mirror. She's looking at Griff, and reluctantly, I turn. He isn't watching Bren. He's watching me, and when our eyes meet, he touches one bandaged thumb to his lips.

I know the gesture and it still cracks me open rib by rib. He's thinking about what to say, and as the silence stretches, I know he doesn't know where to begin.

That makes two of us.

"What happened to you?" I manage and the words make my stomach sweep low because I'm pretty sure I already know the answer.

"I had to pay for what I did."

"The narcing?"

A single nod.

Exactly what I was expecting and it still makes me want

to vomit. "Did . . . did *he* hurt you?" Suddenly, I can't say Michael's name. I can't push it past the thickening in my throat.

Another nod and I have to squeeze both hands together to steady myself.

A smile pushes across Griff's mouth. "He caught me after I contacted you—a parting gift before he blew town. It could've been worse."

Yeah, it could. Because Griff could be dead and he's not and the gratefulness flattens my astonishment.

I inhale hard against sudden tears. "How . . . how . . . ?"

"How did he catch me?" Griff looks away, watches the cars we're passing. "I was in the wrong place at the wrong time."

"And . . . and your hands?"

Bren glances at me, skin between her eyes knotted. She doesn't understand what I'm really asking. Doesn't matter though because he does. Griff holds his palms up so I can see the way the bandages twist across his lifeline . . . or maybe he's just staring at the backs of his hands. Maybe he can't believe what he's seeing either.

"Torn-up wrists," he says at last. "Second-degree burns on the palms. I lucked out. It could've been third-degree."

But this is bad enough and Michael knew it. Everyone in our neighborhood knows Griff is an artist. He was—*is*—so talented.

"They'll heal eventually." Griff's hands drop to his lap.

"In the meantime, I can do almost everything."

"Except?"

"Draw."

Two sharps breaths in and still, *still* the tears burn my eyes. "Does this mean no more art school?"

Griff's smile overreaches his face, but there's nothing real in it, not anymore. "I knew the price, Wick. When I took that job informing on Michael and Joe, I knew what would happen if I got caught. And I paid it."

We stop at a gas station and switch seats. Griff goes to the front. I go to the back. Bren says just because Looking Glass knows I'm home doesn't mean everyone else needs to know too, and I totally agree.

I am slightly surprised she thought of it though.

Maybe even a little uneasy.

Definitely sad. My life isn't the only one that's changed.

I lie on the floorboard and watch the treetops pass us. We swing right and then left as she winds through the neighborhood, eventually pulling into our driveway. The garage ceiling passes above me as she parks, none of us moving until the door is firmly down.

"It's okay, Wick," Bren says, twisting around and putting one hand on my knee. "It's okay."

Too bad she doesn't sound like it is. I climb out of the car, stand in our garage again. There's my car next to Bren's, the boxed-up Christmas decorations on my right. It still smells like fresh paint.

Our house always smells like fresh paint.

Griff steps around me, my bag on his shoulder. I wince. "I'll get it! Your hands—"

He stops, so close I can *feel* him. Griff's warm. Being next to him is like lying in a patch of sunshine; I want to curl up and sleep forever.

"I've got it," he says softly and his eyes travel past me, pin to something beyond my shoulder.

I turn, see Lily standing with both hands clutched to the frame. My knees crumble.

"Wick? Oh God!" My little sister flings herself across the garage and grabs me. We slump into each other. She's almost as tall as me these days, but somehow we still fit each other.

"I missed you," she says into my neck.

"I missed you too."

"Come inside, okay?" Lily drags me toward the kitchen, all chilled hands and huge eyes. Bren's waiting inside. She pushes away from the counter, arms crossed against her chest like she's holding herself together.

"You have to tell me what's going on, Wick."

I shake my head. "You have cameras in your house; probably bugs too. I need to do a sweep and then . . . we'll talk."

"Cameras?" Bren puts one hand on the counter, parts her lips like she's going to argue, and then shakes her head.

"I'll help you look," Griff says, putting my bag on the kitchen table.

"You don't have to."

He doesn't respond, just walks out of the kitchen. I hesitate for a heartbeat, then follow.

We start on the top floor, taking screwdrivers to all the usual targets—smoke detectors, electrical outlets—and we hit pay dirt. It should feel satisfying, but it's not. There are cameras in each of the upstairs smoke detectors and in two of the bathroom electrical outlets. Not only has Looking Glass been watching my family, but they've been watching them in their most private moments.

I know how that feels.

Griff holds up the latest discovery, examining the wiring. "How did you know?"

"One of the other hackers told me. It's a long story."

"We've got time." He pauses, studying me. "Why'd he—"

"She."

"Why'd she tell you?"

"She wanted my help. It was a . . . bargaining tool." I

sigh and rub my eyes against the painful heartbeat in my head. Migraines have the worst timing. I'm struggling to keep everything straight, and in the blur, a sudden question powers to the surface. "Did you send me those viruses? The worms with the embedded messages?"

He shakes his head. "What viruses?"

I cringe. If Griff wasn't behind them, then that leaves . . . Michael? Michael trying to get me to leave Looking Glass, get out into the open so he could find me and get to his money? I don't want to think about it. Can't.

"Someone was trying to warn me about Looking Glass," I say finally. "Whoever it was alerted me to what really happened with Bay. I just don't know why they would."

For a long moment, neither of us says anything.

"Okay," Griff manages at last. "First things first. Let's finish the cameras. We might have them all. We might not. You have any flashlights?"

"Yeah." I walk into the hallway and check the closet. Always prepared, Bren has extra blankets, candles, and flashlights lined up in neat, little rows. It's like if Martha Stewart decided to take up disaster planning. I grab two flashlights, turn them both on, and pass one to Griff.

It's awkward, but he manages, sweeping the light across the walls to test himself. "This'll work."

I shut off the lamps, the overhead lights. The sun's so low I don't have to pull the shades. The rooms dip into dark and we start the sweep, moving so easily in the shadows it's like we were born for this.

And for the briefest second, I'm in that church again, chasing down Todd and searching through the dark for Lily. Griff was with me then too.

"Ready?" he asks.

"Yeah."

It feels like an eternity in the dark, tracing the flashlight beams over the walls, the picture frames, the furniture. We're trying to detect any points of light bouncing back to us, one of the few clues that a pinhole camera's been installed.

I take Bren's office, her bedroom, and Lily's bedroom. Griff sticks to the hallway, the bathrooms, and my room, eventually making his way to me. I've gone through Lily's room three times now and I still can't get myself to leave.

Looking Glass spied on my sister, my adoptive mom. When they thought they were safe and alone, they weren't. I'll have to tell them and I don't want to. I don't want to ruin what's left of our lives before Looking Glass. Or were we even safe before Looking Glass? Not really. There was Joe. There was Carson. Before them, Michael. Maybe we were never safe. Maybe the safety was always an illusion.

Griff's shadow stands in the doorway.

"There's a good field of vision from this angle," I say. I'm in the corner of Lily's room, and from here you can easily see my sister's bed, desk, and closet. If I were installing a camera, this is where I'd put it—maximum coverage for minimal investment. I turn around, run the flashlight along the wall. I don't trust myself not to miss something.

"Do you think we should do another walk-through?"

I feel Griff before I realize he's moved. The heat of his chest—suddenly so close—makes me shiver.

"Let's try this," he says, holding up his cell. The pale light splashes across his cheekbones and the line of his nose. "Advantages to owning a crappy phone," Griff says and it's the first real smile I've seen from him in . . . ages. Long before I went to Looking Glass.

Griff labors through someone's number and puts the cell to his ear. Downstairs, I hear Bren's voice lift in answer. "Just stay on the line with me, okay?"

I guess Bren agrees because Griff begins to slowly pace Lily's room, gliding the phone past her walls, her furniture, her stuffed animals. He's testing for electromagnetic fields, trying to see if the connection will buzz or click. After finishing the room, Griff looks at me and shakes his head.

The relief makes my head go fuzzy—or maybe that's the simmering migraine; either way I'm glad for the shadows. I'm glad no one's going to see how close I am again to tears. Griff walks across the hall and opens the door to my bedroom again. I should be right behind him and I'm not. Here it is, my first time really home again, and my feet drag against the carpet.

"Wick?"

"Coming." I stand in the doorway, take a deep breath to get me through. Even in the dark, I can see Bren hasn't moved a thing. My bed is made. My clothes are hanging. My computer . . . my computer's gone. Unease prickles the base of my skull. When Lily moved my stuff to keep it safe, did she move my desktop too?

"I checked the air vents," Griff says. "They're empty."

"Thank you."

He laps the room, slow and deliberate, as I twirl the flashlight up and down the walls. Nothing . . . nothing . . .

Light.

It's only a pinprick, but that's all they need.

"Got one," I say, approaching the wall near my computer desk. I pull the screwdriver from my jeans pocket and dig the head into the drywall, listen for the tap of metal against metal. "Yeah, it's definitely a camera."

"Okay, let me see where they came in from."

"Maybe from the crawl space?"

Griff disappears down the hallway and I wait, trying not to think about how Kent or Hart or Norcut could be watching us right now. There's a bump on the other side of the wall, scratching like skeleton fingers clawing through, and then silence as Griff searches. It's tricky installing cameras into already finished spaces. You have to come in from behind, usually by digging or drilling into the drywall. Sometimes you can do it from the outside, but for a second floor like ours, they'd have to use the crawl spaces. The camera's body and the damage to the drywall would stay hidden, leaving only the tiny lens visible.

Still no sounds from Griff. The silence has seeped from

seconds into minutes and I stand, ready to go after him.

"You were right." I can't see him in the doorway, but Griff's suddenly there. "I found two more. I think we've got them all."

"Good." I sound as calm as he does, but I have to push one hand against the wall to get my feet moving. I shuffle into the hallway. Downstairs, someone's turned on a light and I can make out the pictures hanging on the wall . . . the staircase ahead of us . . . Griff watching me.

We are inches from each other and the space feels suddenly like velvet.

I could touch him. I could—my fingers are already seeking his skin. They brush bandage instead and we both shudder.

"Why did you apologize?" I have to force myself to face him. "At Joe's, you apologized. Why?"

The question's so sudden he should be surprised. I'm acting like a total weirdo, but Griff exhales like he'd been holding his breath. He turns his attention down, not at me, but at the floor.

"Because I owed it to you. Look, Wick . . . I was interested in you way before you ever noticed me. It's the way you handle yourself—the way you never back down. I'd never seen anything like it. You amazed me and I wanted you because of it and then, when you got tied up with Carson again, I resented you for it. I thought you were self-destructing and really . . . really you were just standing your ground.

I should have been in awe of you. I should've helped and I didn't. I was stupid. I confused you with . . . other people in my life."

Griff's eyes lift to mine. His tone is so soft, the kind of voice you save for confessions. "Do you understand?"

I shake my head. I want to look away from him and I can't.

"I hate myself for abandoning you," Griff says at last. "You didn't deserve the way I treated you."

"And you didn't deserve the way I treated you." I have to haul the words from me and the force spurs me forward; my hand finds his arm . . . and tightens. "I should've told you, Griff. I should've trusted you to understand."

"But that's the thing, Wicked." His smile is bitter. "I wouldn't have understood. I didn't get it."

He stares at me the same way he stared at his webcam the day before, like there's something else he wants to say, but I don't have the courage to hear it. I start for the stairs and Griff follows.

"How much do they have on you?" he whispers.

They. Norcut and Hart. Just thinking the names makes the floor of my stomach wobble. "I killed Alan Bay," I say at last. "Norcut told me it was an assessment test, that I was hijacking some remote computer, but I was actually turning his pacemaker on and off. If she turns over the log reports to the police, it'll look like I did it on purpose."

"Shit. What do you have on them?"

"Not enough." I pause, push my knees straight before

saying, "But Norcut offered me a deal. That money my dad had? He *stole it* from Looking Glass. He was working for them and made off with eleven million dollars. Then Lily took the money from Michael and someone else took it from her. Now I have to get it back or Norcut will retaliate and—"

"Eleven. Million. Dollars. How did Lily . . . ?"

"She took the money from some account Michael had and transferred it into my offshore account. That's why Michael's after me; he thinks I have his money and I don't."

"And you still won't if you find it and give it to Norcut."

"Pretty much."

"Right. Bottom line, you're screwed either way."

"Yeah." I look at Griff and try not to laugh because it really is kind of funny. I'm not being a bitch here. It's kind of hilarious. Or I'm exhausted.

Or going crazy. It's entirely possible at this point.

The edge of Griff's mouth spasms once like he might be biting down a laugh too. It's what I've always loved about him. He can laugh in the dark too. "What are you going to do?"

"Fight."

Two hours later, the house is clear. Griff and I drag our-selves into the kitchen, where Bren's had dinner ready for ages. The whole house smells like lasagna and there's the faint "wah wah wah" of the living room television.

It's all so freaking normal.

Except for the small pile of cameras now on the kitchen table. I collapse in the closest chair and pretend not to notice when Griff takes a spot by the counter, keeping half the kitchen between us.

Bren doesn't say a word as she fills two plates, and maybe it's the clink of dishes that draws my sister into the room. The television goes silent and Lily materializes in the doorway. She walks straight to me and drags a chair closer. I eat and my sister sits, watching me with our knees touching.

"Are these all of them?" Bren runs her fingers through the cameras I dumped on the kitchen table.

"Yeah," I say and force another mouthful of food into me. I'm not hungry, but I know I need to eat.

"Can you tell how long they've been here?" Bren asks.

"Hard to say." I draw my fork through the meat sauce on my plate. "They were probably installed during your last bug inspection."

"I've used that company for years."

"That's why it was a good cover."

For a very long moment, no one says anything. I take my plate to the sink and Lily follows, watches me scrape what's left of my dinner into the disposal. "It's not your fault, Bren. You couldn't have known."

Bren's still staring at the cameras. "I want to know everything."

The whole kitchen goes quiet. Lily shrinks into me, putting her small body between us. I know what my sister's thinking: Don't. Don't. Don't.

Can't.

Because if I tell Bren everything, there's no going back and I'm afraid. Everything I've done? She wants to know all of it? Now I'm cringing. Those confessions would be a minefield. I'd blow everything to pieces.

I meet Griff's gaze and nod to him. He pushes to his feet and extends one bandaged hand to my sister. "C'mon, Lily. Just give them a few minutes, okay? Wick's not going anywhere."

He smiles and she relents. It's like magic the way he handles people, the way they trust him. It's thoughtful too, but part of me wishes he hadn't taken her and that he hadn't left. Would it be easier if Griff and Lily were standing next to me while I confessed?

I flick my eyes to Bren's and she's still watching me, waiting. No, there is nothing easy about what's coming and there's no getting past this anymore. We have lived with so many lies and secrets. If I blow those apart now, maybe whatever's left will be real?

"It started with my dad," I say, pushing each word. "Remember how they said I couldn't have been involved in his scams? Well, I was. I'm the one who made Michael's scams happen."

Bren nods—jerks her head up and down, really—but her eyes never leave mine, and when she sits next to me, I tell her the rest.

How I worked for Detective Carson.

How Milo destroyed Detective Carson.

How Lily stole eleven million dollars and I have to find it.

Then I tell her about Judge Bay and Joe Bender, and honestly . . . I should finesse the story. I should tell Bren I had a slip of the tongue when I told Michael what Joe did to my mother and that I made a terrible mistake and that I was sorry. Bren would believe I fell from grace, but I didn't fall.

I jumped.

"I knew what would happen," I say, watching Bren's face and waiting for the revulsion. "When I told Michael what Joe did, I knew he would kill him. It's my fault."

"You didn't pull the knife."

"No, but I feel responsible."

"There is a world of difference between what you did and what your father did, but you will have to live with your actions—so will Michael. In the end, we all have to live with what we've done."

We study each other for a long, long moment.

"Is that everything?" Bren's voice is scratched and frayed, just like everything between us now.

I nod, feeling light-headed. "I think Michael is far more than a small-time redneck with credit-card scam ambitions. He was involved with Looking Glass—so was Judge Bay. But I don't know what that means and I don't know what to do about it and maybe it doesn't even matter anymore because I need that money and I don't know where to find it."

"Anything else?"

I shrug, shake my head.

"I wish you had told me," Bren whispers.

"I wish I had too."

"I'm glad you didn't until now." Bren's breath catches—or maybe it was mine. She stands, turns to the sink, and spends several seconds moving dishes around until finally saying, "I wouldn't have understood. Being a mom . . . wasn't like I thought it would be. You were getting bullied at school and you were sneaking out and I didn't know what to do. I screwed up."

I can't see her face, but I can hear the tears. They always make her voice slide Southern, diluting her vowels until they spread like butter.

"I screwed up being a daughter," I whisper. "I didn't know what to do either."

Bren sniffles. I still can't see her face, but I know she's smiling and this one will be lopsided, and somehow, that gives me hope. We can't be truly broken if I know this about her, right? Surely I wouldn't have learned those details if this was never meant to be mine.

"Do you want to try again?" she asks.

"Yes."

"Wick?"

Lily. She stands in the kitchen doorway, half hidden in the dark. It's late. I hadn't realized how long we'd been talking, but exhaustion has hollowed my sister's face.

"You're going to want to see this," Lily says. Based on her flat tone, I highly doubt it, but Bren and I follow her anyway. Lily's pale hair makes her a candle in the dark. When we reach the dining room, my hand gropes for the wall, ready to turn on the light, and she grabs my fingers. "Don't."

"Why?"

"Look who just joined us."

My skin prickles. Lily points to a computer setup—*my* computer setup—that's arranged on the dining room table.

She resurrected my security camera feed.

"What is it?" Bren asks.

"It's Hart."

"Well, this feels familiar," Lily says, picking at the table's edge.

Not quite. Where Carson stuck to the shadows, Hart's standing in the streetlight. He's staring straight at the house. He's waiting.

"He knows we can see him," I say, and as if he heard me, Hart smiles. He slides both hands into the pockets of those always perfectly pressed dress pants and walks away.

Lily opens another camera angle, checking to see if Hart went around the side of the house. The yard's empty though. He's gone. "That was awfully easy," she murmurs.

I suck in a breath. "He'll be back."

"It's only beginning," Griff adds. We talk over each other and it should be kind of funny, but both of us look away.

Bren shakes her head. "I can't believe this is my life."

"I'm sorry." Again with the apologies. It's like I'm filled with them, like they're all I am anymore.

Bren's hand snakes into mine. She squeezes until our fingers are tight tight tight. "I was never sorry you came into my life. Ever. We'll figure this out."

And for the first time tonight, Bren sounds more like Bren, like the woman she was before I exposed Todd. She takes a deep breath and it sounds only the tiniest bit shaky on the exhale.

"I wanted to believe Hart. I thought he was good, that he was . . . I believed him because I was scared." She's crying, but the tears are silent. They drip down her chin and it's like she doesn't even notice them. Because they've become so common, so everyday? You don't brush away what belongs to you.

"I *am* scared," she continues. "He said he could help. He said he wouldn't tell anyone what he knew about you. I wanted to fix everything. I wanted to make your lives perfect because mine wasn't. I wanted to give you what I never had. But there's something very ugly in the perfect, isn't there?"

"Yes," I whisper and I didn't know how true it was until now. We both spent so much time trying to make our lives into something they weren't. And in the end, all we did was feed each other lies.

"I wanted to save you," Bren says. "I knew whatever you were involved in was bigger than anything I could ever fight and I wasn't going to risk you. I couldn't." Her smile is razor-blade straight and just as sharp. "So when Hart came along, I was ready to hear everything he wanted to say. I was the perfect target."

"It wasn't your fault."

Bren shakes her head. "I don't know what to do, Wick. About the money, about Mr. Hart, about any of it. If I go to the police, I'll have to give them you too and I *won't*. We deal with this together. As a family." She sniffles and turns to Lily. "You have practice in the morning."

Lily rolls her eyes. "I know. I know. I just assumed we would—"

"Like they said," Bren continues, straightening her shoulders. "This is only the beginning. There will be plenty of other nights. He's gone. The alarm's set. Let's get your gear ready for tomorrow."

Yep, much more like the old Bren. But she can only drag Lily upstairs once I swear to stop by her bedroom before I crash for the night.

"I so missed you," my sister whispers as we hug—hard enough for her fingers to leave marks on my skin—and, somehow, it still isn't hard enough.

"I so missed you," I echo. Lily's smile is watery and I promise her we'll talk more. "We have forever, right?"

"Right." She squeezes my hand one last time before following Bren upstairs. Briefly, I'm grateful. I need a minute. I need more than a minute. My brain is overstuffed and fried. I'm too big for my skin and too small for the room and I'm grateful for the space to breathe again.

Until I realize now I'm alone with Griff.

For a long moment, neither of us moves. Then he limps across the living room and takes a seat on the couch. I wish I could do the same thing. Right now, I'm glued to the floor. I need something to say and I have nothing. Wait. For once, that's not actually true.

"Thank you for taking care of them, Griff."

He nods, looks away. I'm sure it's so I can't read his expression. Too bad I can still see how his jaw flexes.

"Why did you?" I shouldn't ask, but I'm done with all the not-askings and the not-tellings and the silences I bury myself in. Especially with him.

And when Griff faces me, I think he feels the same way. It's simmering in how his eyes bore straight through me, in the way his right hand twitches once.

"I took care of them because they're yours."

It's so honest and raw I feel like I should avert my eyes. "Why were you at Joe's?"

A smirk. I recognize it. There's always a bitter bent to his mouth when he's disgusted with himself. "I was looking for Michael."

"Why?"

"I needed to know his plans." Griff rubs one bandaged thumb against his lower lip. "No one could figure out where Michael was—my cousin, his team at the police department, *no one*. I knew Michael hadn't run. I knew he was still a threat. Problem was, I needed better proof than rumors."

My stomach dips. "Is that what got you in 'the wrong place at the wrong time'?"

"Pretty much. I confirmed with my contacts though—his people are running. He won't be far behind."

"You should never have looked for him."

"I had to."

"Why?"

"For you." His eyes travel past me to the darkened hallway. "And for them."

"You shouldn't have risked it! You knew what would happen if he caught you! You knew what you had to lose!"

Griff tilts his head ever so slightly, almost as if he's trying to hear me better. "As long as he's loose, you're not safe. You'll never be safe."

"That's not an answer." Except it is. Griff knew what he stood to lose and he did it anyway. I feel like I'm spinning, but the room doesn't budge. He sacrificed himself for me.

I sit down. Hard. "Where are you staying now?"

"Here. Guest room. Bren is . . . really generous. I can't go back there. Even if I hadn't worked for Carson and my cousin . . ." Griff shakes and shakes his head like the words are something he has to loosen. "I can't take it there anymore."

There. Our old neighborhood. Funny how a place can be so much more than a location. Griff and I have been defined by that neighborhood for years. It's what people think about when they meet us. It's what *we* think about when we look at ourselves.

I pluck at the braided trim on one of the couch pillows. "What's going on with your mom?"

"Ran off with a trucker." Griff's smile is so white against the bruises, and everything I remember about him sweeps over me. Through me. I have to look away. "Who'd have thought that would be such a good thing?" he asks.

"I'm sorry. I know you miss her."

"Yeah, but I'm trying to kill that."

I wince. I shouldn't because I understand what he means. It killed me how much I missed my mom too. It killed because she left me, because she left Lily, because she left us with *him*. I thought if I smothered her memory enough, I would be whole again.

Correction: I would be whole for the very first time. Eventually, I discovered my mother was taken from me, and maybe Griff will discover something took his mother too. Booze, men, *something*.

But it won't ever replace this: Neither of us was ever enough for our parents. Life would be so much easier if you always loved the things that would love you back.

I clasp both hands together. "I know it's a stupid question because I know you're not, but still . . . are you okay?"

"Are *you*?"

Once, that would've been sincere. Now, it's a challenge. We look at each other, and this time, Griff's the one to look away.

"I'm glad you told Bren everything," he says to the kitchen beyond me. "I had no idea . . . until it was too late."

My throat funnels shut. "Griff, there were all these things I couldn't tell you. I wanted to, but I couldn't bring myself to do it."

"So you just what? Buried them inside you? Let them hurt you instead of me?"

For a second, I'm suspended above us, and then, suddenly, I crash into me. "Yes."

His laugh is so soft it should sound sweet. Instead, it makes all the hairs on my arms stand up. "You don't get it, do you, Wicked? When you hurt so do I."

He says it like he hates it. Again. We're staring at each other. Again.

Or we are until my eyes swing to the carpet and stick.

"I couldn't watch you destroy yourself anymore. You're demanding, difficult, sensitive, *difficult* . . . and so incredibly perfect."

His breath catches and I glance up. This time, I don't look away. I can't.

"And you're so far into this," Griff says softly. "I'm going to have to watch you drown."

My vision blurs. Tears. He's not going to make me cry. He's not. "Then leave."

"I can't."

"If you want to play the tortured hero, go somewhere else." Blurry. Blurrier. I blink and blink. "It won't work for me. I don't need it. But—" I force myself to meet his eyes. "I'm sorry I let you down and I'm sorry about what happened to us."

For a long moment, neither of us says anything. Tears are sliding down my face and I'm pretending they're not there. Stupid really. I know he sees them and that's worse.

Griff's bandaged hands go to his knees. "I'm sorry too. I wanted you for you, but I didn't fully understand who that even was and I punished you for . . . well, I had my own shit that I didn't come clean about. I just didn't want to talk about it. I wanted to pretend it was happening to someone else."

"I get that."

"I know. I understand that now. I wish I'd understood it sooner."

More quiet. It makes fresh tears crowd my eyes. This is all that's left of us: awkward pauses and broken promises and realizations that come too late to save anything.

"You went so dark, Wick. Where you were . . . I wanted

to reach you and I couldn't. I don't think anyone could."

"You're right. I didn't know what I wanted or who I was."

Or maybe I did.

"Maybe," I say, rolling the word carefully because this feels so true and so foreign. "Maybe what you find in the dark is what you really are? Maybe it's what's really there?"

His jaw tightens and his eyes narrow and I don't care because I'm picking up speed and this needs to be said. Not for him.

For me.

"How do you find your way when you can't see through the shadows, Griff? You grope. You stumble. You feel for every crack, every hold, every edge. I know all of my broken places now. It used to be something I was ashamed of, but now it shows me what I want."

His eyes briefly widen and that beautiful, ruined mouth opens. Shuts. Griff shakes his head. Because he doesn't understand? Or because he doesn't want to hear?

"How much did you find out about Looking Glass?" I ask and I know I've broadsided him. I need to. I need to wrench this conversation somewhere else, anywhere else. "Did you know Milo is Dr. Norcut's son?"

"No." There's a long pause. "Shit. Are you sure?"

"Yeah."

"Then that means . . ."

"They were engineering my arrival for a while. I have no idea how long they've been watching—long enough, I guess."

Griff examines his hands. "Did you really torture Bay?"

"I thought it was a training exercise."

"Anyone willing to back you on that?"

I close my eyes, shake my head, but I can still feel Alex's hands on mine just before she slipped. "My roommate would've—Alex—but she ran. I helped her escape. Considering her skill set, she's probably halfway across Europe by now. At least, I hope she is."

"Good for her, not so great for you."

"No."

"I need some time to think—" Griff pushes to his feet, wincing, and I'm moving before I even realize. I have both hands out ready to help and he dodges me. "And you need sleep," Griff says. "Do you think you can?"

"No."

Griff swallows, swallows again. "You know I kind of admired the way you went dark. I could never do that."

"Why?" I whisper. Griff's only a foot away—maybe less. I could touch his hand. He could cup my cheek. Except these are things that belonged to other people, not to us, not anymore.

"Because I'm afraid of what I'd find in me. 'Night, Wick."

First night home and I sleep with all the lights on. So much for progress, right? It's so bright that, when I do wake, I almost think it's morning. It's not of course. The sky beyond my bedroom window is still dark. The streetlamps are still lit.

I scrub one hand across my eyes. How can I be this tired and still not be able to sleep? I got maybe four hours? Five?

I stretch my arms above my head until my shoulders pop. Coffee. I need coffee. I drag myself into clothes and pad into the hallway, listening. Everything seems quiet. Bren's and Lily's bedroom doors are shut, no lights underneath.

In Lil's case, I'm not surprised. We must've talked for more than an hour last night. It was good. Better than before I left. I'm glad for that. Grateful.

Maybe even hopeful. If I have my sister again, I can do this, right?

I head down the stairs, my fingers finding the dent I left in the wall when Todd chased me all those months ago. You can barely see it anymore—Bren had the whole stairwell repainted a blinding white—but you can feel it. Seems like that's true about everything these days; we keep painting over ourselves, but the damage is still underneath and you can feel it if you know where to touch.

I drop my hand, promise myself that if we get out of this, we'll move and start fresh. Maybe it would help.

Or maybe the damage will just follow.

Downstairs, the security feed is still running and the yard is still empty. I sit in the dining room and take a couple minutes to check my bank and email accounts. I can't risk using them again, but I run through everything just the same.

Because I'm looking for Milo?

Possibly, but it doesn't matter. There's no contact from him. Anywhere. Does that mean forever? Or just for now?

I want to punch him for what he did, but I also want to know he's okay. He would have to be, right? That's his mom. His *mom*.

It should be a comfort and it's not.

I push to my feet, shuffle for the kitchen, where everything is shadowy and I have to grope to find the switch.

"Can you leave that off?"

I jump. Griff. "I'm sorry. I didn't realize you were—"

My eyes have adjusted now, coaxing out the lines of his profile . . . his shoulders . . . his chest. He's shirtless, bent over the sink with one arm angled against his chest. It makes my mouth go dry and hot.

Griff shifts from foot to foot. "I couldn't sleep any longer. The pain keeps me up."

"I'm sorry."

He shakes his head—jerks his head, really. Every line of him is angry. "It's no big deal. I needed to change this anyway." Griff lifts one hand, tugs at a twisted bandage. Even from here, I can see it's not working. He turns away from me, yanks at it again. "Do you think . . . could you . . . ?"

Help him. He won't say the words. Because he can't? Or because it's me—because it's *us*?

I join him at the sink, untangle the gauze in silence. "You know, it would be a lot easier if I could see." And I turn my face toward the pale light, smile so he knows I'm teasing.

He doesn't smile back. "It's better this way. It's not really that hard to rebandage; I just can't look at it."

"I get that."

Griff goes still and I pretend I don't notice. I unwind the gauze and rewrap it over his blistered palms, careful to keep everything smooth. It still hurts him though. His exhale is harsh. It brings him closer. Or is that just me? Am I leaning into him? I can feel his heat. Everywhere.

"There," I say, pushing away from him. "You're done."

Griff doesn't respond. The tips of his bandaged fingers

touch the thin skin of my wrist. He traces up, up, up until his thumb is in the crook of my elbow and my legs have gone loose.

I feel like I'm moving underwater when I lift my face to look at him. We are so close. Closer than even when I was doing his bandages. Closer than we have been in months.

My eyes drop to his lips and linger. I could kiss him. I *want* to kiss him. I force myself to meet Griff's eyes. He hasn't moved.

"Griff?" I whisper and I'm not even sure what I want to ask. Or maybe I am sure, because my fingertips find his skin. He's warm, so very warm. How could I have forgotten that?

Griff goes still and I can't stop. I trace the line of his hip . . . the hardness of his stomach . . .

"Please," he whispers and I'm gone. I pull him to me and my arms can't tighten around him enough and my mouth can't taste him enough and he's grabbing me the same way.

Griff's hips press hard into my stomach and his hands go to my face. The bandages are rough against my cheeks, but he holds me softly like he's trying to spare me.

It's wonderful and perfect and not enough and completely enough and . . . and it feels safe. Griff makes me feel safe.

I didn't realize how much I wanted it, how much I missed it, until now.

And I don't notice how Griff's stiffened until his

hands circle my upper arms. They graze the scratches still left from the car accident and he pushes me back a step. "Wicked . . . I can't do this."

Can't do this? I snap my mouth shut and taste him on my lips. "Oh. Right."

We're both breathing hard. Griff takes two deliberate steps away from me and I struggle not to follow.

"I'm sorry," I say.

He jerks like I bit him. "No. No, not like that. I can't kiss you yet because I haven't . . ." His teeth click together and his jaw flexes once. Again. "I haven't told you everything. Wick, I . . . I'm still working for Carson."

My whole world tilts sideways. "What?"

"He came to me after they took you in. That's how I knew where you were. He told me you were in danger and you needed help. I've been pulling whatever information on Looking Glass I can—working through their online presences and some of their customers."

"Griff, do you even know what—" I shake my head, but everything still feels like it's spinning. "You can't *trust* him. He's a danger to you."

"Is that why you broke up with me?" Griff takes a step toward me and I retreat. "Were you trying to protect me?"

I can't breathe. I inhale hard and it's still not enough. "Yes. Carson had video of you following me into the court-house. He said he'd get you prosecuted as a domestic terrorist. He was going to go after your computer, search for anything incriminating."

"And you figured since I'd been helping you, I was at risk."

"Yes. You had—*have*—a future, Griff. He could have taken all of that away. I couldn't let him. The only thing you've ever wanted is to get out, to get away. He was going to take that from you."

Griff starts to speak, stops. I know how he feels. I don't have anything else to say either. Dawn light is leaking past the drapes, turning the shadows lavender and gray. There's a thump from upstairs and the shower cuts on.

My sister's awake. It won't be long before Bren and Lily are downstairs.

"Why didn't you tell me this sooner?" I ask suddenly. "I mean, *God*, Griff, you could have told me last night."

"I know. I'm sorry. I just . . . I didn't want you to look at me like—"

Like I am right now. Like Griff looked at me before we broke up.

I pass one hand over my hair. "No, I understand. I couldn't talk to you before because I was scared you'd see who I'd become."

"I think we're both seeing each other pretty clearly now." Griff pauses, watching my face, my mouth.

"What kind of work did you do for him?"

"Research mostly. Names. Places. I think he stays on

the move a lot. He's afraid of getting caught, Wick. He's afraid for you." Another pause before Griff says, "Carson says he can help you. It's worth a shot."

"No way."

"He says he'll back you, says he knows about Looking Glass and will testify. He knew about Hart. Carson said he knew the guy was watching you way before they took you in. He said he had evidence against them."

"Carson had dirt on everyone. Blackmail was his favorite skill."

"But if you two came forward, it would be . . ."

"A teen hacker and a disgraced police detective. You think a jury would really buy it?"

"What other options do we have?"

I don't answer. Then again, no answer kind of *is* an answer. We have a big, fat nothing. Alex is gone. If I don't get Norcut's money, she'll have me prosecuted for premeditated murder. I glance at Griff, who still hasn't taken his eyes from me.

"After I went to bed last night, Carson contacted me and said he wants to meet you—*us*."

"Where?"

Another pause. "Your old house."

I can't swallow past the knot in my throat. "No good. It's being watched."

"I'll pay some neighborhood kids to distract them. Carson says he knows about the missing money."

"How?"

"No idea. Isn't it worth asking him though?"

I shake my head. "I still don't understand why Carson would help. He has his own crap going on."

"Exactly. Carson wants to clear his name and he'll have more leverage if he can prove Milo planted those explosives in his storage unit. If they go to jail, it helps both of you."

My laugh is a sputter. "What if Carson figured out I was behind it? He could want revenge. I took everything from him. When Milo called in that bomb threat and they found all that evidence he'd been hiding, it *ruined* his career. He's on the run because of me."

"Which means he doesn't have anything left to hurt you with. You're on equal footing now. Better than equal, actually, because you know that neighborhood better than he ever will. If we have to run, he won't catch us."

Everyone gets caught in the end. The thought is sudden, suffocating. I cling to this instead: Carson knows about the money. Carson also had my computer. Could he have come across my account? Was there an undeleted keystroke—something—that led him closer?

No, that's stupid. If Carson stole the money from my account, he wouldn't need to talk to me, but he does want to talk and he does know about the money.

And it's not like I have any other brilliant ideas.

"He can't run, Wick. He can't get out. It's a good thing. He needs us. He needs *you*." Griff extends one bandaged hand. "Come with me?"

"No."

We both jump, turn to see Bren in the doorway. She's fisting her bathrobe tighter and tighter and has eyes only for Griff. "The *hell* you're taking her anywhere close to that man."

"If you have a better suggestion," Griff says, leaning one hip against the counter, "I'm all for it."

Bren glares at him, the veins on her hands standing up as she twists and twists the ties on her robe. "I don't and you know it, but for you to even suggest this without telling me—"

"I would've told you." I step forward, put myself between them. "I'm done sneaking around. I would've told you, Bren. I promise."

"You're not going."

"Yeah . . . I am."

Bren gasps, jerks like I bit her. "Wick—"

"Griff's right," I say, sighing. "It's not like there are a ton of options to pick from. If Carson wants to talk, let him. We'll see what he brings to the table. Maybe it'll help."

"I don't see how it could," Bren says.

I shrug. "Carson's a survivor. He deals in useful things."

"Is that what you were?" My adoptive mom's question is soft for something so sharp.

"Yes. . . . If anyone can do this, I can, Bren. It's what I do. It's what I am."

"I don't believe that." She readjusts her robe, concentrating on the long ties around her waist. "I'll drive you."

"You don't have to."

"I'll *drive* you. Both of you." Bren switches her attention to Griff. "Tell the detective you'll meet him. I'll give you one hour to find out what you can. After that, I'm coming for you."

I let Griff contact Carson. It only takes a few minutes, a few texts, and just like that, I am dipping into my old life. Or at least, that's what it feels like.

It makes my stomach lurch.

I haven't faced Carson in over a month, not since that last night, when he warned me about people who were worse than he was and gave me back my computer. Not that he'd really had a choice about that.

The detective still wants to meet tonight at my old house, which bugs me. Why there? Why not somewhere else? It doesn't feel right, but Griff has a good point about it being more our territory than the detective's. If I need to run, I'll be able to do it.

"And I'll be right behind you," Griff adds.

It reassures me far more than I would've expected.

Bren takes Lily to school. Afterward, she'll go home with a friend. I kind of hate it, but she'll be protected and I'll be free to meet Carson. Griff, Bren, and I spend the rest of the day holed up at the house. The hours drag past, giving me plenty of time to stress. I pace. Griff watches movies. Bren checks on us between conference calls. No one says much of anything. We've talked plenty, I guess, and eventually I drop onto the couch next to Griff, watch *The Lord of the Rings* instead of the clock.

"I want that," I say as he turns off the television when the credits roll.

"What?"

"I want a Big Moment—like the kind people get in movies. I want that decision that forever divides you into Before and After, and if you make the right decision, your After is amazing. But life isn't like that. Your Big Moment is really a billion tiny moments and decisions. You're constantly deciding who you want to be. That's freaking depressing. You're never done."

Griff shrugs. "True, but that means you can always start over. It's never too late." He checks his phone, hesitates before looking at me again. "Time to go. You ready?"

I don't answer. I can't. I go get Bren instead.

After a fair amount of arguing, Bren drops us at an abandoned field on the other side of the neighborhood. Yeah, it's a bit of a hike to get to the house, but we're way less conspicuous, and if any Looking Glass security is still hanging around, we should be able to slip in undetected. Bren says she understands, but I know it still kills her to drive away. Her eyes linger in the rearview mirror.

When her car turns the corner, I look at Griff. The early evening light slants through his hair. "Let's go."

We keep our heads down and stick to people's overgrown yards, weaving behind the trailers and houses until we reach my place. Then we stand in the woods, waiting, watching. It's all kinds of uncomfortable. The temps are still high and the humidity makes me feel like I'm breathing through a wet towel. My hand is slick as I text Bren, telling her we're here and we're fine.

The immediate response?

Hurry it up

Not likely. We're deliberately early for the meeting. Griff and I wanted to be ahead of Carson, to let him come to us.

"I don't think Bren understands this is going to take a minute," I say.

Griff looks at the text and shrugs. "When all this is finished, I bet she gets you one of those toddler leashes."

"Hilarious."

"It's funny because it's true."

And it is, but I concentrate on the house so he can't see my smirk. As far as I can tell, the place is abandoned as ever. The windows are dark and I don't see anyone circling the perimeter. The roofline is patchy, but seems to be clear of cameras.

He wouldn't have had the time to install pinhole cams, right? I guess if he had scoped the place before—

"Now or never, Wicked." Griff takes a step toward the darkening yard. His hand brushes mine and my stomach flips.

Griff grins when I hesitate. "What? You wanted to live forever?"

I roll my eyes, but I follow him. The low sun turns our shadows long and lean as we head for the back door. I work the lock while Griff gives me directions—lift and turn, a little to the right, lift again . . . click.

And then we're in.

There's a heaviness to the air in the kitchen. I feel it as soon as we walk through the door. It's like a breath being held or a scream being swallowed. It's stuffy, dusty, *familiar*.

Everyone's house has a scent. Bren's house smells like fresh paint and orange cleanser. The house I grew up in?

It smells like decay and clings to me like flypaper.

Or maybe that's just the memories. They return with the smell and erupt under my skin. Michael shoved my mom into that wall. He threw her down those stairs. Gave her a concussion. Two days later, he did the same to me, and Lily cried. Right there.

And over there.

And there.

"You okay?" Griff's words slide against my ear in a whisper and I shiver. "Wick?"

"Yeah." I shake myself, force my right foot forward, and then my left. "Yeah, I'm fine."

We circle the downstairs together. Pretty easy since the place is so small. No one's hiding in the kitchen, living room, or dining room. It's empty and yet someone's been here.

"Are all the electrical switch plates down?" I ask as Griff nears me. There are gouge marks in the drywall. Whoever opened them was in a hurry and didn't care about being subtle.

"As far as I can tell, they are," he says. "Weird, isn't it? Why would you take off the plates and not take them with you?"

"Why would you take the plates down in the first place?"

Griff shrugs, looks toward the hallway. "The kitchen cabinets were all open and there are scrapes on the shelving backs like someone took a screwdriver to them."

It's warm in the house, but my skin is going colder and colder. "Same deal with the bathroom cabinets."

"Kids having a party?"

"Nah, there'd be beer bottles or cigarette butts . . . I think someone was looking for something."

"Like what?"

I shrug to hide my shiver. "Beats me. Ready to do the upstairs?"

We take the stairs as quietly as possible, dividing our attention between the windows, where we might be seen, and the bedrooms, where we might find someone. It's the same deal as downstairs. The bathroom cabinets are wide open, the vents are down, even the closet doors are unhinged and left on the floor.

There is a loose board in the closet my mom used. The fake wood paneling pushes aside to reveal a thin coating of insulation and there might—*might*—have been an indentation, like something had been stored there. But, whatever it was, it's long gone now.

Another one of my mom's secrets?

I'll never know. There were so many things we didn't say to each other and this one feels like it's just one more. I replace the panel and stand, forcing myself to move on.

Griff's in the bedroom Lily and I used to share. He's bent in half, checking an exposed floor vent. "I don't like this. I can't figure out the angle."

"Me neither." I check my phone. We're still fifteen minutes away from the meeting time, but it's weird Carson isn't already here. He would've wanted to scope the place as well.

Surely he wouldn't *trust us*?

I pocket my cell and look at Griff. "I mean, obviously, someone was looking for something, but what? And *why*? There's nothing here."

Griff stands, cradling his right hand like it's bothering him. "Wick?"

"Yeah?"

"Do you . . . hear that?"

My heart double thumps. "No."

Griff slowly pivots, expression frozen, watchful. "It's like . . . tapping."

"I don't hear anything."

Griff walks past me, loops through the bedrooms, and pauses next to me again, listening. "I thought . . . I could have sworn . . . never mind."

His attention is now trained on the street below. From this angle, we can see the neighbors across the pitted street and most of the front yard. A car drives past, stirring the brittle pikes of grass.

"Think Carson'll come through the rear?" I ask.

Griff thinks for a beat and then nods. "He'll have to. Can't risk being seen by the neighbors any more than we can."

We start for the stairs and Griff stops, checks his phone. A text message from Carson has lit the screen:

Almost there. House clear?

I stiffen. "Why would he ask that?"

"Part of my job to check the meeting sites. More natural for me to be seen around the neighborhood than him. I checked Joe's house for him too." Griff's eyes lift to mine and he grins. "Who do you think was living in that nasty sleeping bag?"

"Carson?"

"Fallen pretty far, hasn't he?" Griff puts the cell in his pocket.

Tap . . . tap . . . scraaaatttccchhhh.

Both our heads snap back.

"Tell me you heard that," he whispers.

"Yeah. It's rats." I swallow. "I used to hear them in the walls all the time."

Griff makes a disgusted noise. "Let's do this in the kitchen. If we make him face us, we'll be closest to the door. Anything goes to crap, we'll be first out."

I nod and Griff follows me downstairs. It's a decent setup for the meeting. I know my ground. I know the exits. I'm as in control as I can be . . . so why does something still feel wrong? Is it just because the house has been searched?

My foot hits the bottom step and I stop dead. "Electrical sockets."

"What?"

I turn to Griff. "All the spaces that someone's searched. They're all *small* spaces—the gaps behind cabinets, the spaces behind light switches. Whatever they're looking for, it's small."

He nods. "Yeah, you're probably right."

"And they know it's here."

"Or they *think* it's here."

I spin and start running, Griff close behind me. "They just didn't know where to look."

"Do you?"

Yes. Maybe. I think so. I round the corner into the kitchen. The door to the garage is still closed. Griff's half a step behind me and I can feel his scoff against the back of my neck.

"The garage? Where would you hide something out there? Under all the concrete?"

"Exactly." I pretty much hate the house, but the garage is a special sort of creepy. We weren't allowed in there because Michael used it for cooking meth and God knows what else.

In the interviews with my mom, she mentioned trying to get in and how he kept it locked. The officers wouldn't listen. They kept pressing her to get inside.

Now that I'm standing in the middle of it, I wonder

what she would've found. A meth lab? Servers and computers? Nothing?

There's a whole lot of nothing right now. The garage door has droopy black plastic garbage bags taped to the windows, letting in more light than they block. The small side door is ajar, a slice of sunlight appearing and disappearing as the door wobbles in the breeze. There's a jagged crack in the concrete floor. It follows the far wall, forking through dark paint splattered in the corner.

"Okay," I say slowly. "Whoever took the house apart knew Michael's hiding spots. They knew him or, at least, they thought they did, but . . ."

"But?"

"But they should've known most of what Michael did took place in here. Check the walls." I veer right, skimming both palms along the cinder blocks and digging my fingernails into the chipped concrete. Griff takes the other side, and for a few minutes, we work in total silence. There's nothing but the scuff of our shoes and the tap of the side door as it swings against the frame.

"Holy shi—" Griff kneels and scrabbles at the wall. I turn, watch as he drags a cinder block to the side . . . then another . . . and another.

There's a darkened space behind the wall.

"Huh," he says, rocking onto his heels. "Did you know about this?"

"No, it was just a guess. Joe and Michael spent a lot of time out here."

Griff shifts the blocks around, lining them against the wall. They fit together pretty neatly, and in the dim light, you'd have to be fairly close to realize the grout was loose.

In other words, you'd have to know where to look.

I lean down and stick my hand inside. My fingers graze rough concrete . . . rough concrete . . . plastic?

It's a balled-up plastic baggie. There's a small black case inside of it and inside the small black case is an SD micro card.

"Here." Griff passes me his phone. "Access my Google drive. See if you can upload the files and then we can read them from there."

I slide the SD card drive into the cell's base, praying the phone will recognize it. The screen illuminates and a green bar expands as Griff steps me through his Google drive passwords. A few minutes later, I'm thumbing through the files. "Looks like . . . spreadsheets . . . and PDFs . . ." I scroll farther down. "Audio files?"

I select the first and bump the cell's volume a little higher. The speaker crackles.

"Can you get to her?" I stiffen. It's Hart. Even on a bad recording, his voice is assured, almost lazy, like he can't be bothered.

"I've already gotten to her. Look at me." Milo's words are a blow.

Please don't let them be talking about me.

Please don't let them be talking about me.

Please don't let them—

There's noise on the recording. I can't tell if it's static or some sort of movement until Hart says, "Ah, Detective Carson. I'm so glad you could join us."

"Is that . . . ? *No.*" Griff's feet don't move, but he leans away, sucks in a single breath. "Can't be. He said they were *after* him."

"I don't have time for this, Hart," Carson continues. "Part of your job is to handle these things."

"And by handling it, you mean take Bay down?"

"He's a loose end."

"Because you don't like sharing the profits with him?" Even in the recording, I can hear the smile in Hart's voice. "Or because you don't like that he outranks you? We *need* Bay. Without him, we can't source the jobs. Without Norcut, we can't source the kids. Without the kids, we don't have a front."

"And in six months, a year, that won't matter."

Static again. No one's saying anything. Because they're

staring at each other? Because they left? Why wouldn't it be a big deal that Looking Glass "won't matter" in a year? Suddenly, Hart asks, "Who told you that?"

"No one," Carson says. His voice is louder now, but it's not like he's yelling, more like he's moved closer to the microphone. "Put that one together myself. Why? Were you planning on leaving me behind?"

Static—a long stretch of it.

"You sound worried," Hart says, laughter beneath his words.

"Hardly. I know where the bodies are buried around here."

"Unfortunate choice of words, my friend." This time, it's Milo who speaks. Like the detective, he sounds closer. There's a whispery noise now too. Maybe papers moving? "Remember what happens to people who cross us."

Carson makes a strangled noise. "Is that a threat?"

"It's an observation," Milo says. "You'd do really well to remember it."

"Where do we stand with the money?" the detective asks. "Have you tracked it yet?"

"We will," Hart says.

"Which means no. Tate is in jail. He's immobilized. This shouldn't be so hard for you."

Hart grinds his words through his teeth: "We *will* find it."

"And the girl?"

"She's not going anywhere." Hart. Again, I can hear the

smile in his voice. "Don't worry."

Chills again. The girl. That has to be me. I glance at Griff and his face is anguished. He knows it too.

I jam my thumb against the back button. The audio file resets and I mash play. We listen to the whole thing again, staring at each other. With every word, Griff goes paler and paler.

The recording clicks off. There's nothing left and I'm half tempted to replay the conversation once more, but I don't have it in me. We're not any further ahead. If anything, I'm behind a step. Or ten.

I had no idea Carson was involved. None. God, I feel stupid. We're about to meet him.

"They cut him out," Griff says at last. "Carson. He worked with them and they cut him out. Why would they do that?"

"Less people to split the money with? It sounded like they're preparing to close the whole thing down anyway. Milo said Norcut and Hart knew they were being watched. Maybe they were getting ready to run?"

"But they couldn't run without the money your dad stole. When was this recorded anyway?" Griff's mouth slackens as he counts backward. "They said they needed Bay because of his position so that would be when? Earlier this year, right?"

I nod. "Would have to be. After his sons . . . after all of that, he withdrew from everything, pretty much disappeared."

"So that means *what*? This was recorded sometime around when you got the first of your mom's interviews?"

My stomach squeezes. "Probably. It was the same night Bay announced his intention to run for office again."

Somewhere outside, a woman laughs and we both stiffen. There are two slams and a car engine starts. Not good. We need to get moving. Leave, meet Bren, and make a plan.

What a joke. What kind of plan do you come up with for this? I want to put my head between my knees.

"What are you thinking?" Griff asks.

I drag my attention to him. "Nothing. Everything. It's a lot to take in. . . . Milo planted that bomb evidence at Carson's storage unit. He said he did it as payback for me. What if he was really doing it just to get Carson out of the way?"

"It worked. He's definitely hosed."

"Just like Bay. Carson was determined to bring him down, kept saying how Bay was corrupt." I'm staring at the stain on the garage floor again. The car and the laughing woman are long gone, and in the silence, I keep hearing my father say: "It's a matter of knowing people's pressure points. You can bring down someone far more powerful than you are—if you know where to hit."

"Hart and Norcut," I say slowly. "They knew where to hit Bay. They couldn't have anticipated Ian and Jason, but what if they knew there was a secret? What if they knew by pushing it, they would make Bay's takedown look natural?"

"No. No way. That's a huge stretch."

"True, but still . . . it feels like there's something there."

"No one anticipated Ian Bay and Jason Baines trying to kill their father for Ian's inheritance."

"For an inheritance or for money Bay already had access to because he was an owner?" We'll never know the truth—Ian's still in jail and Jason's dead—but if they knew anything about the kind of money Bay might have had access to as an owner . . .

I study the file listing, opening the first few Excel documents. They're filled with Looking Glass information—customer accounts, billable hours. If this is true, Norcut and Hart were bringing down millions.

Or they were until my sister helped herself to some of them.

I pass the phone to Griff, watch him grimace as he scrolls through the same information.

"All of this is about money," I say. "Carson told me he knew the judge was dirty. He said taking Bay down would be a public service. Maybe that's how he justified it to himself. But, bottom line, Hart and Norcut sicced Carson on Bay. They knew where to hit the judge and then they knew where to hit Carson. When Milo planted those explosives, it was never about me. It was about Looking Glass. It was about making sure Carson didn't get up again. Bay was a problem and then so was Carson."

Griff's gaze lifts, meets mine. "And now you are."

Outside, the wind blows harder and the side door presses against the jam, smothering the sole source of fresh air and making the garage's heat even more unbearable. In a heartbeat, everything goes even more stagnant, smelling of dust and dirt and . . . copper.

Something smells metallic.

"Wick?"

I didn't even realize I was moving until Griff spoke. I pick my way carefully across the garage, toward the door, toward the stain. My tennis shoes stick to it and I have to hold my breath as I crouch, touch my fingertips to the concrete. They come away tacky and rust-colored and I gag. That's not paint.

That's blood.

"Griff." I shoot to my feet so quickly my head goes

woozy. "Someone was hurt here."

"What?"

"This is blood. When we came in, I thought it was paint, but it's *blood*." I turn to him and stop. Griff's gone pale, almost gray, but he's not looking me. He's looking at his cell again.

"What is it?" I ask.

"I don't know. It's Carson again. He should be here by now, but . . ." His gaze flicks past me and lingers on the stain. In the dusty half-light, his eyes are antifreeze green. "But why would Carson send me this?"

He holds the phone toward me and I cross the garage to take a closer look.

There's a single text on the screen:

Did she find my present?

The back of my skull prickles and I pass Griff the phone. "Is he talking about the drive?"

Griff shakes his head. "He wouldn't *want* you to have that drive. He doesn't gain anything from showing us this. If anything, it makes us less inclined to help him and he told me he needed us."

"Griff . . . how do we know it's Carson on the other end? What if someone took his phone? That's a big stain. What if it's Carson's blood?"

"No. No way. He's more useful alive . . . I think."

I close my eyes, take a breath, and when I open them,

Griff is watching me like he already knows what I'm going to ask and he's dreading it. "What if someone wanted us to find this? Why would someone want us to know?"

"I have no idea." Griff sighs. "All the information here? It's really confidential stuff. You don't just download it by accident and you damn sure don't hide it in an abandoned garage."

"Unless you're leaving it as a present—a really specific present because it's filled with stuff I could use to take down Looking Glass. Hart gave me my mom's interview videos because they wanted to see how I would react, what I would do with the information. Is this the same deal?"

"Maybe it's a plant. If you use this information, they'd know how you were coming, how you were going to hit them." Griff stops, shakes his head. "No. They'd also have to know you're here. Carson would've had to tell them and he sounded seriously scared when he talked about Looking Glass."

It's a good point. Before he skipped town, Carson told me there were people who were worse than he was coming for me, but . . . "He's a really good liar," I say at last. "It's not much of a stretch to think he could pretend. Maybe he really does want to help us. They definitely burned him. But why catch me here? It's not like they don't know where I live." I summon a smile even as cold sweat leaks between my shoulder blades. "If you're going to kill someone, Griff, you don't do it where everyone can see you. You kill them in the dark."

Or you make them jump off buildings.

Or you have your father slide a shiv into their side.

Griff pockets the phone and looks at me. "If he did tell them, they're waiting."

"Then let's get the hell out of here."

I pivot toward the kitchen and Griff catches my wrist. He winces, but doesn't let go, holding me softly like he's afraid I'll bite . . . or break.

"Me first," Griff whispers.

"You always want to go first." It's meant as a joke, but my timing (as usual) sucks because now we're both thinking of how we chased Todd through the dark to save Lily. Griff leans into me, pressing a quick kiss to my forehead, and then eases us into the kitchen, spends a few moments staring through the window above the sink.

The yard looks the same as it did before. No matter how hard I hunt the tangled woods at the dead grass's edge, I don't see anyone. We're still alone.

"Stay here, okay?"

He's gone before I can agree, disappearing into the front of the house. I lean against the countertop, both arms folded against me, and listen to his soft footfalls. He's in the dining room. Should be able to see—

Tap . . . tap . . . scraaaatttccchhhh.

I freeze, listening. That's not Griff, but it's not rats either. The sound's faint, easily buried under whispers, but now, in the silence . . .

Tap . . . tap . . . scraaaatttccchhhh.

I hold my breath and force myself around. Griff's standing in the kitchen doorway and his eyes are huge. He heard it too.

Did she find my present?

"Anyone out front?" I whisper.

He shakes his head and we both pause, listen.

Tap . . . tap . . . scraaaatttccchhhh.

"Then what's that?" I point to my left, not really because the noise is coming from the left, more because I'm scared and I need to do something and yet . . . wait a minute. "Griff," I say. "When you checked the kitchen, did you open the hatch in the pantry?"

He stares at me.

Oh God. This cannot be happening.

I cross the kitchen and nudge open the pantry door. The pantry itself is empty, but there's a four-foot-high panel by my feet and a pretty big space behind the panel. I think it was originally supposed to house the water heater or something, but Michael walled it in, used it to store stuff occasionally.

Lily and I used to hide there, which was pretty stupid because he always knew where to find us.

I'm sweating *and* shaking now. I kneel, work slippery fingers around the edge. The panel falls away too easily, and suddenly, I'm staring at him.

Carson's smile is a smear of blood. "Hello, Wick."

Carson's crammed into the space, knees tucked under his cheek, left arm lying in a horrible angle at his side. It's useless.

No. Not entirely useless.

Tap . . . tap . . . scraaaaatttcccchhhh.

Carson's patting and then dragging the top of his class ring against an exposed pipe. That's what we were hearing.

"We need to call nine-one-one," I whisper, and yet I'm not moving. Can't.

"Concerned for me now?" That horrible red smile widens, but each word is labored.

"Griff, please!" I can't look away and Carson chuckles like he knows.

"You feel guilty for what you did to me yet?" he asks.

I swallow. "You mean planting the explosives? You had it coming."

"Does that make it right?" Carson inhales. The breath rattles and I cringe. "You're not the one who got branded."

"Wasn't I?"

Carson doesn't answer, but there's another rattle deep in his chest. It's terrible and horrifying and more than enough to get me going. I rock back on my heels, looking for Griff. We have to call the police. We have to call an ambulance— Carson's fingers seize my wrist, haul me closer.

That's when I notice his jacket. It's the same leather jacket that guy from the SUV wore. Carson was at the car accident. Carson tried to kidnap me.

I gape. "It was you. *Why?*"

"Leverage. You know he's coming for you, don't you?" The detective smells of sweat and urine and blood, and when he closes his mouth to swallow, he gags. Carson's grip slackens. His eyes go flat, vacant.

"We need to call an ambulance," I manage and I can barely squeeze the words past the roaring in my head. "We need help."

"We need to get out of here." Griff grabs my arm, bandages flexing. "An ambulance can't fix *dead*. Let's go!"

"We can't leave him like this!"

Griff tenses, swings his head to the left. "Did you hear that?"

He tugs at me again and I struggle to my feet. "I don't—"

I do. A car door just slammed. I suck in a breath as Griff disappears down the hallway again, sticking close to the wall.

Another slam. It's not from one of the neighboring houses though. It's closer. Like right out front.

My heart leaps behind my teeth as Griff spins, charges toward me. He hooks one arm around my waist and hauls me to him. "Run. It's Hart. He's found us."

Griff shoves through the back door and I match him stride for stride. We dash across the yard and we're just past the tree line when I hear the first shout.

"Go!" Griff drops back a stride and pushes me forward. Two more shouts behind us. We tear through someone's yard and I hit their fence at a dead run, scramble over the top, and land with my legs pumping.

Another shout.

And a crash.

Are they coming after us? I glance behind me and nearly trip. No good. Keep going. I hurl myself across the next fence, my stomach scraping painfully across the chain link top.

My sneakers kick dirt into the air, but my lungs are already burning. I can barely breathe. I move my feet faster. I am *not* getting caught because I spent too many hours behind those damn computers instead of in gym class.

Griff grabs my arm and yanks me sideways, almost off my feet.

"But—" I splutter. The car is *that* way. Escape is *that* way.

Griff hauls me between two trailers, curves one hand against the top of my head, protecting me as we crawl underneath someone's porch, scramble until we reach the trailer's metal skirting. Griff leans against the trailer and tugs me closer and closer until I'm pinned between his knees, my shoulders against his chest. He braces one forearm along my collarbone, I press my head against his cheek, and in the shadows, we wait.

But we don't have to wait long.

Two men tear through the yard. They're fast black blurs against the humid green. Watching them through the spaces in the porch steps makes the whole thing feel like a movie.

Or a nightmare.

"We can't stay here," I whisper. I'm breathing through my mouth because everything around us smells like damp dirt. It's like I tunneled inside a grave.

Griff's chin brushes against my hair in a nod. We can't look at each other. We can't take our eyes off the yard.

One of the men whips back through, stops, looks around. It's the town car driver—the second one, the one who showed up after Hart and I were attacked. He spends a moment watching the woods he just came from. Then he studies the yard.

Then he notices the trailers.

"Shit," Griff breathes. "Come here."

He leans to one side, taking me with him. Our hips and shoulders connect with the ground, and for a second,

I freeze. He's taking us *under* the trailer, shimmying us through a small space in the trailer's skirting. We push past spiderwebs, going deeper into the dark. The trailer's floor is inches above my head and something crunches under my hand. I whimper.

"You can do this," Griff whispers. The words lift sticky hair from my neck, make me shiver even though it's stupid hot under here. There's a single patch of sunlight on the dirt and I focus on it as Griff repeats, "You can do this. You can do this. You can—"

The scuffle is soft, but it keeps getting closer. Footsteps. He's coming for a closer look.

Scuffle. Scuffle.

Stop.

He's standing by the porch and I hold hold hold my breath. Is he bending down? Is he looking underneath? Does he see the hole we crawled into?

He does. A shadow slides into that square of late afternoon light and I grind my teeth together to keep myself from breathing. I desperately need to, but I don't dare. I don't trust myself not to gasp.

We wait . . . wait . . . He moves away and my brain goes fuzzy.

I turn my head toward Griff, rest my cheek against his shoulder, and feel everything in me come down one notch and then another. I close my eyes and we stay put, listening. The SD micro card's case is digging into my side and I let it, hoping the discomfort will give me something else to concentrate on beyond the fact that Hart is hunting me.

And Carson is involved.

And dead.

We give it twenty minutes before crawling toward the opening again. Griff goes first, waiting just beyond the line of sunshine as he listens. Finally, he looks at me. "Ready to go?"

"God, yes."

We crawl out from the trailer and then scoot to the opening underneath the porch. Griff struggles to his feet, then offers me his forearm, drags me upright. I squint in the sudden sunlight and check my pockets again. The case is still there.

"That sucked," I say and Griff laughs. He shakes dirt from his clothes, dashes one forearm over his head before turning to me. I've banged off most of the spiderwebs, but Griff keeps checking and checking me like he's convinced I missed something.

"I'm okay," I tell him. "I'm okay."

Griff finally looks at me. "I'm not."

He touches his fingertips to my stomach and I look down. My T-shirt's torn and bloody. I examine the skin underneath, discovering two long, thin scrapes. I must've cut myself on that chain link fence.

Griff curves one bandaged hand against my cheek, and for an instant, I see Alex in him. It's in the way he's tired, beaten-down. I know it because I feel it too.

"What are we going to do?" he asks.

I shake my head. "I honestly don't know."

Griff looks at me then looks away. He's waiting for me to say something and I have nothing. Well, that's not entirely true. I have pocketfuls of apologies, an entire lungful of excuses, a handful of enough bravery to say, "I don't have that answer, but I do know this: If every moment is a potential Big Moment, then this one's mine. I want you."

Griff stares at me in a way that should make me back down and I don't. I've backed down too much to do it anymore. "I wanted you even when I couldn't say the words, Griff—*especially* when I couldn't say the words because they were too big and I didn't know how. I want you."

I swallow and taste tears. Now would be a really great time for him to say something. Anything.

And he's still staring at me.

Until he jerks, blinks. "I want you too," Griff says. "For what you are and what you will be."

I stuff down a hysterical laugh—or was it a sob? Either way, my arms are around his neck and his arms are around my waist, and when Griff's mouth meets mine, I know there's no getting over this and I'm glad, *grateful*, because this is the boy who saw me when no one saw me, who knew I had good in me when I refused to believe it.

His hands frame my face, and panting, we break apart. "Text Bren, okay?" he whispers.

I nod, already reaching for my phone.

"Good. Let's get the hell out of here."

Griff tangles his bandaged fingers in mine and we dart between the trailers, casting one quick glance down the street before bolting for the abandoned field. The setting sun has turned the weeds to gold and we're running hard, but my brain's going even faster. With this information, I could leverage myself against Looking Glass. Norcut and Hart could take me down, but I could take them too. They wouldn't dare risk it. All I have to do now is return the money—or whatever's left of it—and we can call it even.

I'll make them call it even.

Satisfaction makes me run faster. We explode from the grass, sneakers hitting the pavement, just in time to see Bren's car approaching us. It's coming fast.

Is something wrong?

I squint. The shape . . . the shape is wrong. That's not Bren's car.

Click.

I go cold and Griff's hand tightens. There's only one sound in the world like that: a gun. Slowly, we both turn, watch a figure push up from the ground and the thickening shadows.

"Do not move," it says. Orange sunlight slants through the trees, hitting his shoulders . . . his face . . . his pistol.

"You drove me to Looking Glass," I say.

"Turn around," he says.

We do. A black BMW purrs toward us and I have to struggle not to sink to my knees. Every last bit of my energy is gone. That's not a town car, but it's close enough. Looking Glass always liked their shiny, black vehicles.

The car pulls to a stop a few feet from me and I watch

the door open. The driver stands up, walks toward us.

Dark suit. Dark sunglasses.

He pulls them down with a single finger and an animal howl fights into my mouth. It's not Hart.

It's Michael.

"Hello, daughter."

I take a step back and cold metal presses against my skull.

"Don't even think about it," the guy says, nudging me forward again.

"This feels familiar." Michael taps his knuckles against the Beemer's hood. "How're you doing, Griffin?"

Griff doesn't answer and Michael walks around the car, stops so close I can smell the sweetness of his aftershave. "You two look awfully close for someone who's taken up with a doctor's son."

"It's not like that," I say.

"Pity."

"Let him *go*."

Michael faces me. "Gladly. I'm not here for him anyway."

Chills ripple through me. "What do you want?"

"You, but I admit he is a problem." Michael's attention drags to Griff and lingers. "Earlier, it was useful having him with you, made texting you so much easier, but now . . . ?"

"You have Carson's cell?" I ask.

"I'm presuming you found my gift, yes?"

I don't answer, but Michael nods like I did. "Good," he says. "I went to a bit of trouble to kill him, but I won't say I didn't enjoy it. I'm also presuming you found that micro card. Hold on to it. We're going to need it."

"You need to leave." Griff eases closer to me, and Michael's guy switches the gun from my head to Griff's temple. "We're about to have a ton of witnesses."

"'A ton'?" Michael laughs. "Or *one* extremely stressed lady? Your Bren is still miles away. Got caught on her way here and is getting a ticket for failure to maintain lane and speeding."

I swallow. "From the same officer who got you out of jail?"

"No, but nice guess. I use a variety of contacts. It's important to give back to the community, you know?"

Michael glances at me and I flinch, biting down on my tongue.

"But it's not like we have time to mess around," he continues. "We're leaving, Wicket. Get in the car."

Griff stiffens. "Wick."

"No," I say.

Michael's smile slings wider and he nods to his guy. The man steps closer to Griff and we both tense. "This is how it's going to go," Michael says. "In return for good behavior, Wick, I'm going to let Martin here knock your boyfriend out. He'll go down. You'll come with me, and in a few hours, he'll wake up with a hell of a headache."

And we'll be God knows how far away. I look at Griff. *We'll be long gone, but he'll live.*

The relief is a rush until I realize Michael will also have leverage on me. Forever.

Our eyes meet and he smiles like he knows what I'm thinking.

"How do I know you're telling me the truth?" I ask Michael at last.

Griff's eyes go wide. "I'm not leaving you alone with him!"

Michael laughs. "You *don't* know that I'm telling the truth, but I am. Martin"—Michael gestures to his gunman—"could've killed him when you two came out of the field, but he didn't because I told him not to. Consider it a show of good faith. I know how you feel about the boy and I'm going to let him live."

"What do you want?" I ask.

"Your cooperation." Michael bends down, swipes a long piece of grass from the ground, and begins to shred it. "We have things to discuss."

My head goes light, woozy. I don't want to discuss anything with him.

"Let him," Griff whispers and I whip toward him, convinced I couldn't have heard right. Michael and Martin both stiffen, straining to hear Griff's words. "Let him hit me," he repeats under his breath. "Wherever he takes you . . . I will find you."

"I'm so sorry," I whisper.

Griff shakes his head. "I trust you."

My breath hitches, and for a very long moment, all I can do is stare at him. "I love you," I whisper and the words should feel like a bomb because I withheld them for so long, but they're suddenly easy to say, like they belonged to him all along.

"I love you too." Griff's words are a confession and a promise. Now I just have to be brave enough to see this through. I swallow, swallow again. I'm struggling to breathe, but I force myself to look at Michael. I nod.

"Good," he says. "Do it farther in, Martin. I want Bren to have trouble finding him."

I wince. It's another delaying tactic. When Bren finally gets here, she'll wait and wait, never knowing Griff's unconscious body is only a few strides away.

Griff keeps his eyes on me as he backs into the waist-deep grass. "This far enough for you?" he asks finally.

"Watch your tone." Michael flicks the grass bits from his hands. "It'll do. Come here, Wick."

I turn, take an uneven breath, and force myself forward. One step. Two steps. There's the most awful thud behind me and immediately a rush of grass as Griff hits the ground.

Michael extends one hand, palm up. "Cell."

I give it to him. Michael pops the battery off the back and smiles at me as he pitches the pieces in two different directions. "Now we don't have to worry about being interrupted."

Or being saved.

"See how pleasant things can be when you cooperate?" Michael grins and I follow him to the car.

We leave Peachtree City by back roads. Michael drives. Martin sits behind me, keeping the gun trained on the back of my head. I try to concentrate on the passing houses and cars instead, but I don't recognize any of the surroundings. Thanks to the navigation system, I can tell we're headed south, but beyond that it's just long stretches of darkness punctured by random porch lights. I have no idea where we're going, but then the car's headlights hit a reflective green sign and I have to press both feet into the floorboard. "Are you taking me to the airport?"

Michael makes a left, maneuvering us down a long, paved drive. "Aren't you the smart one?"

Not nearly smart enough. I can't think past the whistling in my head. I put both hands in my lap, twisting my fingers together. It's one thing to drive me somewhere. It's totally different to fly. Griff won't find me. By the time he wakes up, I could be halfway across the country.

So what am I going to do? Run for it?

Impractical. We're at least two miles off the main road and the woods will slow me down. Even if I did reach the road, the likelihood of flagging down a car is pretty much nil so that leaves . . .

Hell if I know.

It's a small airport—we're passing mostly private planes, puddle-jumper stuff. Michael drives us to the tarmac's far end and parks by the very last hangar.

"Get out," he says, unbuckling his seat belt.

I fumble with mine. My fingers have gone numb. *All* of me has gone numb. Michael keeps one hand on my arm as Martin walks away, heading into the darkened hangar. We follow and my eyes adjust slowly. I can see shapes on either side of us. Boxes? Equipment?

Farther ahead, it's easier to see what's waiting under the moonlight: a plane.

I don't understand. Is Michael escaping for good? If he is, why would he take me with him?

"What do you want?" I ask.

"To talk."

"About *what*?" I turn and it's a mistake. Michael's in my space now, breathing the same air. He traces one finger along my cheekbone and I struggle not to shudder.

"All this time," he says softly. "They told you I wanted to kill you, right? That you were mine? That I knew you had the money and I would come for you?"

I nod. I'd forgotten the sound of his voice, how smooth it was, how every word felt like the promise you'd always wanted. He used that voice with addicts looking for a fix and with my mother when she was looking for an escape.

"Norcut and Hart were half right," Michael continues. He pulls me deeper into the hangar by my elbow. We walk just outside of the moonlight as Martin jogs back and forth ahead of us, readying the plane. "I was coming for you. You *are* mine. You aren't just my daughter. You're my creation, my right hand. But I knew you didn't have the money."

"How's that?"

"Because I did."

"*You* have the money?"

He smiles. "Aside from that minor lapse with your sister, I've always had the money. I stole it months and months ago—just before my first arrest. Why do you think Norcut was always so quick to keep any appointment with you? Why do you think Carson stayed so close to you and your sister?"

"Because he wanted to arrest you."

Michael gives me a pitying look. "Or is that just what he told you? I didn't expect for your sister to find the money, but thankfully, I knew exactly where she would put it so I waited. Then I took it back from your account. I needed to panic them. Fear makes for an easier target and I knew the dear doctor was seriously terrified when she started having my old contacts killed."

"They were going to *kill me* over that money." I take a

deep breath, smelling fuel and oil. "If I don't deliver, they'll kill Lily and Bren. You have to return it."

"No, I don't. By the time I'm finished, there won't be a Looking Glass. I created it and I can destroy it and they know that. They fear me."

"*You* created Looking Glass?"

Michael shrugs. "What did that bitch tell you? That I worked for her? Bay found us clients. Norcut found children with the right skills and Carson handled security. Eventually, Hart became the face of Looking Glass. He has that . . . approachable look people love so much. Hart helped Bay find the right companies to hire us and I test-drove several of our"—Michael grins, his teeth flashing in the moonlight—"sales pitches? You remember that last scam before I was arrested?"

My stomach squeezes. "Yeah, we were asking people for donations and then stealing their credit card information."

"And it worked beautifully. We took money from the marks and then we took money from the credit card company."

"You mean you sold the credit card company a solution to a problem you created. They never realized they were paying the people who ripped off their clients in the first place."

"Nicely done, wasn't it?"

I stare at the plane waiting for us on the tarmac, force my heartbeats to slow. I've been working for Looking Glass for years, I just never realized it.

"All this time," I say, dragging my head up to meet his eyes. "All this time when Carson was chasing you, it wasn't because of the drugs or the credit card scams. It was because of Looking Glass. It was because of the money."

Michael nods. "They wanted to cut me out and he made it happen. Or he tried. Carson was supposed to tip me off about that raid and he didn't. He thought—they all thought—by catching me in the thick of it, I would go away for a very, very long time. One less person to split the profits with."

The raid. The one Griff kept me from, the one where Joe and Michael were caught, and I thought my father was gone for good.

There's a sharp clang behind us as Martin unhooks the plane's tie-downs and flings them to the tarmac. Michael's watching him, but his eyes are glazy. "Then Norcut sicced Carson on Bay. And what a beautiful job you did on that judge for the good detective too. Well done. Would've worked out beautifully for Carson if Norcut and Hart hadn't turned on him, gotten that boy of hers to plant those bombs. He must've been desperate for leverage when he tried to kidnap you. Something to remember here, Wick. You can't trust anyone except yourself . . . and me."

"Then why were you chasing me?"

"Because we're family. We're supposed to be together." His grin is boyish and sickly in the pale light. "Yes, I was pursuing you, but I never wanted to kill you. Ever."

"Throwing me around was what then? Because you love me?"

The smile drains from his face. "Because I want you to become the person you're meant to be. I saw what was in you at an early, *early* age. I saw what you would be capable of, but it wasn't until you asked me to kill someone that I knew you were ready."

"Ready for what?"

"To join me."

Join me. Michael says it like it's the easiest thing in the world and maybe it is. Maybe it's always been. Fighting against who I am is what got me here, isn't it?

I study him, look at his suit . . . his shoes . . . his car. Even with the pretty clothes and the prettier vehicle, he still looks rough. In the dark, Michael's blond, short-cropped hair is almost impossible to see, turning his head into a skull, his cheekbones into pits.

"You think I should join you because I lashed back at Joe?" I ask at last.

"Ah-ah." He wags a finger at me. "Be specific. You had me kill him. You knew what you were asking."

"I had to save Lily. He was going to hurt her to get to me."

Michael nods. "Absolutely. Love is leverage, Wick.

Joe understood it. Carson understood it. Norcut and Hart understand it. But look how that worked for them. Look what I've done for you. I've moved worlds for us and I would do more too. That woman who adopted you, she can't give you what I can."

I stare, feeling like I'm seeing Michael for the very first time. Is that . . . *jealousy*? He's watching me now too, and even though his eyes are smudged with dark circles, they're still as blue as I remember them.

Michael and I have the same eyes, the same hair. We are so alike in so many ways.

But it doesn't matter anymore.

There has to be another way for me. My entire life everyone has told me who I am: I am my mother's daughter. I am my father's right hand. I'm not decent. I will *never* be decent.

They told me evil's in my blood and I believed them. I acted like it was my destiny, but it was my choice. *My* choice. I didn't make it before. I could now. Maybe, just maybe, it isn't about what I've done, but what I'm capable of doing.

If I let myself.

Michael's palm curves against my face and my stomach threatens to heave into my mouth. His eyes inch across my face. Can he tell he makes me sick? Can he tell I'm horrified?

"You used to flinch whenever I touched you," he whispers and there's something awful underneath his words. It sounds like awe. "But you don't anymore. You are stronger than I ever believed. Aren't you tired of being everyone else's weapon, Wick?"

"Yes." And I'm telling him the truth because suddenly I understand how lies aren't the only things that can protect you. I know who I am now. That's going to have to save me.

"Then stop letting them use you," Michael says and his fingers dig into my cheek, finding the soft spot beneath my eye. "Take control, and come with me."

"No."

Somewhere outside the hangar, Martin slams a door shut. Michael leans in close. "Are you sure? I want you to think very carefully, Wick, because there is only one right answer here."

I shudder even as pity chews through me. For all my father's talk of love, he will never understand it. "I am not a thing to own."

Michael's fingers arch into claws, igniting my skin with pain.

"It's ready." Martin appears at the hangar's opening, one hand against the metal frame . . . the other hand pointing his gun at us. At me. "We need to go."

"A minute," Michael says, digging in further. My vision blurs and I blink away tears.

"We don't have—"

Pop! Pop!

Martin's knees hit the concrete and his body slumps forward, splays flat. Michael drops his hand and we both shrink away. Blood seeps from underneath Martin, expanding in an ever-widening pool, and all I can think is: *Martin's been shot.*

And immediately afterward: *They're using silencers. This isn't just catching us. It's an execution.*

Pop! Pop!

I throw both arms over my head as bullets hit the metal siding. Something next to me shatters and I duck.

"Run!" Michael shoves me toward the hangar's other end. "Get to the car!"

I spin around and take off, my sneakers slapping against the concrete. Behind us, someone yells and someone else answers.

Two of them. There are at least two of them.

Pop!

I jerk to the right and my hip collides with a sharp corner—table? Can't tell. I stagger sideways and Michael gives me another shove. "Go!"

Pop! Pop! Pop!

Something heavy collides with my lower back. I make it one step, two steps. Down. I'm down. Am I hit? Both hands skid in front of me, both knees stutter against the concrete, and I twist, ready to wiggle to my feet.

But Michael wrestles me to the floor.

My spine hits concrete. My head follows. There's a starburst of pain and I start swinging. I get in a hit to his face and one to his ear. Michael hisses and clocks me, catching my right temple and spraying colors behind my eyelids.

"Stop it!" He shakes me hard and pries open my fist.

Something scrapes my palm. Paper?

"Take it," he hisses and I thrash. I slam the heel of my other hand into his nose, feel it crack. Blood spatters my cheeks and Michael rears up, grabbing his face with both hands.

Pop!

Michael shouts, grabs his arm. His face is anguished and astonished and so very red.

I gape . . . gape . . . kick to my feet, feel the swipe of his fingers against my ankle.

Only helps me run faster.

I lift my knees and hit another box, have to splay both arms wide to keep from toppling. I stab one hand against the wall and keep going.

Almost there.

I can see the car! I can see the car!

I'm nearly to it when I realize Michael's not following me and I'm already in the driver's seat when I see him stagger from the hangar . . . and waver.

Two more flashes of light from inside. Two more shots. And he falls.

For a heartbeat, I hesitate. I'm gasping and gasping and I still can't get enough air. They shot him. Michael's down.

He's *down*.

There's a roaring in my head now and I jerk the driver's door shut, slap my palms across the dash, leaving sticky, bloody prints. Michael's paper scrap unglues, flutters to the floorboard.

I grope along the console. Nothing. Nothing. Noth—
keys!

I jam them into the ignition and jerk the car onto the road, flooring it. I keep both hands on the wheel and my eyes straight ahead. I don't trust myself to look back . . . but I do stray once. I check my rearview mirror and I recognize the man standing in the road behind me.

It's Hart.

Eventually, I stop in the darkest corner of a Winn-Dixie parking lot, check my bad arm, feel the rest of me. I'm in one piece, but why is the front of my T-shirt so wet?

Carefully—*slowly*—I open the car door and push to my feet. It's kind of amazing when the world doesn't wobble. I'm steadier than I expected. I stand in front of the head-lights and survey the damage.

The front of my shirt and shorts are damp with blood, but it's not mine.

It's Michael's. The thought is so far away it feels like someone else's whisper. When he hit me from behind, it must've been because he was shot.

Then they got him in the arm . . . and then I remember the two flashes of light.

They killed him. My father's dead.

I rub a cold, sweaty palm across my face, smell the oil and dirt on my hands. It makes my breath catch again and I have to remind myself to stop, to *think*.

But all I can think about is this: Everyone's gone. Joe . . .

Michael . . . Carson . . . every tie to my past is gone. The only thing left standing between me and the rest of my life is Looking Glass. I need to take care of that, but *how*? They're expecting me. They'll see me coming, and if I don't move against them, they'll move against me.

Someone's going down, and considering Looking Glass's resources, it's a pretty good bet that someone will be me.

"I'm finished," I whisper, trying the words aloud. It actually helps. A little. "So what am I going to do about that? I need a plan . . . I need a plan . . ."

I don't have a plan.

I wish I still had my cell. I'd give anything to call Bren right now or to hear Griff's voice.

I climb into the car again and something crinkles under my foot. I peer down at the floorboard and see something next to my sneaker, something like . . . paper?

Yeah, it's paper. And suddenly, I remember Michael shoving something into my hand. It's a note—definitely a little worse for wear now. There's dried blood on the bottom and one corner is torn. I fold down the edges and angle the writing to catch the overhead light. It's four lines of numbers and twenty-one numbers per line. If I had to take a guess, it's four bank accounts.

Presumably, *Michael's* bank accounts.

He wanted me to have them.

I don't know what to make of that so I stare at the numbers instead. I stare until they swim together. I think of the SD card Michael secured for me, how I could take down Looking Glass. I think of the bank accounts.

I think of the money.

With enough money, you can disappear. I know that. Of all people, I know that so well. I could threaten Looking Glass with what I have and then I could get Bren, Lily, and Griff and we could run. They'd never find us. I could make sure of that.

I take the SD card from my pocket and roll it around in my palm, all of Michael's carefully curated leverage. My leverage now. It's the only thing standing between them and me and Michael made sure I had it.

He took care of me. This was his legacy, and his love, and he knew I would know what to do with this. He knew I was ready.

And I am ready because, suddenly, I know what I'm going to do, what I *have* to do.

I put the SD card onto the console between the front seats and tuck the paper with Michael's account numbers under it. I'm ready, but it still takes me a minute or two before I can put the car in drive. Once upon a time, Griff told me you can't save everyone, but if you're lucky, you can save one person. I've saved my sister, Bren, even Griff, and by giving me this money and leverage, Michael saved me. I don't know what to do with that, but I do know what I have to do next.

Maybe I've always known.

But do I really have the courage to do it?

"Yes," I tell myself, and tug the gearshift down. The car purrs forward. I keep one hand on the steering wheel and one hand on the paper as I turn onto the main road. I head north. I don't stop and the moon is low in the sky when I pull into the parking lot.

I park under the glare of an overhead light and something beeps. I tense, peer down at my legs . . . the console . . . the passenger seat. There's a soft yellow glow in the shadows. It's a cell phone—a burner most likely. Michael or Martin must've ditched it when we got out of the car.

I run my thumb over the keypad. I shouldn't call. I shouldn't. I do. I dial her number and a sob catches in my throat when I hear her voice:

"Hello?"

"Lily?" My voice cracks and I have to clear my throat. "Haven't I taught you anything about answering strange phone calls?"

"Wick!" Lily's crying and laughing. "Where are you? Bren's coming to pick me up. She said she took Griff to the hospital!"

I close my eyes and take a deep breath. "Is he okay? I mean . . . do you know anything?"

"Yeah, she said he's going to be fine. He's been admitted or whatever, but it's just for observation. Where are you? She's freaking out."

I lean my head against the steering wheel. I can't tell her. It's not fair for Bren and Griff and Lily to hear second-hand what I'm about to do, but I'm doing the right thing. I know I am. "I'm safe. Promise. But I have to finish something first."

"And then it'll be over?"

Tears sting my eyes. "Yes. Definitely. I love you."

"I love you too." Lily disconnects and I heave myself out of the car. I lock the doors and then wonder why I bothered.

It's not a far walk to the main office building, but by this time, my head's throbbing, counting every heartbeat. I shuffle along, making it, maybe, ten steps before a beaten-up Crown Vic slows along the street and stops at the curb. No passengers. I can't make out the driver. He or she is just a black shape, a shadow.

Then the headlights flick once and I get it. I almost laugh.

Milo. That's Milo.

He came for me—not so close that he could get caught. It's pretty damn obvious where I am, after all, and he's not going to get too close. I know that about him because I know that about myself. We are alike.

Only, we really aren't anymore. If we were, he'd be down here too. I stand under the yellow parking lot lights, waiting to feel something . . . and there's nothing. No, that's not totally true. There's some pity and some sadness. Milo was right: We are the products of our parents.

But that doesn't mean we stay that way. You can choose your family. You can change your destiny. It's the easiest and hardest thing in the world.

I hope Milo realizes that one day. I lift a hand in a

half-assed wave and the headlights flick again and again. Is he frantic now? Worried? It would be so easy to go to him, but it's not what I want anymore.

I turn around, walk the last twenty feet or so to the door, and open it, squinting under the fluorescent lights. Full-blast air-conditioning hits me and I shiver.

Or maybe I shiver because I know what's coming next.

The officer at the front is half asleep, but by the time I put my hands on the desk, he's sitting straight.

"Can I help you?" he asks, eyes dancing up and down my face. He's trying really hard not to look horrified. It's kind of hilarious.

"Yeah," I say. "My name is Wicket Tate, and I'd like to confess my crimes."

What Happened After

Norcut and Hart never saw it coming. That probably doesn't say anything great about me, does it? No one ever thought I'd come clean. It was the one piece everyone counted on.

But I was able to use it.

Funny how that's kind of my life's theme until this point. People have used me and I've used them and now it stops. With me.

I gave the first set of officers my story and all the Looking Glass paperwork. They looked at me, looked at the files, looked at me, and started making phone calls. Or, at least, I guess that's what they did because fifteen minutes later I had a set of detectives to talk to . . . and then another set . . . and then came the Feds.

I'm not sure who called Bren, but she showed up about two hours later with an attorney. After that, everyone started shouting. Did the police realize I'm still a minor? Why hadn't I seen a doctor? How much longer was I going to be held?

Had I been arrested?

Bren's attorney had a lot of questions. Four days later, we're still figuring out the details. There's a slew of stuff the government could charge me with, but as my lawyer keeps reminding them, I'm the one who came forward. I'm the reason they have this information. I didn't have a legal guardian present during questioning. The police didn't offer me a doctor right away. Was I even in my right mind when I came in?

Blah blah blah.

Bren sat with me during the interviews. She kept one arm around my shoulders, and somehow, it was enough to keep me going—even when they told me I'll be facing charges. We still don't know what kind or how many, which means we also don't know how long I'll spend in prison.

Yeah, I said prison. If it had been other crimes, I probably could've scored juvie. Being that the government is terrified of hackers, I'm looking at a trip to Club Fed. Ten years. Minimum.

The detectives initially thought I'd get a few days to prepare myself, "to get my affairs in order" is what one of them called it, but because I'm considered a flight risk, they're holding me indefinitely. They did let me be the one to tell my family, which was nice of them, I guess. Bren, Lily, and Griff filed into the interview room to see me, and when I told them I wasn't leaving, Bren wobbled like she needed to sit down. She got on the phone with another lawyer instead.

Probably just as well because, right then, I didn't want to talk. I didn't want to hear about our next legal moves. I just wanted to be next to Griff, and when I squeezed my hand around his, it felt like everything wonderful in the world when Griff squeezed back.

"Please," he whispered.

I didn't understand, and then he kissed me and I did. Griff kissed me with a mouthful of forgiveness and forevers and I promised him the same. This is how I am with him. This is *always* how I am with him, and when we broke apart, I realized this is how he is with me. They cannot take it.

Lily struggled with my decision. She was pretty angry with me. It hurt, but I understood. We worked so hard to keep me from getting caught and now it feels like I was always destined to be. Except it wasn't destiny. I chose what would happen to me and I made the right choice.

She says she understands, but it's hard. For both of us.

In the meantime, I answer police and Fed questions while I wait for my transfer to a full-time facility. I'm trying to be helpful, but I might have forgotten a few things.

Things like Milo.

Things like Alex.

She sent a postcard to my house. I didn't see it, but Bren told me. There wasn't any note, but the picture had two old ladies laughing and leaning against each other. The caption said "We go together like drunk and disorderly." The postmark was from Paris. I'm not sure why, but I really like the idea of Alex living the rest of her life in Paris. It's the City of Light, right? She'd never have to be in the dark again.

Mostly, I've given the agents and officers names, locations—basically, everything I have and everything I know about Michael's operations. The officers are calling him a monster and I agree. He is. It's my heritage, but it's not who I am. It might not be Michael either. In those last moments, my father was someone else. He was human. True, his love was twisted, deformed. He was violent. He used people. But he was also lonely. Normal people aren't the only ones searching for someone who understands them. Monsters search too.

The morning my transfer comes in, the guards take me through the rear entrances, and as I wait for the van to come around, I notice the figure at the fence line.

Griff. He came to see me off.

Immediately, the guards start yelling and threatening and he's smart enough to take off, but not before I see his grin. It's for me alone and I almost laugh. Amazing how his smile warms me like sunshine.

He's attending community college in the fall and will transfer to art school after his hands have fully healed. Bren's pretty much insisting he stay at our house. She wants to make sure he'll be okay. I'm not worried though.

Griff's going to be brilliant.

He's *already* brilliant.

But right now, Griff's running hard in the opposite direction with two heavyset guards in pursuit. They're never going to catch him, but they're hoofing it anyway. The van comes around for me and the remaining guard opens the passenger door, motions me inside.

The driver looks at me and then looks at his clipboard. The name on his shirt says Baker and the badge underneath it is scratched.

"Tate?"

"Yeah."

"Okay, let's go." Baker heaves himself around and shifts us into drive. We pull away and my stomach clenches so hard I feel like I'm going to be sick. Terror has a way of doing that to you. It fills you up, makes you feel like it's the only breath you'll ever take.

But it isn't and I know that now. I'll get through this. Somehow.

"Charges like yours," Baker says, watching me in the rearview mirror. "Usually you go away for a long time."

I flick my eyes to the windows, try to memorize every pine tree we pass. It's going to be a while before I see stuff like this again. I want to enjoy it while I have it.

"Like *decades*," he adds, and it's funny how the statement curls into a question. I lean my head against the glass and look up. The sky is a bowl of sludgy gray. It's going to rain later. I wonder if I'll be able to see it from my cell or if the windows will be too small.

Or if there will be any windows.

Either Baker gets the hint or gets bored because we drive the rest of the way in silence. It takes us over an hour, but it feels like only minutes, and when he drives the van behind the chain link and razor wire fencing, I have to swallow and swallow to keep my stomach where it belongs.

Baker parks and climbs down from the driver's seat, wanders around to unlock my door. "Welcome to your happily ever after"—he checks his clipboard again, grins at me—"or however long you make it."

He's trying to scare me and I grin. That was the wrong thing to say to me or, maybe, the perfect thing to say to me. All this time I never believed in happy endings. Life wasn't a fairy tale. Love won't save you. No one gets out alive.

And it's true.

Or, at least, it's partially true because love *can* save you. That's the crazy thing about it. All those sappy stories and Top 40 songs, they're so cheesy and stupid and *right*. Love is everything the fairy tales say it is.

Maybe that's why I was so sarcastic with the whole thing—because I didn't want to fight for love, for what I really wanted. I didn't want to be brave. I wanted to run. I wanted to hide. I wasn't willing to risk anything for it.

But the problem was, by not risking anything, I cost myself even more. Griff would probably call this a Big Moment, right? I am now the heroine of my very own romantic comedy. Although considering I'm about to walk into prison, romantic tragedy is probably more appropriate.

But one day I'll walk out, and when I do, I'll have my second chance.

I just have to get through this first.

Baker stands with me while we wait for my transfer. Eventually, another uniformed woman comes to get me.

"Tate?" she asks.

"Yes."

"You'll be debriefed first," the guard says. "After that, we'll bring you to intake."

Nausea rolls through me. Intake. That's a mild word for getting my prison-orange jumpsuit and a cavity search.

"Great!" I say and make sure to smile. The guard rolls her eyes and motions for me to follow her. We make a right down a fluorescent-lit hallway, and when we reach the first door on our left, she opens it.

"Sit down. Don't move."

There's a table with two chairs on one side, one chair on the other. I take the single chair and fold my hands on top of the table. It feels too formal so I put them in my lap. That doesn't feel right either, but I leave them there and wait.

It's only a few moments before the door swings open and a woman walks in. Our eyes meet and my heart double thumps.

"I know you . . . you were the social worker at Looking Glass—the lady taking notes during therapy," I say.

"I'm Special Agent Bennett," she says and looks into

the hall, waiting. "And this is Special Agent—"

"Hart," I say. He stands in the doorway, both hands braced on the frame. He's still perfectly dressed, perfectly polished, and I don't think that hair would move if I blasted it.

"Actually, the name's Larkin," he says. "But if it makes you feel better we can stick to Hart."

Hart—Larkin, *whatever*—shuts the door and takes the closest chair. His feet slide so far under the table he accidentally kicks my feet. Special Agent Bennett stays standing, arms crossed. Her attention is trained on Hart and his attention is trained on me.

"Hello, Wick," he says. It could be that day in Bren's living room instead of today, like nothing's changed except for me. "You've been busy."

I nod. "You too."

He smiles and I lean back. I'm ready to get this over with. I've about had all the fun I can stand with these people.

"I always knew you were special, Wick."

"You know that sounds creepy, right?"

"Sorry. It's true though."

"What do you want?"

Hart studies his hands. "I wanted you to know the truth. I've been in deep undercover for years now. Those men watching you from the building opposite Looking Glass? They were mine." He pauses, waiting for some response from me, and when I don't say a word, Hart continues, "I knew your mom. I knew what she went through. Losing her . . . they told me I couldn't save everyone and I know that, but I still carry the guilt—probably will for the rest of my life."

For something offered up so freely, the words are scraped and raw like Hart excavated them from some part of his soul no one was ever supposed to see. I want to look away and I can't.

"I'm really sorry for your loss," he says softly. "I wish your mom's life had a different ending."

"Me too." I take a deep breath against the sudden ache in my chest. "And Bay? What about him? What I did . . ."

"You had no idea what was going on, Wick."

"Doesn't make it right."

"No." Hart's sigh is long and heavy. "I had no idea what she had you doing until it was too late. I'm so sorry, Wick. I never would have let that happen if I'd known."

There is the softest cough from Special Agent Bennett and Hart nods at her, squaring his shoulders.

"I started my undercover work with your dad," Hart says. "I won't say I know what you went through, but I think I have a pretty good understanding. My team and I have watched for a long time."

"Did you make that deal with Joe? Were you the ones behind his plea bargain?"

Hart nods. "I was trying to bring all of Looking Glass down."

"Great job of that."

He grimaces and there's something of the old Hart that peeks through. He's irritated I beat him to my dad and I like that; means bringing down Michael and Norcut and Looking Glass was personal.

"Fair point," Hart says finally. "Thanks to you, Dr. Norcut will go away for a long time—as will her son if we can ever find him."

You won't.

"So how long have you been watching me?" I ask.

"Awhile now." Bennett steps away from the wall. "Those viruses at Looking Glass were from me. We weren't sure if you were working for your dad or if you were really on board with Dr. Norcut. Larkin and I were fishing, thought you would be an ideal inside source for us if we could bring you to our side, but things . . . got out of hand before we could loop you in."

"'Got out of hand'? That's what you're calling it?"

"I'm sorry," Hart says.

I take a deep, deep breath and let it escape slowly. "Aren't you supposed to be debriefing me?"

"We are debriefing. Ten years here"—he shakes his head—"is a waste for someone like you."

I wait, watching Hart, watching Bennett. She's looking straight at me now. She's holding her breath.

"Oh yeah?" I ask at last.

"Yeah." Hart leans forward, and this time, I don't lean

back. "I'm sorry I couldn't tell you the truth about who I was and what I was doing. I wanted to. I think you have a lot to offer the world."

I stare at him, searching for the bullshit. But there isn't any, and I should be sarcastic because that line is *so* cheesy, but I meet Hart's eyes and nod. "I know I have a lot to offer."

"Good. Because I want to give you a job, Wick."

"I've heard that line before."

"Yeah. True. But this time it's your choice and it's the real deal: paycheck, W-2, taxes. It's a desk job, but you'll work with us. . . . So what do you say? You want to help the government catch some bad guys?"

Hart grins and, after a beat, so do I.